AFRICANA

By William Harrison

AFRICANA

ROLLERBALL

LESSONS IN PARADISE

IN A WILD SANCTUARY

THE THEOLOGIAN

AFRICANA

WILLIAM HARRISON

WILLIAM MORROW AND COMPANY, INC.

New York   1977

Printed in the United States of America.

1   2   3   4   5   6   7   8   9   10

Library of Congress Cataloging in Publication Data

Harrison, William (date)
    Africana.

    I. Title.
PZ4.H3223Af   [PS3558.A672]   813'.5'4   76-49494
ISBN 0-688-03166-8

BOOK DESIGN   CARL WEISS

FOR
OLD FRIENDS
AND
COLLEAGUES:
JIM,
MILLER,
AND HARRY

CONTENTS

ONE   **BACKGROUNDS**
KENYA, LONDON, TEXAS, WALES,
KOREA, DREAMS, CREATURES,
PERSONAGES   *13*

TWO   **THE CONGO**
ANIMALS, ANECDOTES, POLITICS,
ENCOUNTERS SEXUAL AND
VIOLENT   *51*

THREE   **BIVOUACS**
SWITZERLAND, SPAIN, CHILDREN,
GAMES, WEAPONS, THE DOLDRUMS   *119*

FOUR   **BIAFRA**
PUBLICITY, REFUGEES, STUDENTS,
DEALS, DEATH   *165*

FIVE   **OBLIVION**
THE SOUTH SUDAN, NAIROBI,
LONDON, MOMBASA, LAST MOVES   *235*

Kuna wageni shambani. (There are strangers in the field.)
Watu wamelewa. (The men are drunk.)
Pana watota mlangoni. (There are children at the door.)
Je, mbele hakuna hatari nyingine?
(Say, is there any danger ahead?)

—lines from a Swahili grammar textbook

AFRICANA

PART ONE

BACKGROUNDS

KENYA,
LONDON, TEXAS,
WALES, KOREA, DREAMS,
CREATURES, PERSONAGES

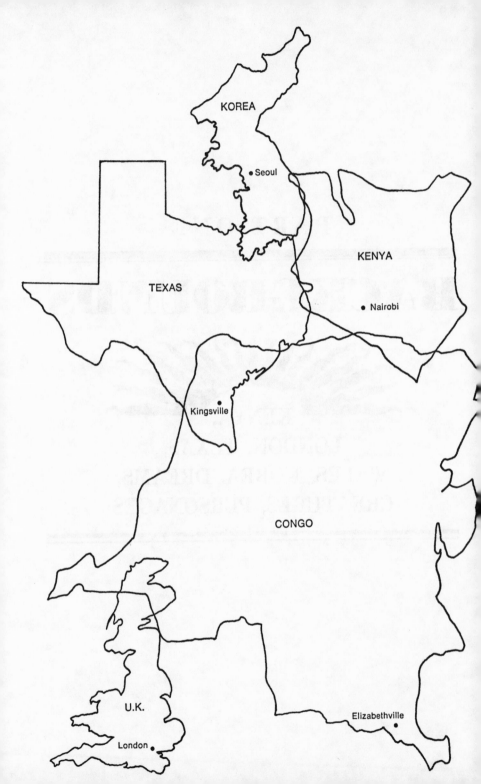

THERE WAS ONCE A SOLDIER NAMED LEO WHO WAS ALSO a philosopher. He had a small private army of mercenaries in Africa, was in love with a woman named Val, and had a friend named Harry of whom he was afraid.

Leo was from Wales, Val was from London, and Harry was from Texas.

They went to Africa because that was a well-known place for savages. There they met many people as well as various ghosts and shadows.

Leo thought about many things and made speeches. Val, who was once a writer, was too beautiful for ordinary men. Harry was courageous and insane and had disturbing dreams.

† † †

A haze of very fine dust covers the jungles of central Africa, a dust blown down from the Sahara called the *harmattan*.

Europeans go around with handkerchiefs over their mouths. The air is dense with this hot, sticky haze, and beyond—always out there somewhere—trouble is about to erupt, wars are being fought, massacres have occurred, and the drums and animals signal a constant distress.

A few farms have been hacked out of this middle jungle that goes around the continent like a thick belt; the farmers beat back the undergrowth long enough so their crops of yams and bananas and cocoa come up, then the forests grow back, orchids creep in like delicate killers, the great ferns sprout up again, grass higher than a man's head reclaims the furrows, and the paths and narrow streams are inundated with feathery bamboo, flowers, and fierce weed; one can see the growth and feel it. One's relationship to it, as Leo once said, becomes episodic, like war; the creature of the field survives only one embattled day at a time.

Then into the jungle itself: the streams turn into rivers, then go back into swampy streams again, the water in them so still and smooth that the overhanging foliage is reflected in their mirrors. Water lilies are white as snow—and from some of them poison is extracted for arrows. Creeper vines. Dazzling unknown butterflies flitting in the interlace of branches. A land of parrot, monkey, hippo, ibis, centipede, firefly, kingfisher, killer ant, wild duck—and off in the hills, never seen, the leopard.

Then back into a patchwork of farms and villages. The traveler comes on them suddenly: weird little clearings with their mangoes, guavas, avocado pears, or thatched huts surrounded by goats. The farmers come out to say hello in Efik or Swahili or some Bantu dialect never before recorded. An endless maze of bush trails, many of them old slave routes. Where the paths of different tribes meet and join, villages grow up; they are like anthills, endless as mangrove forests, no more than a bowshot away from each other, on and on, each one arranged in its own maze like the trails surrounding it, so that a traveler has to search his way into the center, where, if he bothers, he becomes a guest. Giant cotton trees—not unlike the cottonwood trees of Texas—send airy particles floating in the dusty haze of the landscape. And in the fallen, rotting tree trunks by the water's edge or along the paths the endless orchids grow: lovely markers in the mulch of the centuries.

Everything a maze: the villages, the crisscrossed trails, thickets and forests. In the high grass one sees nothing; one path looks like another and purpose becomes lost, nature overgrowing all strategies and directions and claiming everything while the *harmattan* obliterates definitions, and men and animals become one shape, trees and time become dreams, and the maze itself becomes engulfed with all its starting points gone.

† † †

Leo sat on the porch of his bungalow, the main headquarters building of his ranch near Ndola. He drank a lime cooler and wore his new chocolate-colored tailor-made jungle outfit from Bernard Weatherill of London. His men—called his Elite Rifles, though they were a somewhat grubbier group than this name implied—sat around him like schoolboys. He entertained them with historical anecdotes and lectured them.

His great white falcon, Dorothy, glared over his shoulder from her perch on the back of his rocking chair.

At the battle of Cannae, Leo told his men, Varro put his strongest warriors and armor in the front line of his Roman legion and Hannibal replied to this juggernaut with his weakest forces. The result was that Varro pierced into Hannibal's army deeper and deeper until Hannibal's soldiers collapsed around the Romans, surrounding them, jamming them close, and butchering them.

Leo's men listened and sipped their own lime coolers—which contained a weaker ration of gin than the commander's.

As shadows grew long across the savannah, Leo went into the same speech he had delivered years before in Kenya and many times since.

Civilization has its rules for war, chivalrous ways of harming people, but piss on that. The rules are always broken and in terrible ways which when the rules were drawn up nobody even guessed to make a rule about. Civilization always starts out to make itself less guilty and ends up more guilty, so let there never be any rules, nothing too bloody or horrible. Go mad and get creative with madness, if possible, because such madness will finally be healthy.

Leo's men didn't altogether comprehend his speeches, but they always tried to remain respectful. Even so, some of them farted and the odor of putrid gin rode around in the heavy air of the bungalow porch.

Leo and the falcon looked down on the men with about the same gaze.

† † †

Harry had recurring dreams.

One was an extravaganza, some he didn't mind, and one bothered him very much. It was less a dream than an image: there was a solitary black flag high on the wall of a castle. The castle sat on a promontory of rock. Around it, the land was scrub tree and desert and Harry was lying there below looking up at that flag rippling in the breeze. It was a silent dream, no action, he just lay there, and he realized that this was possibly the last thing he had seen, while dying, in a life he had lived before.

† † †

Val had a desk of beautiful inlaid woods that went with her everywhere. When she traveled around the jungles with Leo and Harry an armored lorry—a Saracen—which Leo bought for military purposes bore her special desk.

She liked the idea of having written something, but didn't much care for writing itself. Who did? There were bothersome spellings, facts, broken pencils, verbs, and an armada of daydreams.

She had come to Africa as a correspondent for *The Times* and she had that to remember and cherish. She had also sold articles to magazines, composed unpublished poems, and considered the lofty novel. But the necessary energies failed her. She read a lot of books, yet understood that thinking of herself as an authoress was a vanity.

Harry wrote every day in a little leather-bound diary. She peeked at it once or twice and it always gave her a laugh. It contained bare entries: dates, fragments of events, names. Harry was never one for elaboration, but he wanted a record kept; he liked to recall what had occurred on a certain assignment, all that. She could recite the data of ancient Egypt or discourse on the various schools of painting or list the American presidents or trace Cicero's thoughts through Karl Marx, but Harry had his odd patches of memory jotted down in his pocket diary. A second-rate intelligence, Harry, but endearing. Val decided that he was poorly educated. He had attended a university in Texas, played football, and studied engineering. Yet there was none like him for sudden odd intuitions and moments of daring.

She sat at her beautiful inlaid desk and let the daydreams come.

She wondered if Leo would kill Harry or if Harry would kill Leo.

Then, as usual, she began to think about herself.

She wasn't beautiful until her late teens when she lost her fat. Before that she was large and awkward and prepared for a career. All her savvy, Harry once said, probably came from those years.

Her father, Edgar, was in Whitehall for thirty years and provided her Fleet Street contacts.

They lived in Hampstead Garden Suburb, not far from Spaniard's Inn and the Heath where they took weekend strolls.

On her desk at *The Times* when she was a mere research girl was a silver ashtray, presented to her by her father, engraved with the sentiment, "Ask no questions and you'll be told no truths." She loved it. She thought of herself as an idealist set to brooding by the Dark Continent.

She and her father played the horses. They had a Turf Accountant in Hampstead High Street and at the various tracks sat in the best boxes with her father's cronies.

When the old widower died he left her a portrait of her grandfather done by Winterhalter.

She became the lover of a senior *Times* correspondent and accompanied him to the Congo. She met Leo in Katanga during the uprising.

Once she discovered she was attractive to every man who met her, she used her good looks like a weapon. "It's immature, I know it is," she told Leo, "but I love to walk into a room and stir them up!"

Leo asked her to please bear a child for him. This was two days after they first met.

Her poetry had lots of French phrases.

At the height of the Katangan hostilities she published an article on the many pleasant river voyages of Africa in *National Geographic*.

She usually wore low-slung jeans and a blouse with a button missing.

She and Harry had a joke between them. She would stand on the porch of the Ndola bungalow, jut out her hip and imitate Mae West, breathing out, "Hey, Tex, you carry a pistol?"

† † †

Does the karoo bush grow only in the Congo? No, it grows on the slopes of Mount Kenya, too, and in the rolling hills of the Calabar region; it grows in the flats of Mombasa and on the highlands of South Africa, on the purple rise of the Cameroon range and far up the White Nile into the Sudan. And memory, what of it? Leo sometimes remembered a patrol beside a river, but was it the Itsava, the great Congo, the mighty Niger, what water? And what mountain? Kenya, Elgon, old Kilimanjaro? He remembered himself dressed in a monkey-skin headgear like a Masai chieftain. Or in a mangrove swamp, trapped, movements of the enemy out there in the high grass.

Leo went to Kenya—the details blurred and ran together as his life ran on—hired by an estate owner so British that his name was actually Sir Reginald. Leo's duty was to patrol with his men in a couple of Land Rovers. Seven big blacks and a crazy Belgian comprised that first tattered unit. They were officially called a Mobile Intelligence Outfit and were paid jointly by Sir Reginald and nine other feudal lords in that northern district of Kikuyuland, but they were clearly, eventually, the white man's terror unit. Mau Mau was loose: a special African madness. The followers drank blood before battle like their ancient ancestors, remained more marauders than revolutionaries, stormed the white *shambas* burning and looting, and needed—to coin Sir Reginald's phrase—a hard hand.

In Leo's little mercenary force the pay was poor, the risks high, but Leo saw a future in it. Every morning he met his men in front of their trucks, had the Belgian chivy the men into two neat ranks, and walked around making his daily speech. He had his first falcon on his shoulder, a Black Shaheen named Daphne.

Already he had learned something from the native chiefs: he went down the lines, looked each man in the eyes, and had each one speak his name; this was a private morning ritual with each soldier—and hardly within the western tradition of making obedient men through a process of humiliation and the obliteration of personality. A blood rite of brothers as the names came back, instead: Gandiri, say, or Preston or Mewishi.

He touched a button or a man's sleeve.

They worked like coolies, fought his fights, and became extensions of his brain. If they could figure out what he wanted they'd do it in advance; they struggled to please him. In pay, they each received fifty pounds a month and Leo's particular brand of dark adventure.

He kept all spoils himself.

Out of his treasury, he hired more men and sought new assignments.

The Simbas didn't just shrink into the bush and their anticolonial movement didn't just sputter and die for lack of enthusiasm. They were beaten, badly mauled and beaten, and

Leo, the surprisingly tough landlords, and the Kenya Regiment did the whipping up.

He took his 11 A.M. tea with the ladies on the verandah of the old Norfolk Hotel in Nairobi when he visited the city.

He learned Swahili and studied Arabic.

He set himself rules. Never wear a bush jacket or any clothing of the hunter. Never fight or kill with the methods of the native. Never be called *bwana.* Establish eccentric personal habits.

His outfit escaped ambush four times. Meanwhile, he took photographs and geological and floral samples. He studied the myrrh bushes, the rhinos, the nomads, the scorpions. He put a grenade in the belly wound of a famous rebel leader and blew him to pieces—which was considered by Simba standards pretty uncouth and insulting to the great warrior. But he also told Sir Reginald and the others to stop flogging their natives, though they argued that the Wogs preferred this to any docking of wages or the more civilized forms of punishment. (They stopped flogging until Leo finished work for them and left the region.)

In the back of his Land Rover there was always Carlsberg beer and Worcestershire sauce. Everything Leo put in his mouth was awash with one or the other.

He hired Weldu, the son of a noble Dinka witch doctor, an expert game tracker, gun carrier, and valet. (Weldu, in turn, taught the Commander to tell the difference between a Mau Mau signal and the genuine bark of a zebra.)

Leo's photograph appeared in the *East African Standard* and was toasted by the landowners gathered at the Long Bar in Nairobi and also stuck on spears in villages along the Northern Frontier where magic rites were performed as they cursed his image.

And Weldu—with modest skepticism—asked, "Do you yourself believe that God lives up above the tree line on Mount Kenya?"

To which Leo answered, "What do you think, Weldu?"

"I confess I'm a heretic. But cautious. Better to believe in almost everything like a simple Christian—for safety's sake."

"Right you are," Leo agreed. "That's why I drink honey and blood, same as the true Masai. And pray in the mosques whenever possible. And keep both hawks and rosary beads. And spit on my bullets."

"You do all that, Commander?"

"Yes, and always believe whatever my servant believes," Leo lied, "or else I'm a fool."

"In that case," Weldu concluded, "we are only servant and master for this short life. After death we are brothers forever, correct?"

"If you follow my example as I follow yours," Leo amended. "And I've promised to lead you through the great darkness, Weldu, remember."

On the side panels of his infamous Land Rovers were falcons stenciled in black. *Goats, pigs, men and women, you're all dirty out here in the bush, but terribly civilized among your farms and I mean to show you that,* he told those terrorist encampments and villages. These were black men who practiced all the taboos and wild fancies of a mysterious jungle protocol, who thought it more criminal to mutilate the dead than to kill, who honored warriors by covering them with their shields; these were a people to whom the white man had sent missionaries and clothes. Now the outside world had sent its other manifestation, Leo.

With Harry—as Leo would sometimes note—shadows of temper came over him. As if in a rapture. Harry's meanness was like a bad drunk, spewing out of him, passing away, leaving him a little disgusted with himself as he settled back into normalcy. But Leo worked deliberately, as if he were constructing an awful mosaic, a piece here, a piece there, all this will fit in. Not much spontaneity from Leo even in those first months out there in Kenya, but lots of surprises.

The men in his Land Rovers moved in the swoon of his command. No telling how many renegade bastards might swarm out of the bush, they knew that; they were rightfully afraid to disobey any strategy, but Leo kept them inebriated with his own strange lust, go here, do that, and they kept their victims half alive, fed renegade farmers to their own swine, and worked out the Commander's patterns. Welcome to real savagery: play this on your drums village to village, he was saying to the continent. Beat out the news of my arrival and get my name right.

A few years later Leo would have Sergeant Major Hicks (Sandhurst educated) and a company of men with a slightly greater military demeanor. There would be artillery, a demolition squad, bazookas, Sten guns, a flame thrower, and his men would all wear those chocolate-colored uniforms from Savile Row.

As Leo would say, however, the greater the order the greater the chaos and madness.

And what are the reasons, Commander, sir, a man goes to war?

First, to get away from home. Then to dress up in uniform. Then to be in foreign places with exotic women and purposes. Then to live a neat existence with simple duties and a simple chain of command. And to some, Weldu, to stare over the edge into the fucking abyss.

† † †

Wild Bill Donovan went to Africa only once, shortly after World War II, and he wondered why there were so many kites in the sky.

He was a large man, Donovan, with a reputation for being fearless. During the war he headed the OSS—the military intelligence unit which later became America's CIA.

He was also nearsighted and too vain to wear glasses.

"What're all those damned kites?" he asked Leo. "Do Africans all fly kites?"

"Those aren't kites," Leo told him. "Those are vultures."

† † †

After her father's death Val began to dislike London. She decided it was a city of owners and talkers. If one went to Burke's for lunch or to Corfu for holiday it was to say one had gone. One kept score of books read, wine stored, concerts heard, names dropped, friends screwed.

She took up with Bedford of *The Times* because he had the seniority to help her promote herself beyond that little research desk with the silver ashtray. Also, somehow, because he had a flat on St. John's Road overlooking Regent's Park.

"Why did you choose me?" Bedford asked her those nights they were alone on the balcony above the park and zoo. He wasn't sure he possessed Val, though he wanted to. He wanted them to marry, then she would have legal right to his stamp collections and he would have her, the Winterhalter portrait, and the inlaid desk.

"I chose you because of this flat," she said.

It was an answer Bedford admired. He assumed this meant she approved of the furniture and appointments.

"What do you like best about my little place?" he asked with some coyness.

"The zoo across the street," she answered absently.

"The zoo?"

"The odor of tiger and hippo shit. Your place always smells like a lovely cage, Bedford, you can't help it. It's the way the wind blows."

"You like that?" Bedford asked, confused.

"I want to go to Africa," she announced. "Get us both an assignment, will you, Bedford? You can, you know."

"There's no reason to go."

"There should be a war soon," she said, leaning against him. "Surely."

Bedford stared beyond the park toward the skyline of London. Val adored him, he felt sure of that. And, yes, the wind blew right up from the zoo into his nostrils.

† † †

Malaria: a strange fever. It both causes and cures madness.

Leo had it a few times. In Biafra he was out of sorts with it and once traded some guns to a competitor just to get some needed drugs.

T. E. Lawrence had malaria. His gentler critics say that's what made him such a liar—about what happened in Deraa and such.

In 1927 the Nobel Prize in medicine went to a doctor who treated insanity by raising the body temperature and that same year the Nobel Prize for literature went to a Greek woman who wrote a poem about a warrior wandering the swamps of Macedonia after a battle who was cured of madness when he took a fever.

The candelabra tree of Africa—not usually exotic lilies, also poisonous—gives the milky white sap from which poison is made for most poison arrows. The juice from that tree heats

up the body, the blood almost boils in the veins, and before
death the brain burns up with visions.

Valencia in Spain has the annual festival of the fires, Las
Fallas. Giant papier-mâché figures are built in every plaza,
then set ablaze. Fireworks and flames everywhere, fires rising
to the tops of the cathedrals, then a litter of ashes.

Even cities are known by their forms of fever and madness.

All this in Val's notes.

† † †

When Harry arrived in Korea to begin his service, the
Eighth Army had lost its morale.

In Tokyo, General MacArthur insisted that the UN forces
needed to cross the Yalu River and bomb and invade China,
but President Harry Truman still wanted a limited war. In
Korea itself, General Ridgway had given up trying to moti-
vate his men on an ideological basis and was appealing to
professional pride, the ability to fight, and toughness. Harry
was assigned to help in this morale-boosting exercise. Because
he happened to believe in all that, he sold it to others. He
was young. He was a new captain, eager, hopping around as
an intelligence gadfly, catching choppers and gathering reports,
a sort of armed messenger radiating the new vision—much
to the disgust of a few old troopers—and with a general faith
in the UN, the war, American innocence, and masculinity.

In January, 1951, Operation Thunderbolt began—which
was unlikely behavior, suddenly, for an army that had been
chased all the way down to Seoul. Backed up on the frozen
banks of the Han River, the old Eighth Army had decided on
an offensive. It moved sluggishly forward and occupied Wonju
(a single line of entry in one of Harry's little pocket diaries,
dated the twenty-second) and with light opposition moved
on up to Hoengsong later. It was bitter cold and Harry was on

his own, mostly riding around in windswept vehicles or choppers, trying to find out anything he could; the Eighth Army's
intelligence was nil, Seoul had already exchanged hands three
times at this point because nobody ever knew where the Communists were, there was rampant black marketeering and
vice and all the usual human waste of a long, bogged-down
war, and the enemy was still floating around somewhere out
there.

In Seoul itself there were at least four conflicting ideas on
how to run headquarters and the urban emergencies, so Harry
kept clear. He decided to go up to Hoengsong because he
might find out something more about the North Korean regulars face-to-face than by filing reports and hugging the HQ
fires.

Operation Roundup had started when he arrived.

The South Korean forces (ROK) were circling from Hoengsong toward Hongchon in a wide arc trying to throw a net
around several pockets of Communists. But things were wrong.
There were more Communists inside the circle than anyone
had guessed. Also, the two groups forming the net weren't
moving toward each other at the same pace.

Harry joined X Corps—which chugged along across the
frozen ground as fast as possible just to keep warm. They
finally moved so fast that they exposed their flank and allowed
the Communists to counterattack. During the opening minutes
of that attack Harry jumped on the last available chopper
and went off to find out, if possible, where other ROK troops
were. He found them cut off north of Hoengsong. The enemy
had set up a road block and everyone was confused and
scrambling.

There was a dapper South Korean general named Roon.

"Shall I try to get a message to General Ridgway?" Harry
asked him.

"He already knows," the General answered in his Oxford accent. "And who would you be?"

"Captain Marvel of Intelligence," Harry snapped back, feeling exhilarated because they were all trapped.

Shells were exploding not too far away and the General, cool and detached from such annoyance, was drawing heavily from a flask of liquor—either because he was very cold or wanted to get exceedingly drunk. It turned out that he was also hip to comic books.

"Then say *Shazam*, young captain, and get us out of this. Or we're going to have to actually fight our way out of this pocket—which I'm fairly certain we're not mentally prepared to do."

General Roon emptied the flask while Harry, embarrassed, gave his real name and duties.

"You ever fought?" the General casually asked.

A shell landed about sixty meters from the roadside where they stood chatting.

"In South Texas where I was raised," Harry related, "we hunt the javelina. This is a fierce wild pig. One day I chased one into a ravine. I followed it in, but couldn't find it. Looked behind every rock and mesquite tree. Then I felt these hairs on the back of my neck standing up and I turned to face it. We looked into each other's eyes, this old boar and me, and I saw something I didn't understand. A shadow inside him. He bared his tusks and attacked and I killed him—gut-shot him, then finished him with my old bone-handled knife. As I did this, I felt the shadow move inside me."

"Into your body?" General Roon inquired with about the tone of a skeptical don.

"Yessir, and that shadow is still there."

"Do you feel like Achilles, then?" the General asked. "Dipped in protective water so you'll never fall in battle?"

"I can't rightly say, sir. Maybe like that."

General Roon's eyes glazed slightly—perhaps from weariness or too much of the flask. He drummed his fingers thoughtfully on the top of a jeep while his men jogged by on the road. General Roon knew his men had a long way to run. Most of them would run for a day and a night, never slacking the pace; they would eat and defecate on the run, they were doomed otherwise. The General drummed his fingers.

"Get in the jeep," he told Harry.

They drove along the frozen road. Their driver gripped the steering wheel so hard that his knuckles turned white.

"Where're we going?" Harry asked.

"You have told me a wonderful story which I believe," the General said. "I am taking you with me like a rabbit's foot."

That night they were at Wahling Crossroads and a roadblock manned by thousands of Communists. The ROK generals were trying desperately to call X Corps on the phones, everyone was numb with fear and cold, and everyone around General Roon asked questions he couldn't answer. A light snow fluttered down and sniper activity had picked up.

General Roon and two of his colonels huddled under a blanket in the jeep on that moonless night trying to study a map by flashlight. Harry stood around flapping his arms against the relentless chill. Not far down the road a soldier had been picked off by a sniper—who probably used an infrared scope. By daybreak, Harry reckoned, the Communists might have the entire battalion between lines of fire.

General Roon came out from under the blanket, strolled around in the darkness, and bumped into Harry.

"Ah ha, the intelligence officer," he remarked, his Oxford accent deepening. "Say something intelligent, won't you?"

"Call in some napalm," Harry suggested.

"Napalm would be like a Biblical rain," General Roon philosophized. "It would cover the just and the unjust."

"A good pilot could lay it on just right," Harry argued.

The General considered this plan in silence. "They know our position," he said, finally, "but we don't know theirs. Too risky. I have to reject napalm."

"At least it would warm things up," Harry offered.

Another hour passed during which time the General retreated underneath the blanket once more. At last, Harry was invited underneath, too. He received one rice cake and a shot of tasteless booze.

Because of this hospitality Harry volunteered.

"Do you plan to send your demon shadow or go yourself?" the General asked with a smile there in the flashlight glow.

"I won't attack single-handed," Harry said. "That would be excessive. But I can creep through their lines and give a pilot a nice target."

The colonels agreed immediately that this was indeed a wonderful plan.

"My specialty is crawling around in the dark," Harry drawled. "It really wouldn't be too much trouble."

"Never in my military experience," said the amazed General Roon, "has anyone volunteered to do anything the least dangerous."

Harry knew he appeared young and silly, but felt a strange electric confidence. He had heard of a foolish sergeant on Hill 786 who had fallen on a grenade to save two officers nearby and had told them before he died that he somehow didn't think the explosion would hurt all that much. But Harry only felt a sort of pre-game jitters, as though he was old Number 54 playing for the Longhorns at linebacker again.

He heard the distant thud of a Bofors gun.

One of the colonels offered him the last rice cake.

An hour later he was inching along, trying to move without rattling his gear or grenades. The nerves in his stomach had tightened—he knew he'd have to kill any sentry who stumbled onto him—but he enjoyed these moments of pure concentration. He crawled through snow bearing the odor of the enemy's urine. He talked to his body. Leg, I will pull you up here just so. Ass, I will scoot you just over here a bit.

The first encampment was thick with the smell of opium and nervous sweat. Everyone seemed very quiet. They're listening for the enemy, Harry decided. They're listening for me.

Rolling off one of his elbows, he checked the sleeve of his quilted jacket and read the luminous dial of his watch. At four-fifteen, Roon and the colonels would direct a false charge, then pull back in a hurry; Harry would deposit his grenades— preferably in something combustible—and set off the two flares which were weighing him down. The planes should be right on the horizon after that.

Naturally, he would be in the target area himself.

He lay still. He felt like a man swimming to the surface from a great depth. It was a feeling he would have in Katanga, later, and in Biafra, and in so many of those years after this when he wouldn't exactly be an American anymore, just one of the world's mercenaries.

He thought about the javelina. It was a true story.

Women, too. He considered why he was usually unsuccessful with them.

He held his breath so much that he got a headache.

My name is Harry Veer. Twenty-three years old. Six-foot-three and two hundred pounds. Already a captain in intelligence. Yes, I was good in school. Read my tags for yourselves.

Torture me all you want, I don't care, I'm like Brer Rabbit, I love torture.

At the appointed time he heard the ROK's distracting advance, the crack of rifle fire followed by the heavier stuff. Men jumped up all around him. He hadn't realized how far into their lines he had gone until they began to run around chanting and clattering. They drummed on metal as they revved themselves up, chanting, "Kill GI!" like boys at a pep rally, giddy, and they kept running and jumping and diving all over as shots whistled through the air.

Harry set off the first flare and ran, too. In the darkness, no one seemed to see any difference as he clomped along in a crouch, running like a fullback, shedding grenades, while his enemies rushed forward toward the barricades, drugged and dazed, where they expected an attack. Harry found a darkly ramshackled truck and popped a live grenade into its gas tank. Soon after he set off the second flare. As he did so, a man jerked his shoulder and spun him around.

There was a moment of uncertainty.

Harry drove a pistol butt into the man's face, fell atop him, groped, and gouged behind the soft neck muscle to get the carotid artery. The man seemed willing to let Harry do this. When Harry got off the body a few seconds later he could feel the shadow inside him grown hot. The fever was on him.

The planes came, Harry survived, and he was awarded a Silver Star. He was invited to General Roon's home in Seoul where the general's wife served rolled beef and rice.

The strategy in Korea after that night became simple: drive them back hill by hill, river after river, kill as many as possible with superior fire power until the 38th Parallel is reached. Operation Meat Grinder, Ridgway called it. For Harry, then, it became the limited war in which he enjoyed unlimited personal fighting.

His situation was unique: he was an intelligence officer assigned to a special group which often got into the field. He enjoyed considerable autonomy after Wahling Crossroads, had a jeep and driver, room on anyone's plane or helicopter, and a growing collection of weapons and skills. He took another field promotion. He knew where the action was and how to get there. Mercury with a sword, that's how he saw himself.

Occasionally he settled down for a few days in Seoul. There were rats everywhere, human dregs, helpless children. He watched the last of the pontoon bridges blown up during a counterattack, thousands of frightened families screaming to get across the Han River and out of the city, then the ice on the river itself being mortared so they couldn't cross. Such nightmares, then boredom. When he tended to his bureaucratic duties at HQ a deep almost frantic boredom took hold—so depressing that it made him angry and drove him back up-country.

He also became terribly lonely.

In February, 1952, a shell fragment got him in the left buttock. Shot in the ass and no laughing matter, he wrote home. He was in the Seoul hospital until April when he went over to join Ridgway's staff in Tokyo. Then—not recovering too well—he went back to Texas. MacArthur was gone by this time, victim of a politician's prudence, Ridgway was the new Far East commander, and General Van Fleet was mopping up Korea.

Before Harry left Seoul he limped into a bar.

"You are going to kill me," a frightened bar girl accused him as he offered to buy her body.

"Don't be silly," he argued, manufacturing a laugh.

"You will take me upstairs and kill me," she whined. She was a slender girl, not particularly pretty, who had entertained scores of men, soldiers north and south, Harry knew, at that same hotel bar.

"If I'm acting weird," Harry said, "it's because I'm flying out in a few hours. I'm going over to Tokyo headquarters where I know I won't like it."

"You are a man of bad temper," she said.

"We'll have a bottle of beer together," he said. "Just stay right here at the bar and drink. We won't go upstairs, okay?"

They drank beer for a few minutes and everything seemed better. But then the girl began sobbing. Harry tried to comfort her, but she folded her face into her hands and wouldn't let him touch her.

"I want to go away from you," she whimpered. "It is rule of establishment that I stay and drink, but I want to leave."

† † †

A travel note among Val's papers. The cheetah of the great Serengeti are dying of heart attacks because they are being chased around the reserve by tourists in cars. Tourists are also giving the lions such close and constant observation that many mother lions have become restless and nervous and won't lie down for their young to suckle. The cubs are dying of malnutrition.

† † †

Leo's father worked on the docks at Cardiff, drank gallons of stout every day after work, and beat Leo's mother. She left the brute and put her clever son in school in the town of Caerphilly where she became secretary in the school office.

The town of Caerphilly is noted for its ruined castle. Playing around the walls of that castle young Leo—who was pudgy —invented his dreams and future. Since he and his mother were so poor, he decided early that the army life was suitable.

One day the boy made a discovery. He ran home to tell his mother who was ironing and listening to the radio to see if the BBC would play another song request she had sent in.

"Mother, I figured something out all by myself! Guess why the stairways inside the guard towers and turrets of castles always go up clockwise with the wide part of the stair on the left side?"

"Why is that, Leo?"

"So the man defending—at the top—can use a sword in his right hand! And have the widest part of the stair to stand on!"

His mother gave him a blank look and then smiled without any real comprehension.

† † †

Leo served in Libya, then Sicily (the Italy Star, 1943), and for his services on the African continent received a grant of land given away "to men and women of pure European descent who are eligible to farm the area reserved for Europeans in Kenya and whose war services a grateful country wishes to recognize."

He never farmed. Instead, he sold the land and with his money earned and stolen during the Mau Mau campaigns purchased the ranch near Ndola in the middle of the continent. He built up his little army with new assignments. He advised the Kabaka, head of Uganda. (The British government paid him a handsome bribe to keep him from any actual participation on that ruler's behalf.) He received a mysterious grant of arms and cash from Sir Roy Welensky in South Africa. He established credit at a military warehouse in Lusaka. He was paid a retainer to advise the heads of the Ewe tribe in Togoland. And so on.

But Kenya: there, at the beginning, he became himself.

In those days gazelle and zebra strolled casually along the

Great North Road as his Land Rovers chugged from encounter to encounter. A strange and awful beauty everywhere. A delicate herd of bushbuck standing in the midst of wild jasmine. The White Highlands with their streams swollen and booming after the monsoons of April. Clouds lying in the bowls of lonely, unnamed craters. *Nyika,* the wilderness. The sky filled with a flight of white egrets turning toward an uncharted lake in the mountains. The evening silence: a forest holding its breath so that one could hear echoes of the Pleistocene. The deadly extravagance of nature all around.

Leo and his men were also some of the last to chase the notorious Kimathi and his remnant Mau Mau band as they fled higher and higher into the Aberdares.

"Where do you think they are now, Weldu?"

"Deep in the mountains."

"What are they doing? Won't they starve up there?"

"They wear the skins of the leopard, Commander. By this time, maybe, they have turned into leopards."

"You don't really think that, Weldu."

"Some of them will turn into trees. Or rocks. They won't necessarily become leopards, sir, no, I'm not saying that."

Weldu stood on one leg, like a heron, when he conversed.

His drink was Sloan's Liniment—which he took internally as a caution against bites, nausea, fevers, worms, arthritis, and fear. The liniment was precious to Weldu. He usually bought it in large quantity from Somali traders when the Land Rovers swung north into the brush country on the rim of the desert. Except for this, Weldu was strictly an antimaterialist. His disdain for loot was considered a tribute to his father, the witch doctor, from whom he had obviously learned spiritual values.

At one of the little trading posts on the frontier Leo discovered a present: an old Masai war rattle left there by the fleeing Kimathi and his band.

"What's this for?" Leo asked Weldu. "Is it cursed? Should I touch it?"

"It's a tribute, Commander," Weldu explained, balancing on one leg. "Kimathi is saying you are *mangati:* a worthy foe."

Leo gazed off toward the mountains and thought about all the killings. Weldu, like a slender black bird swallowing, took a sip of Sloan's—his throat stretched upward, his head tilted back, one leg tucked up in the folds of his khaki britches.

The war rattle bore bright yellow feathers and scratches from continuous use.

Leo hefted it and listened to its sound.

It was a nearly natural thing, as if it had been born in the bush; alive, beautiful, exotic, with some horrible odd purpose all its own.

† † †

Moise Tshombe, head of Katanga, richest province of the Congo, had a deep bass voice, but wanted it deeper.

He also wanted Katanga to be a nation, not simply a province. So he spent his days sending messages and talking on the phone to Patrice Lumumba, Cyrille Adoula, Joseph Kasavubu and various Belgians—all of whom considered they were running matters in that country. He spent his nights before a great ivory-trimmed mirror speaking in deeper and deeper tones. The timbre of his voice already hurt sensitive ears, but he wanted a lion's roar.

One day Moise Tshombe called Leo on the phone. The connection—as usual—was imperfect. Leo thought it was an Italian actor, the one with the very deep voice who dubs in Italian for the American movie heroes.

"This is Moise Tshombe," the statesman said. "I'm inviting you to a party."

"Where?" Leo inquired.

"In Elisabethville! I have a big house! Ask anyone, you can't miss it!"

† † †

When trouble started in the Congo, Bedford of *The Times* created an assignment for himself and Val. They flew to North Africa, then down to Leopoldville where they met both the wiry Lumumba and the zombielike Kasavubu. Then they started out with a guide touring by jeep across the muddy backcountry roads.

Val wanted to copulate out in the open where nature would offer the python, the mosquito, or some great jungle beast as interference. This mystified poor Bedford, who considered even the best African accommodations rough enough.

They stopped for a night on the banks of the River Kasai at an old hunting camp. The guide suggested a *boma:* one of the cup-shaped jungle tents made of a thatch of thorns and heavy vines. Natives tied gazelles, say, to the outside walls of *bomas,* so when a jungle cat came to feed they could shove a spear through the small holes of the thatch and kill it.

The guide locked himself inside the jeep for the night and Val and Bedford entered the *boma.* He was armed with insect repellent and a vague lust (she hadn't consented to sleep with him since their stop at Morocco en route), and she tingled with an odd excitement which came mostly from the odors of the dirt floor and the sounds of the surrounding bush. Soon, Bedford's senses were waylaid by the joints of her naked body, the swell of her breasts, and the way her hair shone in the dappled moonlight inside their thorny cage.

Then the leopard came.

At first it paced around the *boma*. Bedford tried to see what was out there, but Val knew.

Then it pounced on the cage; the vines trembled. Bedford hurried into his clothes. "Ah!" he cried. "Ah! Ah!"

Val, naked in the moonlight, tried to touch the leopard. She reached through the holes after it, so that Bedford had to pull her back.

The leopard tried to chew through the vines and thorns. Bedford froze in fear.

Val seemed to writhe in a way which terrified him even more. She danced in strange, wanton undulations.

Bedford tried to calm her, but his voice only said, "Ah! Ah!" as the leopard snapped a limb of thorns in its powerful jaws.

Another vine snapped. Val danced, thrusting her hairy mound toward the leopard, holding her breasts in her hands.

They heard the guide yelling and banging on a piece of metal, trying to frighten the creature off, but already there was a hole in the side of the *boma* large enough so that Bedford could see the eyes: large, yellow, awful.

Val still danced, she had gone crazy.

At last, more out of desperation than ingenuity, Bedford let go a blast of insect repellent. He held the aerosol can right in the leopard's face and pressed the red button. The animal roared off into the night.

Val pushed her arm through the hole where the heavy thatch had been gnawed away. Her fingers splayed open in the moonlight.

† † †

Harry's Uncle Murdock always dabbled in wars and his five active decades as an American agent supplied him with several: he got into the thick of World War I, had something dark and unofficial to do with the Rif War in Morocco in the 1920s, paid his respects to the Spanish Civil War to an extent that he was banned from the country thereafter by special decree from Franco, and by the time of World War II was into espionage. Not long after D-Day he went to work for Wild Bill Donovan and became a maverick within that maverick outfit, plotting and stealing and stabbing long before the computer-styled CIA took over.

Uncle Murdock met an appropriate end: he shouldered down a door in Belgrade one evening and got shot. He was trying to pilfer some agricultural documents which were actually published a week later in all Yugoslavian newspapers.

The body was flown back to Kingsville, Texas, Harry's home town, where the Korean hero was recovering from his infamous wound. Harry had returned to the normal family landscapes—where else?—and was present that April afternoon as the South Texas winds whipped the mesquite trees around the church and as several inappropriate litanies were sung for Uncle Murdock. Since no one in the family really knew Uncle Murdock very well—he was a legend, not too strong on correspondence—there were no tears, but a number of cousins and such turned out in stern Episcopal black. Harry attended out of curiosity; he was looking over the small crowd for anything remotely feminine—old girl friends, wives, anything.

Among the strangers were some gentlemen from Washington, D.C., Uncle Murdock's cronies. They were down for the last rites, Harry supposed, because the State Department said they had to.

Nothing could have been more wrong. The men were there because they loved Uncle Murdock. In sensible terms, they shouldn't have come.

Just before the coffin was lowered there appeared beside

the priest a neon drunk: a red-faced man in a green sports jacket, pink trousers, and a dazzling yellow tie. He moved right up, stood beside the coffin, wet his lips, and delivered an impromptu eulogy to the gathering. He spoke as though everyone else had forgotten to do or say anything very human or touching. The family propped itself up stiffly and listened. They were a pale group and Harry found himself thinking, there, I like this man, and there's my blood in that coffin, the wild strain, wherever it came from, it flows in me as it flowed in Uncle.

The wind blew hard, threatening the canopy under which the family sat. The man in the dazzling clothes raised a fist to the skies.

"I tell you, ladies and gentlemen," he cried. "This man died of a rare disease! Rare among people of the earth! He died—of bravery!"

The speech moved Harry deeply.

"You have seen an eagle! An eagle shot down from the skies!" the multicolored drunk concluded, and the other gentlemen from Washington applauded, including the nearsighted one who stood over by the withered mimosa tree.

Afterward when the brightly dressed stranger was staggering around on top of the nearby graves, Harry walked over and shook his hand. The man smelled like straight bourbon. He said he was tired, that he had just flown into Corpus Christi on a direct flight from Beirut, a special trip just for this. Then the man made a connection and exclaimed, "Yeah, the *nephew!* Harry! The one in Korea!"

He took Harry over and introduced him to Wild Bill Donovan who was standing under the mimosa with tears in his myopic eyes.

The man was Jim Roy Hoskins, but Harry at that time didn't know what that meant.

Harry borrowed his daddy's new Ford with the Rotary Club emblem affixed to the license plate and drove J. R. Hoskins, Wild Bill, and the others back to their plane in Corpus Christi. J. R. Hoskins gagged and nearly vomited. Wild Bill said, "Okay, son, what can we do for you now? What sort of service you want?"

Both Wild Bill and Hoskins claimed they would stay in touch. Harry felt certain they didn't even know his name, but some two weeks later, sure enough, he received a call from Washington. J. R. Hoskins was from Beaumont, Texas—and, later, of Prague, Paris, Istanbul, Zurich, Alexandria, and other sinister points. Friend of Sam Rayburn, Lyndon Johnson, and other assorted Texans, and once, years before, professor of political science at both Rice Institute and Harvard.

When Harry talked to J. R. Hoskins on the phone the man's voice was sober and very different and Harry answered his question with one word.

"Africa," Harry said, and so it began.

† † †

Leo had a catalog of military medals and placed a nice order twice a year. He also had a favorite jeweler in Bond Street who struck original medals and awards for him. Sometimes Leo found old coins or bits of African hardwood carving or broken animal teeth which he had converted into medals for his men.

He liked giving out medals.

Some of his best men—like Weldu or Mewishi or Hicks—sagged under the weight of many decorations.

They stood at dress parade out in front of the bungalow at Ndola in their chocolate-colored uniforms.

Leo always made a speech.

We're not revolutionaries! We are for sport, the sport of

*fighting, and you men are to understand that I mean this in
an aesthetic way! Because only the aesthetic principle itself
matters—and not even who wins or loses!*

After such ceremonies the men always stood around with
their leader sipping bottles of Simba beer. They kept their
usual respectful silence because, of course, Leo was never
quite finished.

*There are no causes! Fighting is always for itself! Because
it's active, you see, men? It keeps you from becoming terribly
pessimistic and cynical! It rejects all the so-called rational
processes which lead men into despair!*

† † †

In *zamani,* the old times, there were never beggars in
Africa. The tribes were much too proud to let that happen.

But when Val got there old men were everywhere begging.
The villages were dying off. The elders were filing into the
cities, gathering insects off the streets to eat, sleeping in doorways, and instead of smoking the great tribal pipes they wore
metal pipes around their necks, little metal pipes dangling
on pieces of dirty string.

They came up to her outside the hotel in Elisabethville asking for tobacco.

It was the same, she was told, from Nairobi to Lagos, from
Capetown to the Sahara.

† † †

Harry trained in Washington and in various centers in
Virginia and Maryland nearby. He frequently had lunch with
J. R. Hoskins or men who said they represented Allen Dulles.
It became clear that foreign policy had complicated itself out
of existence.

"Ideas are to be mistrusted," J. R. Hoskins told Harry.

"They're just tools by which men manipulate other men, nothing else. And you're certainly right: we don't have any idea what we're doing. But I consider that our strength."

One day they went to the Pentagon and played on the handball courts with some athletic colonels.

The colonels and J. R. Hoskins agreed that the important thing, always, was that America should win.

"Capitalism and free speech. Tennessee whiskey and the oil rig and the goddamned hot dog," J. R. Hoskins said without even the slightest trace of irony.

One of the colonels asked why Harry wanted to work in Africa.

"You go there to take your gut temperature," Harry said, and everybody laughed and laughed.

In the locker room J. R. Hoskins showered, then dressed in a blue-green sports jacket with an orange shirt.

"Know why I dress this way?" he asked Harry. "I dress like a burlesque comedian, but it's practical: I'm recognized all over the world, see, for the clothes. It's finally a kind of disguise. I'm an easy man to double. This very minute there's a man strolling down the Mall in London wearing an orange shirt and a blue-green jacket like this. Another man watches him through binoculars from over in St. James Park and wonders if it's me. In the trade, Harry, I'm known as The Peacock!"

They went to that little red and white kiosk which sits outdoors at the center of the Pentagon and ordered sherbets.

"You understand your mission?" J. R. Hoskins inquired with all earnestness.

"I'm assigned to a UN action team, but under my own authority. There are no definite orders. There are no rules. We have no set policy toward anyone and all treaties are null and void. All contact will remain unwritten."

Harry delivered this like a recitation.

"Very good," said J. R. Hoskins, and he spilled some orange sherbet on his orange shirt.

† † †

In Katanga there were always many truths and lies, but one lasting social fact: Moise Tshombe loved the evenings, those talkative political occasions filled with good food, brandy and cigars, and ornamental European women. He wanted more than anything else to turn that resonant and cultured basso of his on those who attended his nightly entertainments in the mansion.

He wanted to be a man of destiny, as Val observed, but more than that he wanted to wear a tuxedo.

Once, years before, the Belgians had cut off his grand-father's head and displayed it around the province preserved in a jar of paraffin. The grandfather—and all Tshombe's ancestors—were from the fierce Bayeke tribe, and Tshombe's most loyal African admirers felt that true savage blood would eventually win out, that his Oxford education somehow wouldn't hold, and that he would get tired of courting the Belgians, the reporters, the ladies, and minor politicians.

At the party that evening were mining executives, a delegate from General Mobutu who carried his pet monkey, Guy Weber of the Belgian army, two businessmen from South Africa, American and European reporters including Bedford, Bjørn Egge of Sweden who was coordinating mercenary activity, two UN officials, assorted spies and diplomats, Leo with his falcon on his shoulder, and the lovely women of whom Val was loveliest.

Val noticed Leo and his bird early in the evening. He was short, sandy-haired, freckled, muscled, and intense; he wore a chocolate-colored uniform which she liked, but stood at the buffet eating with both hands which put her off. She thought of going over and petting the falcon, but it looked too forbidding so she ended up petting the monkey who belonged to Mobutu's man.

There was considerable stuffy talk about business in Katanga: new mines, new shops, new hotels, and airports.

"Soon Katanga will look like California," said one of the American UN officials with pride.

Moise Tshombe had a little cloth skull cap which he kept putting on top of his head then taking off again. A nervous habit. He listened to the businessmen and diplomats discussing the future of his country, leered at the pretty women, jerked the cap off, popped it back on, and boomed out things in his deepest possible voice.

Matters were so complicated that Tshombe had a right to be nervous. He wanted Katanga independent from the Congo, so he played the old colonial Belgians against the official Congolese government in Leopoldville. There in the capital Adoula and Lumumba and Kasavubu argued and tried to gain control from each other. The U.S.A., ever fearful that Communists might be at work, arranged for a United Nations force to throw out the Belgian army and all foreign elements. This forced Tshombe to hire mercenaries. Lumumba tried to use the UN as his personal political tool. General Mobutu waited and watched—with an army of twelve thousand Congolese regulars loyal only to him. There had been conferences and negotiations. At one of the conferences in Leopoldville Kasavubu had taken Tshombe prisoner, thrown him in jail, treated him oddly well, then released him again. Secret deals had been struck. Elisabethville filled up with photographers, spies, and soldiers of fortune.

"It is my intention to get very drunk tonight," Moise Tshombe told Val as they danced.

A six-piece combo belted out a hip jungle cadence as Val and Tshombe tried the Twist. He was soon out of breath.

General Mobutu's man—the one with the pet monkey—held forth on the country's need for a television station. Someone argued that there were only a few radios in the whole country—usually owned by village chiefs—and virtually no TV sets, but the man insisted that his general wanted TV broadcasting in the Congo.

Bedford was trying to hold a literary discussion about famous African writers with some of the reporters.

Suddenly, Leo was making a speech.

The world has lost its capacities for sharp and vital feeling! People are inebriated and captivated by comforts they neither need nor really want! Technology has given us a century emotionally and spiritually lost, the great instincts dying all around us, awe and courage and romantic love vanishing forever! Men have lost the dream of making themselves legendary! We've lost the knack of character! And character has brutal side effects, yes, but we have to find it or die!

He stood at the buffet with an eclair in his hand. It matched his uniform.

The combo was still banging away and nobody much listened, so Leo wiped the buffet table clean with a swipe of his arm. Roast pig, yams, and the imported delicacies such as caviar and prawns all hit the floor together.

General Mobutu's man, a big black wearing two dull-looking conduct ribbons on his jacket which identified him as some species of military, stepped forward bravely to tell Leo he was being a boor.

Leo's falcon—in one quick, neat move—plucked out the left eye of the pet monkey. The monkey squealed, defecated on its master, and leaped to an overhead light fixture.

Moise Tshombe's laughter boomed around the room.

When the combo didn't stop playing soon enough, Leo went over and grabbed a clarinet away from its owner. He broke it in half over a music stand. Musicians and sheet music scattered.

Guy Weber, the Belgian, touched his pistol, but Egge, the Swede, shot him a glance. Tshombe was still roaring with laughter and some of the guests were trying to find this amusing, too.

Leo's perigrine held the monkey's eye in its beak. The eye seemed to stare out at everyone.

Mobutu's man struggled to remove his soiled jacket.

We need men capable of a radiant evil! Leo continued. *Because the world is in its darkness, its deepest darkness, and only a hideous light can make any difference now! Can you possibly understand that?*

Val's lips were parted in awe.

"Let the man speak," Tshombe generously announced.

The monkey still squealed with pain, his cry forming a high descant behind Leo's words.

You're all merchants and consumers! But only speed and power and great daring will be noticed now! All lessons have to be scars, wounds on the world's fat face, so it can't be indifferent!

Not long after this Bjørn Egge offered Leo a glass of brandy and things began to settle down. Even so, the musicians refused to come back into the room.

"I don't know what to say to you," Val gushed. She spoke like a schoolgirl although she wanted to impress Leo.

"You want to tell me I'm the first real man you've ever met in your life," Leo said with confidence.

Their eyes met.

"I think that may be it," Val laughed.

"Come on," Leo said. "Come away with me."

PART TWO

THE CONGO

ANIMALS,
ANECDOTES,
POLITICS, ENCOUNTERS
SEXUAL AND VIOLENT

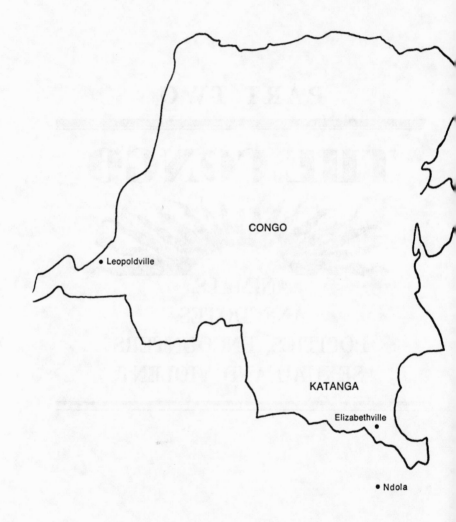

VAL COMMANDEERED THE NDOLA BUNGALOW FOR HER-self and padded around naked inside it day and night. This drove Leo's men wild, but Sergeant Major Hicks, the big whiskey-faced Sandhurst soldier in charge of the force, gave the phenomenon sensible British explanations.

"The av'rage Englishwoman h'aint atall icy like some have it," he said in Val's defense. Or: "Hit's the weather in these tropic parts, lads, nothin' provocative, she's just thick blue-blood!" Or: "Hit's British eccentricity! Just a colonial odd-ment, think of hit that way, lads!"

The men continually claimed to have seen her passing a window. They claimed her breasts were of extraordinary size, the nipples oddly shaped or colored, that there were moles here or there on her, that their wildest fancies applied.

Weldu fell in love and stood on one leg beneath a nearby palm tree watching the bungalow. He consumed all his Sloan's

Liniment in this vigil. Others clustered under the shady porch of the main barracks across the parade ground. They seemed to keep watch in shifts, one group relieving another. Tales of Leo's prowess circulated. Mewishi, the Commander's personal valet, was besieged with questions each time he crossed to the supply store or left the bungalow to fetch Leo's car. Yes, he had seen the mistress naked. No, she didn't seem to wear clothes much. When he explained that he was from a tribe where the women were always naked, the others were furious with him because he was indifferent to the obsession of the camp.

One day Mewishi hung his mistress's undergarments across the bamboo railing of the bungalow porch. Fist fights broke out in the noon mess.

Another day Leo stayed in the bungalow until late afternoon. The men wandered around sick with envy.

The inlaid desk arrived. It was carried from the railway line by sad-faced porters wearing bright red *kangas*.

Then one night the Belgian—the same one who had fought with Leo back in Kenya and who had never been promoted or given a medal because he was a nuisance and a drunk—shot himself while sitting on his bunk. His suicide was discussed at great length. It was agreed that the man had many problems and that Val's presence was only a small part of them all.

† † †

The old Bantu culture flourished between the headwaters of the Congo and Zambezi rivers as far back as the European Dark Ages. The race mined and traded in copper and spread its wealthy influence east and west to both coasts and all the way down to Capetown. The region became known as Katanga and by the time of Moise Tshombe it was richer than ever and still coveted by every foreigner who saw it.

Leo's Ndola ranch was just south across the border. When he went to work for Tshombe he had the advantage of being able to take his Elite Rifles over to Elisabethville, then, if necessary, scurry back to safety in a neutral territory. Usually, though, his entourage stayed at the old Rex Hotel. He wore his best chocolate uniform to various conferences, his men drank and ate and whored, Val went shopping for supplies and became—with Mewishi—the unofficial quartermaster. Then they would suddenly jump in the Land Rovers and head north. There would be a show of strength at some bridge up there or perhaps a skirmish, then they'd come back to the city to the same bars and brothels, leave again for other brief assignments, return to the ranch once more, come back to the Rex Hotel.

Weeks of this. Sergeant Major Hicks recruited seven new men. Paydays were regular and there were bonuses and medals. Leo bought Val a beautiful yellow dress with matching bracelet which all the men liked. She occasionally talked to the men now and they adored her. Even so, she was very different—as exotic as one of the Commander's speeches—and they kept a respectful distance.

Twice she went with them north on assignments, but usually she stayed at the hotel with Mewishi. It was during one of these periods when Leo and the men were gone north that a soldier of fortune calling himself Butler checked into the Rex. Butler was the *nom de guerre* of Harry Veer.

By this time Val knew her strange self-truth: sexuality was her doom and destiny, the energy by which she would stand herself against a pale and bewildered world, the force by which she would deal with men. Leo—who was intellectually stim-

ulating and nearly impotent sexually—had given her an exciting base of operations. The Elite Rifles were somehow charged
by her presence. The jungle spoke directly to her.

One night she came down to dinner. Mewishi stood behind
her, fronds of a nearby potted palm drooping over his
shoulder. He wore a .38 Special in a shoulder holster under
his tunic and she wore the yellow dress and bracelet.

Two or three tables away sat Harry. They faced each other
over the soup, the fish course, the entree, and occasionally
their eyes lingered into wanton public display. She was the
most beautiful woman ever to gaze on Harry in this way. To
Val, Harry looked like a caged cat.

She spoke to Mewishi as she rose to leave the dining room
and, in turn, Mewishi came over to Harry and presented him
the key to Val's room wrapped in the folds of her dinner
napkin. There was a bare trace of ocher lipstick on a corner
of the cloth.

Later, the bolt rattled and the door to Val's room swung
open.

Harry stood in the doorway and surveyed the darkened
room. As his eyes grew accustomed to the pale moonlight he
saw Val sitting cross-legged on the bed combing out her hair
in long slow strokes. She was like a lioness grooming.

Slowly, too, he took off his clothes. He stepped into the
moonlit spill of the window so she could watch and when he
was naked before her, hair and muscle and thick erection, he
began to fasten the claws to his fingers. Silvered talons for
each finger, worn like rings: he displayed his hand in the
moonglow and it flashed like deadly electricity.

Two days later Leo and the Elite Rifles returned from
bivouac in Northern Katanga.

"How's your mistress?" Leo asked Mewishi in the hotel parking lot.

"She has been with a stranger the last days," Mewishi answered.

"Oh? What are they talking about?"

"Commander," said Mewishi with reluctance, "I don't think they have yet spoken a word."

Leo sent word to Val's room that he had returned and that evening when no answer had come back he dined alone.

Mewishi gave the Commander the name on the hotel register: Butler. Sergeant Major Hicks and another were dispatched to search Butler's room as Leo finished dinner, but came back with no additional information. Leo took a third glass of wine and wore a blank face.

Before midnight Harry emerged from Val's room and went down the creaking corridor. The slow ceiling fans above his head beat a steady rhythm as he walked. Danger was in the hotel like a stench.

Two volunteers waited in Harry's room. One was a big corporal named Gandiri who fancied himself expert with a dagger. The other was Weldu, who felt strongly about another man in Val's life. Their plan was simple in the extreme: they would quietly murder this intruder and drop his body out of the window into the Land Rover. Since they assumed that the man who would walk through that door would be a docile civilian, they waited in the dark without much precaution or fear. Even Weldu, who had little stomach for combat, napped casually behind the door.

However, Harry didn't exactly stroll in.

The door flew open—his approach had been silent—and Harry bounded into the center of the room to one side of the yellow slant of light coming from the hallway. As Gandiri lurched forward, Harry disarmed him in a single—almost gentle—move. Weldu stumbled up to assist. Then Harry showed his clawed hand. Weldu's mouth and eyes popped wide open and a tiny cry of terror came from deep inside him. With little hesitation, Weldu skipped to the window and jumped out toward the Land Rover two floors below. He landed on it only partially, then fell to the ground where he broke his leg—the one he usually stood on.

Gandiri thumped down the corridor toward the stairwell. He made a strange sound because a good part of his throat was missing.

Harry straightened things, took a shower, changed clothes. He kept his Astra-Constable automatic pistol beside him through all this. Then he packed his bags and went back to Val's room and moved in with her.

† † †

The morning after all this Leo went to the city market. He visited the stall of a Dutch cloth merchant who also happened to be the best falconer in the region. Leo traded his clever little merlin—he had to kick in a few large rand notes —for a beautiful white Greenland falcon named Dorothy.

Then he went to a café and drank several strong espressos. Sitting at that table near the window where he could watch the pedestrian life of Elisabethville flow by, he wrote out his rules for falconry. His birds were always female, those being the larger and tougher of the species, and females needed rules, Leo told himself, many special rules and regulations.

—never overfly her and tire her out
—remember to treat her with extreme courtesy
—never exhibit her among strangers

—assist her in killing her quarry, so she will realize you are in the game with her

—never return her stare and if she stares at you turn your face away until her mood improves

—never give your attention and training to more than one falcon at a time

Leo sat there drinking coffee remembering all the falcons he had owned. He had a lovely Black Shaheen from India once. And of course several good perigrines. And the little merlin.

His new bird, Dorothy, sat quietly on the leather pad on his left shoulder, her hood in place over her head. Her feathers shone.

I have the true look and bearing of a falconer, Leo told himself. I will keep you forever. I will feed you only fresh lean beefsteak soaked in warm water.

† † †

The big corporal, Gandiri, recovered in a hospital in Lusaka, but never rejoined the Rifles nor was heard of again. Weldu was treated by Tshombe's personal physician. The morning after the incident Val appeared at breakfast on Harry's arm, and Leo, resourceful as ever, went over and joined them, ordering eggs and chips.

"Your name isn't Butler," he began. "It's Harry Veer and you might work for the UN, but the CIA's more likely. You have a high rank in one or both because best I can discover you're your own boss. My men think you're either the devil or a member of the Leopard Cult."

"Sit right down," Harry said politely after the fact.

"Are you spying on me or do you just fancy my woman?"

"I'm nobody's woman," Val interjected.

"My country doesn't really care what goes on here just as long as there aren't any Communists lurking around," Harry said. "You're not Commie, are you?"

"No, not us," Leo said with a smile.

"Well, the other thing is Val. She stays with me."

Harry attended to his omelet. Val watched Leo squirm. Mewishi stood back there against the potted palm listening.

"Why don't you both come back to the ranch with me?" Leo offered. "Then I wouldn't lose face with my troops and I'd have the pleasure of your company."

"Why should I?" Harry asked. He tilted his plate and finished its contents.

"Because I can offer your sort of diversions," Leo answered.

"What *are* your diversions?" Val asked Harry.

"Oh, fighting," he said simply. "I'm good at it."

A day later they packed up the Land Rovers and lorries and bumped back down the muddy roads toward the ranch. Val and Harry took the bungalow and Leo moved into the small apartment above the quartermaster's store. It was a cramped two rooms, especially after Leo moved many of his books there.

Late each morning Leo strolled across the parade grounds to the bungalow, rapped on the door, and took his place in the office just behind the shuttered windows of the porch where the usual paper work required his attention.

Sergeant Major Hicks tried to account for this new arrangement to the disgruntled men.

"England's an island, see, lads, and cut off from normal commerce and such. A weird distant land. And hits men and women 'ave always been bored and played games as far back as bloody Camelot!"

The Elite Rifles were unhappy with such explanations until

Mewishi—who knew such things—confirmed that Val was pregnant. The men quickly calculated that this was Leo's good work and therefore whatever odd arrangement the commander desired was beyond question.

Life at the ranch soon drifted into regularity. Weldu returned. Dorothy, the falcon, was much admired. A rumor began that Leo would be given an airplane. Harry was given a wide berth. The men often gazed at the windows to the bungalow, still hoping Val might pass into view.

Then a call to arms came.

One morning they all started back to Elisabethville again with cooks, demolition team, infantry, armor, and every aspect of a long encounter. One of the lorries carried Val's inlaid desk. The men noted that Val sat between her two men in Leo's lorry and that the three of them laughed and touched each other.

That night they stopped and made camp en route and Leo gave Harry an expensive new Mauser-Bauer rifle and the honorary rank of colonel. At the campfire the men stood at attention, Leo and Harry shook hands, and the commander made another confusing speech. Among other things said was *just as a woman uses love to express violence, so the soldier uses violence to express love!*

The men didn't understand the speech, but felt happy around the fire. Proximity to Val was a bonus. And Harry moved among them like a savage force.

† † †

Ian Smith and Roy Welensky were different types, but both men agreed Leo should have an airplane. They held an afternoon social and business meeting in the city of Salisbury and among other matters discussed this. At all costs, they agreed, African nations run by blacks should be disrupted and mercenaries with airplanes could cause considerable disruption. But Ian Smith wanted to provide a jet fighter and Roy Welensky wanted to donate a sensible cargo plane which would deliver a whole battalion of men and equipment at once.

"A fighter plane could strafe," Ian Smith argued. "Besides, the jet makes a hell of a wonderful noise to scare shit out of the Wogs!"

"But a cargo plane could drop parachutes!" Welensky retorted. "Think of thousands of parachutes floating down on the bloody jungle!"

"They'd hang in tall trees," Ian Smith countered.

"A jet would fly so fast the jungle would just be a blur," Welensky added.

They began to shout.

Ian Smith's thin nose began to bleed in the excitement. He kept his reserve, stretching out on the sofa, dropping his head off the edge, and stuffing Kleenex up both nostrils.

"Sorry," Welensky managed.

Ian Smith lay there thinking of his favorite historical figure, Cecil Rhodes. The tycoon after whom his country was named.

Welensky, who was once a boxer in university, paced around the room shadow boxing.

Soon the Kleenex hung down from Ian Smith's nostrils like red ribbons.

† † †

On the outskirts of Elisabethville there is a series of small truck farms: squares of tilled land crisscrossed by muddy roads at whose intersections are clusters of mud huts and shops. At one such isolated intersection Leo's patrol arrived. The mud building was a Texaco service station, a single gas pump out front. A large red, white, and blue sign adorned the face of the hut reading PEPSI. On the bench below it sat a large calabash of native yams.

As the Land Rover approached, a boy ran out into the road waving his arms. He wore a pith helmet several sizes too large for his little black head and carried an old Army issue .45 pistol.

Leo and Hicks got out of the Land Rover and conversed with the boy in a language Harry couldn't understand. The conversation grew animated and they went inside the station, so Harry checked his gear: his lightweight magnum pistol, his vintage grenade, the wire garrotte, the small dirk taped to his boot, his rounds of ammunition, and the Mauser-Bauer. He half hoped that a lorry filled with Adoula's regulars or a UN platoon or whoever was supposed to be marauding in the neighborhood would wheel around the corner of that field nearby. The morning was hot and indolent. Standing there at the Land Rover, Harry could hear only the buzzing of flies and the muted voices of Leo, Hicks, and the boy still carrying on inside the station.

Leo finally came out and explained. "There are three kids in there with five prisoners," he said. "This morning the sergeant leading this scouting party of kids got killed and somehow the kids got the drop on a whole bloody platoon of marauders. But they haven't been doing so well. The prisoners lured one kid into the back room and killed him. So it's touch and go, the kids in there with their guns trained on the door. A standoff. The prisoners won't come out and the kids are afraid others might arrive."

There followed a discussion of possibilities.

Harry said he would stay with the kids until Leo and Hicks went for help. He pointed out that he possessed a UN arm band—which might be of some use. He would have the mud building as protection.

"The Land Rover needs more protection than these prisoners," Harry said finally. "Take everyone with you and don't worry about me."

"We'll hurry right back," Leo promised.

Harry watched the Land Rover disappear, then went inside the mud building and into his first assignment in Katanga.

Inside was a crude bar: a rickety table with cases of warm beer stacked behind it. The prisoners were in a back room behind a heavy wooden door. The three boys—weighted down with their M-1s and .45s—spoke no English, so Harry settled down with a bottle of Simba beer.

Eventually the boys acted out their morning episode. They pantomimed the ambush, showed how their sergeant got picked off as he ran among them trying to tell them what to do, and explained how they flanked the marauders. The leader of the three, the one in the pith helmet, even managed to convey what had happened to their unfortunate comrade: the prisoners had grabbed him, pulled him into the back room, and slit his throat. The boys had obviously taken the prisoners' rifles, Harry discerned, but had been too small and timid to shake them down for knives.

The flies still buzzed around. After a half hour the boys began to feel more at ease with Harry present, so opened beers for themselves.

The hut reminded Harry of all those dirty roadside service stations and general stores on the outskirts of red clay towns in, say, Oklahoma, with tires stacked up outside, thick grease spots on the ground, and the dung of farmers inside. Somewhere, he mused, there might be a real war going on: grown men, at least, with uniforms and strategies.

The little black soldiers watched him. He reckoned their ages at no more than fourteen.

War is personal, Harry deliberated. Years away from all this one might pick out the grand designs, one might determine that the Congo was part of a so-called Third World, one might regard the ironies of the career of Moise Tshombe, one might watch the fabric of history knit together with all its lies and manufacturings.

Harry, whose mind was stubbornly active and seldom reflective, might have imagined that in time the city of Elisabethville would be called Lubumbashi, the Congo would be called Zaire, Katanga would no longer bear its name, that the statistics of history would have swallowed up all the traces. Future journalists, he might have imagined, would concoct, in general, fair play: a colonel on a hillside, say, with binoculars, mercenaries who came only for money, little black boys in pith helmets hiding behind their mamas' skirts. Few would imagine battles in hotel corridors or goat pens or tiny mud buildings in the suburbs where one disorganized patrol found another.

Harry felt his fevered shadows grow close. He didn't speculate on history. War was a spiritual state and Harry took its encounters personally.

In time he grew angry with those prisoners in the back room. They had murdered one of his little comrades.

Although he was not very good with languages, Harry tried cursing them in French, Spanish, and English. He stood at the closed door shouting obscenities until his little companions, getting into the spirit of things, let fly with a few Bantu epithets.

The boy in the pith helmet—who was full of beer—pissed on the door and this performance was regarded with hilarity. The other two boys laughed so hard they forgot their rifles and duty.

Suddenly the door flew open and the prisoners inside tossed out their victim, the smallest of those small black soldiers. Everyone's laughter choked into silence when his mutilated body hurtled out and fell with a thump.

"Come out of there!" Harry heard himself screaming.

The door had been flung wide, so Harry and the boys could see the black maw inside: no lights, a nothingness, only the sound of the prisoners' breathing.

"Get your asses *out* here!" Harry yelled like a drill sergeant. But there was no response. The boys surrounding him didn't understand exactly what he wanted, but they leveled their rifles at the door and tried not to look at the corpse of their friend.

A chair came sailing through the door and narrowly missed Harry's head. "I mean it!" he yelled.

When they wouldn't present themselves, Harry took out his grenade, pulled the pin, tossed it in there with them, slammed the door and shot the bolt. For a moment he and the boys stared wide-eyed at the bolted door; it was going to be awful in that windowless, solid black room, they knew, and dangerous where they stood. So they ran outside and put their fingers in their ears.

When the grenade went off—a single deep bump of a noise—one wall of the mud building blew out and another caved in. Harry and the boys watched without expression.

Beer bottles and glass everywhere. One of the black soldiers from the back room, his clothes in rags, staggered through the rubble, then collapsed.

Harry went across the road, slumped down underneath a euphorbia tree, and the boys came over and sat around him in a circle. They studied his blank face. The flies buzzed and a soft noon breeze came up and blew away the smoke hovering over the remains of the mud building.

Before long Leo and Val arrived in a jeep. The Land Rover had been sent to another assignment and there were things to do.

"Come on, man, don't sit there like that," Leo admonished Harry, so Harry got up and went with them. They drove back toward the city, the long narrow highway overhung with a deep foliage of trees, and Val and Leo made conversation, saying, see, the old Trans-African road, Harry, it goes from Algiers to the Cape and we're on a stretch of it here, it takes on the character of all the cities and villages it penetrates, then it goes out there onto the raw savannah and into the hills again.

Val held Harry's hand.

"Don't worry about it," Leo told Harry. "You did wonderfully. I'm going to strike a special medal for you and throw a party! Would you like that?"

They drove down a long corridor of trees, passing lean-to shops, mud huts, pedestrians, old buses filled with workers. The bustle of the city seemed normal.

"Would you wear a nice medal if I presented you one?" Leo asked gently and Harry nodded yes.

† † †

The sad elephant.

The Syrians used elephants in battle as far back as the time when Darius fought Alexander.

Ptolemy II had elephants shipped up and down the Nile and both the Egyptians and the Carthaginians used them.

The Balearic Islands got their name from the Greek word *ballein,* to throw, because there were expert slingers who joined Hannibal when he passed through. The slingers became a special unit in his army and rode elephants.

When confused, elephants tend to walk in circles.

A bull elephant after the birth of its young will come take a good sniff, making sure it is his baby, then file away that scent forever so it will never forget.

After much experience in battle, Hannibal removed his slingers from the backs of elephants and imported special Indian drivers. When an elephant became temperamental in battle and began doing damage to its own side, the Indian drivers were armed with little chisels and mallets with which they killed the beasts.

All this once again in Val's notes.

†   †   †

Val became Leo's press secretary and the foreign correspondents adored her. A German photographer for *Der Stern* presented her with an uncut diamond which she in turn gave to Mewishi who traded it for groceries for the Elite Rifles. An aged editor for *Newsweek* sent up a note saying he had returned his mistress to America and was pledging his devotion. Bedford of *The Times* hung out in the lobby of the Rex hoping for some official reason to say hello.

Val wrote a nice press release glorifying the mercenary life.

It revealed that mercenaries had once fought for a pope, help-ing him to regain his holy throne.

Harry was also writing, sending out weekly reports—as cryptic as the entries in his little diary—to both his UN bosses and American intelligence, saying, yes, things are fine, I'm getting leads on military activities and I've been lucky enough to infiltrate this odd little private army. His reports—as a courtesy he showed them to Leo—were answered with packets of information delivered by courier to the hotel every morn-ing. They came in brown wrappers, like pornography. Val, Leo, and Harry sometimes sat around in the evenings play-ing cards, drinking gin coolers, and reading over the packets.

Every night Val and Harry yawned and looked at each other and went off to bed together. Leo's consolation for being left alone was that Val was pregnant with his child. After they retired Leo sometimes played solitaire or read the amusing packets. The material was mimeographed and marked in red SECRET or TOP SECRET and always contained such esoteric information as the recent baseball scores in America.

Leo discovered that the mimeograph paper was highly flam-mable. For quick disposal in the event of emergency, he de-cided. Late one night he made two neat scientific piles: one of the CIA mimeograph paper and one of hotel toilet tissue. Sure enough, the mimeograph secrets went up in a puff and the poor-grade toilet tissue—noisy when wadded up—would hardly burn.

Leo sat pondering this in his room. Before him were the two piles of ashes on his desk and in some profound way all this seemed a measure of western technology.

All African tissue is rough on the bum, Leo allowed, but I'm a generous man, fair, and I credit this marvel to Yankee ingenuity.

† † †

Weldu was left alone in charge of the ranch at Ndola because arthritis developed in his recently broken leg. In the absence of the other men he became restless. He especially missed Val and in his heart knew that Leo had ordered him left behind because he was so transparently lovesick.

On moonlit nights he walked slowly around the perimeter of the compound. He heard—or thought he heard—the faraway keening of jackals or perhaps the pygmies deep in the forest. Pygmies, he knew, were mad and sang to the trees.

Weldu also remembered things: his father the witch doctor, a rainbow in the mountains, the way Val's shirt always missed a strategic button. He had a good memory—all his life pain had summoned up recollection—and a sixth sense. The sixth sense was a small inheritance from his gifted father. When the commander was off on an assignment Weldu could sense his return. Once, he ordered Mewishi to prepare the evening stew for an additional fifty and Leo and the Elite Rifles arrived without notice just in time for supper.

Weldu wandered in the moonlight, stood on his throbbing leg, and listened to the forest. He strained to recall his past, heard the mysterious noises of the moment, and conjured visions of the future. He did everything possible not to think of Harry Veer.

† † †

Everyone gathered in the ramshackle ballroom of the Rex Hotel for a ceremony. Some potted plants were brought up from the dining room, paper streamers were hung, and Leo had three kegs of Carlsberg beer flown up from Lusaka.

"For the bravest of the brave," Leo announced, and he

hung the medal around Harry's neck. No one really understood.

The medal was an antique Roman coin set in silver, very nice. Harry turned it in the light as he inspected it.

The Elite Rifles drank the kegs dry and got into the gin ration, but Leo didn't complain. Instead, he stood on the stage—there was no orchestra, only a dilapidated Wurlitzer jukebox—and made a speech.

Men's loyalties will eventually gravitate to the big corporations, and governments as we know them, men, if they continue to exist at all, might become minor regulatory agencies —courts of arbitration in which the corporations work out their areas of disagreement.

The men poured gin. Val stood beside Harry and looked at the medal.

War of sorts—clandestine business—will go on. But men won't be as emotional about products and companies as they've been about their tribes and homelands in the past.

Sergeant Major Hicks chewed his fingernails. Only Mewishi stood at rigid attention and listened.

Our kind might eventually become obsolete, but make no mistake about it now, men: we're not a vanished breed yet! There are new nations emerging, guerrilla wars, protest movements! The old warrior is still very much needed!

War is still the great education in reality, the way things really are! The children, the professors and priests need to know that! They nourish a lot of vague hopes about man's good soul! But there's no civilization yet, it isn't here! It may eventually come, I'm not saying it won't, lads, but, ah, we're still in the reign of terror!

The men raised their empty glasses and mumbled a salute.

A burly female photographer from *Paris-Match* took a

photo of Val, Leo, and Harry standing among the streamers.

Sergeant Major Hicks, drunk and pleasant, wanted to discuss the nature of courage with Harry, but Harry answered, "Sorry, I don't talk about myself in that way." This refusal impressed Hicks well enough.

† † †

It was arranged that Leo's Elite Rifles would go on patrol for a month in the northern part of the region. Preparations were made and Val, who showed not the slightest bulge, argued that she was going. Weldu returned from Ndola with a pet cobra—the only thing he could devise to impress the mistress. Everyone was excited to be off to the bush and somehow oddly confident with Harry along.

Weldu's cobra intimidated the entire troop—as he hoped it would—and when they got to their first bivouac he kept dumping it out of its basket. It hit the ground with a thump, slithered toward some unnerved soldier, then stopped and coiled—sort of like spin-the-bottle with everybody hooting and jumping. Mewishi got caught in the stampede one afternoon as he was carrying a big calabash of stew from the fire, and supper sloshed out on the ground. Everyone got short rations that night and Leo warned Weldu to stop, but Weldu couldn't. He had seen Val's amusement with his antics.

The next night at supper Weldu's cobra hit the ground just as everyone sat down to eat. Leo appeared with Dorothy on his shoulder, a fierce authority about him, the sort he hadn't displayed since Harry's arrival. Plates of food rose in the air as the men scattered, then Dorothy's hood was off and her eyes fastened on the snake. Leo had opened her hood and had thrust his shoulder forward slightly, so the first thing the bird had seen was its quarry. It swooped down on the cobra, dropping on it like a falling rock, and with a couple of wingbeats the snake was airborne, plucked away like a straw. The men watched, mesmerized, as Dorothy climbed and circled, higher and higher. This was the first time Leo had ever loosed her to hunt since buying her in Elisabethville and he talked to her under his breath as she rose above the clearing, saying, there, there now, do it, dear. Then the cobra dropped. The men scattered again, Weldu too, but no need, it fell in two pieces, one end of it slapping onto the hood of the half-track. By the time the men edged back into the area Dorothy was perched on Leo's shoulder once more.

Leo punished Weldu further with a fixed stare.

Mewishi took the cobra's head and stuck it on the antenna of the commander's jeep, venom still in its fangs. It looked tough, Harry said.

And so the games began.

Val slept with Harry in the back of a lorry and Leo claimed this was embarrassing.

"How's that?" Harry asked.

"This isn't like the ranch or the hotel," Leo claimed.

The Commander, Val, and Harry were eating at a card table set up in the clearing like white hunters on safari: real silverware, mosquito netting, the works. Val smiled into her plate of hash.

"And it isn't good for morale!" Leo snapped.

"Whose morale?" Harry inquired.

"It's—undermining authority," Leo kept on.

"I suppose I could sleep with Weldu, too," Val said, not without cruelty.

Harry paid elaborate attention to his food.

"To make it democratic," she added, "I could pass myself around."

"Don't be a slut," Harry put in.

The argument raged after this, not very well defined.

Every day Leo and Harry took separate platoons and competed, risking men and machines in the bush. Men were led under waterfalls, into mangrove swamps, through thorn fields, and generally abused. Once or twice they ran onto enemy patrols—or facsimiles. Nothing was sure. UN scouts, some of Mobutu's regulars, Lumumbists, Belgians: somebody out there was the enemy and it was Leo's job to see that no major buildup occurred in the northern sector. And there were games within games. Sergeant Major Hicks claimed there was an Irish platoon somewhere out there using Gaelic as code on the radio. Leo offered a bounty on anyone bagging an international reporter or correspondent. Harry ordered himself a new 9mm handcrafted in Brussels and entertained everyone by shooting through trees into targets.

At night they came back to camp where Val—so it seemed—was the scorekeeper in all this. She loved such theatrics and competition and considered—rightfully—they were for her.

One day they took a prisoner who wore a uniform of assorted parts: World War I English doughboy helmet, khaki kilt, big army brogans (USMC issue), voodoo necklace, homemade gun belt.

Sergeant Major Hicks and Weldu decided to interrogate him.

"What exactly do you men want to find out?" Harry asked with a smile. "You want to find out who's out there and where? The answer's simple: everybody's out there and they're all around us! That's what he'll tell you even if you torture him!"

"Always question prisoners of war," Hicks said, as if reading from a manual.

But the man wouldn't even give his name. He was too

frightened of being mutilated—for Leo's old reputation in Kenya had obviously grown with exaggerations over the years. They twisted the prisoner's arm a bit, offered him cigarettes, and offered him the rank of corporal, in turn, but he wouldn't say a word. Sometimes he made a sound—a noise which Leo took to be part of the ancient African click speech—but that mainly in response to pressure. He was an ebony midget under five feet tall. Harry noticed that his odd khaki kilt had a bullet hole in it right over the genitals. The prisoner's hands shook all the time.

Late that afternoon they zipped him into Leo's tent with Dorothy. A magic bird, Weldu assured him; look into her eyes and she'll turn you into a ghost. Before long the prisoner began to sob and wail. The men drew back a flap and looked inside. There he sat on his haunches, eyes clamped tight, not moving a muscle. When the men brought him out of the tent after supper they checked his mouth—just to make sure he had a tongue inside.

Harry decided to take a turn himself.

He spoke through a Bantu interpreter—they still didn't know if the prisoner understood—and told him that Weldu always turned into a leopard with the moonrise. Harry made up a blend of Congolese folk legend and old werewolf movies he could recall. He rips the throats out of his victims, this Weldu, Harry whispered hoarsely, and only a silver bullet fired by an old gypsy can stop him. Harry fitted his silver claws onto Weldu's fingers—to Weldu's great pleasure and the great discomfort of the prisoner. Then Hicks brought some spoor he had seen earlier in the day. Weldu sat down on a bucket, snarled and grunted, splayed his taloned fingers wide, grimaced, bared his teeth, then showed the prisoner the result inside the bucket.

"See!" Harry boomed. "Leopard shit! There!"

The prisoner stared into the bucket, turned pale, gagged, and almost fainted. But he still wouldn't talk—or couldn't—so Weldu took his shoes from him and chased him into the bush.

" 'At 'un's a city boy," Hicks noted. " 'An ee's gonna 'ave a mean time of it out there in the bloody jungle tonight!"

Weldu wore the claws until Leo made him put them away and after this Weldu's regard for Harry altered.

† † †

When the hostilities began in Katanga, Major Mobutu was twenty-nine years old, hard in the gut, and was seen frequently at various government offices around Leopoldville trying to find out what was going on. When he discovered that no one really understood what was happening he promoted himself to colonel.

He also heard of Leo's exciting Elite Rifles and the beautiful Englishwoman who served as press agent, so began to copy some of Leo's style for himself.

He put on weight and hired a speech writer. He enjoyed giving audiences and making speeches, so he rented an abandoned movie house in the center of the capital city for those purposes. In time he met Antoine Gizenga, who was vice-premier and Lumumba's lieutenant and who had never before given him any attention. He also met a Belgian minister, a crazily dressed American who called himself The Peacock, and a native girl known as Rena the Jungle Bunny.

His worst moment came when his representative, one who had gone to Elisabethville to reason with Moise Tshombe, returned to him in tears.

"Be a man," Mobutu scolded him. "Dry your face!"

"A man's hawk ate my monkey's eye!" the representative wept.

Mobutu smirked. The next day he sent one of his trusted majors out to buy a falcon, but the major reported there were no falcons in Leopoldville—only parrots. That is how General Mobutu, head of the great army of the Congo, managed to get a caged parrot in his entourage.

As for Rena the Jungle Bunny, her career was only beginning. After a single night with Colonel Mobutu she fled to take up a profession as a camp follower. She had a lovely raised tattoo on her belly which made her famous: a likeness of the phoenix emerging from the hair of her crotch. This became a matter of debate and discussion among the more educated soldiers and mercenaries; they wondered how such a simple native girl came by such a sophisticated literary symbol.

† † †

While they were in the northern region on patrol they cooked in heavy pieces of tarpaulin coated on the insides with plastic and set on tripods: these odd pieces of gear became home and Harry liked to stand over them staring into their boiling contents. He felt very comfortable looking in at the potatoes or carrots or those giant edible tubers which formed the main part of the native diet. Leo's tent stood nearby. The card tables and netting. Val in the glow of the lanterns with her pencil behind her ear. After the day's competitions and after dinner they played games by the pale camp lights; they went at Scrabble (Harry always got a *Q* without a *U,* so couldn't make a word) and various card games. Harry knew a few tricks with the deck including the Shooting of Dan McGrew, which Val loved, and clever Leo told the history of card games and recited the names of the sovereigns who adorned the face cards.

Harry began to worry in his happiness, afraid that it might go away. He became protective of Val as her stomach began to protrude. He enjoyed Leo who was competitive and articulate. And the evenings were wonderful out in the bush. Yet there was risk: half an army might suddenly roar out at them, might rape Val, might make a drum out of Leo's ample skin. Time, he knew, might be against them, and such rare pleasant interludes might quickly become memory and pain.

He stood out beside those tarps in the evenings, smelling the good food, hearing friendly voices, nightsounds out there beyond the glow of their campfire, the forest creaking and whispering. He felt rapport with the night and with the fierce nature surrounding them and with these two people. It was the first real rapport with anyone or any place Harry had ever known.

† † †

Dag Hammarskjöld's office on the thirty-eighth floor of the UN building was decorated with Danish modern furniture and austere Nordic appointments, but there were a few telltale African items, too: a carved shield on the wall, a primitive ivory sculpture on the writing desk, a leopard-skin rug.

A spiritual man, a poet, a friend of the arts, smooth as an egg, Dag Hammarskjöld: the Secretary-General who relied on logic, fairness, and the integrity of language properly used. But there were those tokens of the dark.

One day the American diplomat came visiting. Dag supposed he would like this man: an intelligent, gentle, educated type with a smile like a Roosevelt. They sat down to discuss the Congo. The Secretary-General shared some cheese which had been given to him by Greta Garbo and some wine which had been a gift from a pal in the Stockholm foreign office. Dag was like this: his acquaintances invariably wanted to give him things.

For a while the two cultured men talked books. They had both read Toynbee and shared a noble historical perspective, as though time was a great pageant on which all men large and small imposed their own myths.

"Now what we want to do in regard to the Katanga situation is simple," the diplomat said toward the end of their visit. There was a soft light in the room: the last dying rays of sunset high over New York City. The wine bottle stood empty. "We will sell weapons to Leopoldville and Spaak in Belgium will sell weapons to Elisabethville. Let there be business as usual."

The diplomat's soft voice bore the modulations of reason, yet Dag sat listening with a growing unease. He listened for a long time, until the room grew dark and there was only the American's Ivy League accent going like music in one corner of his consciousness. "Markets," the voice said. "Balance of power. Politics forever."

That night after the diplomat had gone Dag went to his writing desk and lit a simple candle. The African objects in his room shimmered in its pale glow and the Secretary-General felt a deep tremor: down inside he knew the world wasn't at all like his soul, not at peace, not logical or fair. He fumbled in his desk and removed the current issue of *Newsweek*. It was folded to a photo of Val standing beside a Land Rover, her thumbs tucked into the belt loops of her jeans, her breasts prominent beneath the open shirt, her lips moist. Dag Hammarskjöld peered deep into her eyes. All the zany terrors he had ever imagined were there. Death and sexual madness. The primeval mud-and-blood idiocy.

The Secretary-General rocked back and forth in his chair in the eerie candleglow. Clutching Val's wild image to his chest he hummed a tuneless sound; spittle ran down his chin, his eyes rolled back, his body yearned, his brain caught fire.

† † †

Harry sat outside another ramshackle bar/service station in a small mining town in Northern Katanga breaking down an old motorcycle into all its greasy parts. A broken gearbox spring, that was the trouble, and Harry sat there on the warm packed dirt, his concentration complete, as around him lay the entrails of the machine: main shaft, gudgeon pin, manifold, condenser, flywheel magneto, sprocket, all his tools and a pan of grease.

He was enjoying himself. As the weeks had gone on, the Elite Rifles had mostly concerned themselves with protecting Tshombe's bridges around these towns from which most of the region's wealth flowed. The work had been hard. Everybody was dirty and restless. There had been little combat, but there was always work: quartermaster jobs, repairs, transportation worries, ordnance problems. Harry took interest in all these; better to stay busy, he felt. Leo had his heavy thoughts, Val had her desk, and so on.

He used to be pathologically clumsy—or remembered himself that way—and if he had natural rhythms, as Leo attributed to him, they were a long time developing. Just as Val wasn't beautiful until her later years, Harry's fingers and feet just didn't work for a while. He had his growth early, so knocked over end tables, tripped on rugs, and spilled lots of food in his lap. Then dexterity came like a gift. He could sit there now with all those greasy parts, stare into them like an augur watching signs, and it was a game, just another of the many games he enjoyed playing every day.

Mewishi came over and offered to help, but Harry grinned and said, "Naw, you'd just get yourself all black."

To which Mewishi offered a smile, a big torch of white teeth.

"Do you have a rank, Mewishi?" Harry asked.

"Why, sir, yes, I'm a corporal!"

Harry asked Mewishi to outline the various ranks of the Elite Rifles and it turned out there were no privates. Everyone was a corporal except for Hicks, the Sergeant Major, Leo, and Harry.

"Sergeant Major believes you may be the bravest man he has ever met," Mewishi divulged.

Harry sat back and regarded the poor old motorcycle. Forlorn thing, split in two parts like a good horse cut in half.

"Tell me about Weldu," Harry suggested. "Does he still resent me?"

"Oh, no sir, he admires you very much."

"Truthfully?"

"He considers apologizing for attacking you in the hotel that time," Mewishi revealed. "Especially since his leg still aches. He imagines you may still be working a little juju on him."

"He thinks I have that sort of power?"

"He isn't sure, sir, no, he isn't."

"Okay, tell me about the mistress," Harry said. "Would you die to protect her?"

"The Commander asks me the same, sir, and, oh, yessir, it would cost my honor if I failed to fight! But my honor is also to serve at menial things! The Commander explains that no duty is without importance!"

"Right," Harry confirmed. "Not even motorcycles."

Mewishi nodded and his teeth lit up in another grin.

"And are you the Commander's personal bodyguard, too?" Harry inquired.

"Oh, yessir. The Commander's a curious white gentleman, you see, and not exactly a fighter himself."

"Not a fighter? What then?"

"Well, a great leader of men who fight."

"Like a tribal chief?"

"Oh, no, sir, not exactly like that either. More like—a medicine man."

Harry concerned himself with the gearbox spring. The day had grown hot, yet the warm stench of the grease and the heat rising off the packed dirt beneath them wasn't unpleasant.

He and Mewishi sat cross-legged.

In their silence they marveled at each other.

† † †

Every morning the monkeys began to screech and cry. No one knew why, yet everyone speculated. Finally, Rena the Jungle Bunny, who had joined the group at one of those nameless mining camps, explained that it was well known that monkeys were always filled with terror and didn't enjoy life. Everyday is torture for them, she remarked. "They cry and wail like that because they hate the dawn."

There were always baboons out in the open spaces. Leo knew about baboons and often referred to them in his speeches before the troop. *Baboons are among the most aggressive animals,* he told his men during one of his philosophical pep talks, *but the males—while they threaten each other a lot—have never been known to kill each other except in captivity!*

Harry was fascinated with the mystic leopard. He wanted to get to another part of the continent, he said, where the leopard population was greater.

The leopard had never grown soft like the lion, had never adapted to man's encroachment into the middle jungles, had always feared the intruder enough to keep away, to become a shadow in the hills. All over Africa it had gone to higher ground, leaving the jungles and savannahs and many of its natural hunting areas. The tribes worshipped it, and in one form or another each tribe had its Leopard Cult—always a secret society which generated the creature's power. The Leopard Men settled things: avenged disputes, injustices between families, wrongs between tribes. They drank blood and sang to the moon. And when they put on the headgear and claws they became leopards according to some, their arms and legs actually altering, their eyes turning yellow, hair and spots appearing on their bodies, their voices turning into that cat-like breath.

Harry's claws were from the Leopard Cult.

One of the Elite Rifles, a Masai named Pogo who was a poet, composed an ode to the claws. Pogo sang his poem to the beat of drums and it became the hit song of the outfit while they traveled around the northern provinces.

† † †

The mining towns became drudgery and each one seemed dirtier than the last.

"We need to get back to Elisabethville," Harry told Leo. "Why's that?"

"Because of Val," Harry explained. "She needs a bath. And she's pretty far along now."

In the mining camp they presently occupied there were

an assortment of lice, thorns, leeches, turds, rotting carcasses, and, as the Sergeant Major observed, all the benefits of the unsanitary life. The men suffered from bites from big red ticks hungry for blood. The preventive medicines ran short and some of the troop had stomach pains. The rainy season had left a cloud of mosquitoes over the forests.

There was also the pestilence of industry—which annoyed Leo as much as anything else. The miners were mistreated: miniscule wages, dangerous conditions, poor housing. It reminded the commander of the terrors of Wales.

An American mining firm operated the camp on The Milky Way Plan. This was explained to Leo by a company official in simple terms: the miners tired easily in the heat and production was never very good until the company started providing daily lunches. With good company lunches under their belts the workers overcame malnutrition and worked with greater output, but eventually the company decided the lunches were too elaborate (sandwiches, fruit, candy bars) and began to reduce the fare. Soon it became apparent that the workers needed only the candy—Milky Way bars—to keep their production at satisfactory levels.

"It was worked out scientifically," the official told Leo. "They didn't need or deserve sandwiches. Yet when we took away the Milky Ways their energies fell and production suffered."

"What about their teeth?" Leo inquired.

"Oh, all the candy. Their teeth rot out of their mouths," the official admitted. "But we provide company dentists."

On Saturdays the wives of the miners came to get their husbands' paychecks. They first lined up at the paymaster's table, then went over and lined up at the cart of the Lebanese trader. Before their husbands got off work that day the wives had spent most of the earnings. They were especially fond of the bright materials hung in bolts over the sides of the two-wheeled cart. Lined up to buy, they were a scrawny collection—skinny children pulling at their skirts, wiry little babies in their arms—yet in spite of their undernourishment they were all well-dressed because they couldn't resist the Lebanese trader.

He was a corpulent man with a hooked nose so large that it actually reached his upper lip. His cart was ablaze with cloth and goods. Val bought Crest toothpaste from him.

There he was each payday, rocking back and forth in his old army boots, his robes thrown over his shoulder Arab-style, his hands caressing the bolts of cloth.

"Val does need to get back to the city," Leo finally conceded. "Also, I'm sick of all these bloody mercantile sorts out here in the middle of the jungle."

† † †

Leo addressed the men.

We must pass along a few wild genes to our children! An untamed attitude toward life! Not just a few pieces of family furniture!

Harry and Val were rolled up in the double sleeping bag in the rear of the lorry. The night wore a canopy of bold stars and the men sat around drunk as the faraway whine of a mine-shaft motor mixed with the sounds of the forest. Leo walked among them working out his thoughts.

Fucking youth. Both the Romans and Greeks, who gave us the stupid idea of always working hard and building for future generations, saw their children turn to materialism and the flesh! So now the kids are mixed up, soft, oversexed, inept! Products of a domestic affluence which has overwhelmed

them! They have strong egos, but no identity! They're a
negligible force! And our duty to them, men, is to make them
wild, truly animal, and brutal enough to stand alone.

After a last drink, Leo shuffled over to his tent.

The cold moon rode above the surrounding hills. Only a
few cedars dotted the hills now: the wood supply low, centuries of use eroding the jungle itself.

In their warm sleeping bag, he knew, Harry and Val were
probably making love. Harry was probably filling her insides
with warm fluid, spilling semen over the womb where Leo's
child floated in its prebirth silence, over the loving cunt, the
dainty uterus, the hard heart, the fearsome soul of that
woman, and the limbs, blood, dreams, and first stirrings of
the infant.

Leo stripped himself naked and curled up on his cot inside the tent. He could smell his own dank body odors. Tuck-
ing his legs up to his chin, he achieved the fetal position and
tried to make his mind one with his unborn self across the
way in the truck.

The thought that this might be somehow possible calmed
him and after a while he went to sleep.

† † †

Val rode along in the rattling Saracen truck with Harry
beside her as the streets of tar and sand appeared once more:
Elisabethville. At the edges of the road tufted papyrus, like
soft feather dusters, grew from grass as thick and strong as
wire. Along the horizon huts sat in clusters and the city traffic
increased.

"You had your nightmare again last night," she said to
Harry, trying to draw him into conversation. He was sullen
today and preoccupied. "Tell me what you dreamt."

"My extravaganza," he answered without looking at her. He cleaned his Mauser-Bauer while Mewishi drove.

"Tell me about it."

"I don't understand part of it," he said. "When I understand I'll maybe tell it."

"I could possibly interpret it for you," she suggested, but Harry didn't reply to this. They bumped along in silence until they came to an intersection where a lanky black policeman stood directing traffic with his oversized and soiled white gloves. Across the street bees were buzzing through a giant silver oak tree.

"Tshombe's going to pay us tomorrow," Harry finally said. "Tell me what you plan to do with your money."

"Send it to Westminster Bank," she said.

"No, give it to me," Harry told her. "I'll see it gets into a Swiss account in your name."

The policeman waved them through as Val considered this.

"You can't trust anyone else," Harry said. "And I've got the contacts."

"Very well," she answered.

Her shirt hung open and Harry watched the slow rise of her breast as she breathed; her breasts had grown heavier, lovely, and he stroked the cool metal of his rifle, gently applying gun bluing, as he imagined the touch of her skin.

"I want to go to Switzerland and live," he said to her. "Just the two of us in the mountains. You can have the baby and I'll take care of you both. We'll have money. A nice chalet with flowers. When it snows we'll go skiing. We'll visit the glaciers and such as that."

"Harry!" she said with surprise.

"You can sit at your desk and write while looking out over the Alps. I'll wrap the baby in a blanket and go to the village, so you can have time for yourself. We'll eat fondue. We'll have a car so we can drive up to the high lakes."

† † †

Back at the Rex Hotel, Weldu and Hicks interviewed applicants. Leo sat behind a table in the dining room, his hands folded, watching those who appeared. One was a Spaniard who called himself El Paladín. He was the size of a terrier with arms like thick ropes and a grin full of gold teeth. He spoke both English and Spanish without benefit of grammar.

"Possible I can kill a man with a small piece of seashell, sometimes a Coke bottle, perhaps a matchbook folded just right," he said, trying to impress them. "But mostly I'm a rapist."

"We hain't got need of one of them full time," Hicks managed.

"A folded matchbook!" Weldu added. "Very clever!"

The Spaniard stood there grinning.

"Any rapes to your credit?" Leo asked, speaking up.

"No, truly, no rapes because the girls they don't let me."

"Too cooperative, are they?" Hicks put in.

"I could blow something up with dynamites," El Paladín suggested. "Or stab somebody. No job too small, you name it."

"Can you cook?" Leo asked.

"No, but can medic. I got a special prescription for jungle boils. Sure cure!"

"Hired, then," the Commander said. "Next man!"

† † †

The rooms of the Rex Hotel consisted mainly of a series of shuttered closets large enough to store quantities of gear when the inhabitants of the rooms came in from safari. There were many locks and bolts and the porters always jangled with keys. One of the reasons Leo preferred the Rex was that he could keep his prized weapons, medals, liquors, radios, foodstuffs, and spoils near his bedside. He also had a strongbox—requiring two of the Elite Rifles to heft it—which bore the company's pay.

In the bridal suite, occupied by the Commander when possible, there was also a brightly painted tub, gold and silver, large enough for a platoon. Soon after their return from the north, Val, Leo, and Harry decided to get drunk and take a bath together. They drank gin coolers and undressed, hanging their clothes—chocolate uniform, jeans, fatigues—in the spacious shuttered closet.

They drank a quart and a half of Gilbey's and scrubbed each other. It was a family scrub, nothing sexual, but they enjoyed their nakedness and took care to observe each other closely.

Leo: a thickset tree trunk of a man, fair-skinned, sandy hair on his chest and arms, a sandy-blond mustache, green eyes. Too much belly, a flabbiness in the triceps, but legs like cypress or hard maple. Hair, medium length. Ears, a bit large. Fingernails bitten to the quick. Height, five foot eleven. Penis, stubby but fairly grand in circumference. Balls, bulging. Buttocks, of indifferent quality.

Val: the magnificent female specimen, long and narrow in the waist, ass like a Nile queen, breasts of unusual size and appeal fastened to the slender frame, face of sculptured, candid beauty, full and almost thickish lips. Eyes, soft brown. Skin, the color of caramel. Hair, deepest brown. The bulge of the pregnancy carried low so that she maintained her small waist. Legs, long as a model's. Feet, too big. Cunt, a real bush and dark as the forest of the night.

Harry: dark and blue-eyed, the build of a young athlete,

liquid as a cat in movement, hairy, thin legs and hips but a gorilla across the chest. Exceptional muscle tone in the pectorals, biceps, back, and shoulders. Fingers, long and strong like a piano player's. Hair, black. Face, hard and handsome with prominent brows. Height, six two. Penis and balls, a major weaponry. Buttocks, small and hard, but dented with a scar deep enough to bury the fingers that touched it and horrible to behold.

The bathroom filled with steam as they sang.

Their songs: Yellow Rose of Texas, Galway Bay, Bringing in the Sheaves, Just One of Those Things, Black is the Color of My True Love's Hair.

† † †

The war and its spoils hadn't suited Moise Tshombe.

In the beginning he planned to cheat the mercenaries, but their presence in the capital scared him so he filled their strongboxes and bank accounts as agreed. The Leopoldville factions which had promised to split apart had somehow strengthened against him. His voice had properly deepened, but it sounded less like the lion than the somber notes of a man whose ambitions and lusts had not quite worked out.

"War itself is a disappointment," he told Harry.

He had asked Harry over to the governmental offices for a private conference and had revealed that he knew all about the American: that he was really CIA, that he enjoyed an inflated reputation in Leo's little army, that he was a hybrid spy in a land which was really only a playground.

"It doesn't matter to me," Tshombe assured Harry.

"Good," Harry answered.

"I am a man capable of understanding ironies," he told Harry.

Most African wars were mild, he explained, yet he had hoped for more in the Congo. The Arab word for war is *barouf* —meaning gunpowder—and mass violence on the continent with only a few historical exceptions had been loud and smoky without much injury or loss. In the Boer War, Tshombe said, using his deep voice, there were flags for teatime, time out for burying the dead and caring for the wounded, and no fighting permitted on Sundays.

"Men play at war," Tshombe lamented. "Great battles, the catharsis of true fright, the glories of slaughter are all secondary to preening. Most warriors—like your commander —are strutting actors."

"Leo Rucker?" Harry repeated.

"An elite theorist of the traditional officer class," Tshombe said. "One of an old breed of military intellectuals."

They drank limeade and watched the rhythmic turnings of the ceiling fans. Sounds of cars and hawkers from the street outside.

"He has style," Harry said in Leo's defense.

"Oh, truly," Tshombe boomed, throwing back his head in a laugh. "He does have that. Mobutu wanted to copy Commander Rucker's image, you know, and ended up with a parrot in a cage!"

Harry waited until his host's laughter died down again.

"What is it you want from me?" Harry then asked.

"There's a woman in your camp. An exceptional woman —you know her well. I want to make love to her."

Harry tried to keep a blank expression.

"The war is a disappointment. I could lose my life and my kingdom. It occurs to me that I should have the few small benefits I really desire."

"I agree," Harry answered.

"You do?"

"Prepare yourself for a night of love. I'll see that she's here by nine o'clock."

Moise Tshombe rose and pumped Harry's hand with gratitude.

That night the guards admitted the woman through the doors and down the dark corridors of the presidential rooms. The leader of Katanga awaited her in a brocade robe, a cigar fastened in his smile, his little cloth skull cap in hand.

Rena the Jungle Bunny entered his bedroom with a flourish. She threw open her cloak and revealed her raised tattoo—the one rich with western literary meanings.

"Disgusting," Moise Tshombe sighed. "Repugnant!"

Nevertheless he went to bed with her and was generally pleased with her services.

Afterward he lay there in the semidarkness conjuring up a vision of Val.

He understood clearly, of course, that neither Leo nor Harry would let her come to him.

But he yearned.

Katanga had the smell of carrion.

Barouf, time, ambition, the weary soul.

† † †

Sergeant Major Richard Hamilton Hicks rose from his bed in the Rex Hotel at four A.M. and set about shaving. He liked to be up before his men, although reveille in the hotel was an informal affair, the men drifting down to breakfast with their hangovers while he enjoyed his first tea at dawn and glanced through the morning dispatches. There was seldom anything important in the dispatches—mostly those odd brown packets for Colonel Veer—so he had the cool of the day to himself and time to reflect on his duties.

He worried over the Elite Rifles as he shaved. They had lost their edge up there in the north drifting from one mining camp to the next. Here in the city matters were worse. The Commander was beginning to spend his days with the press, the gun traders, the manufacturers' agents and all those flies who buzzed over the swollen carcass of the war. The Commander had to keep busy, of course, so he wouldn't fret over Val and Harry. Then the town: new brothels everywhere, new saloons, rampant gambling, murders in the side streets, intrigues.

Drying his face with a towel he thought, god, I'd like to get the men out in back of the hotel for drill.

Drill: the beauty of it.

He strapped on his pistol, slipped into his tunic—light cotton cloth heavy with Leo's medals—and laced his boots. When he had fixed his beret over one ear, he clicked his heels and gave himself a salute in the mirror hanging over his basin.

Val, Harry, the Commander: all that popped into his mind again as he went downstairs, but the first odors of tea and toast expelled it.

The porters and waiters stumbled around in their half-sleep as the Sergeant Major's tea brewed. He read the newspaper —the *Telegraph,* one week old—and fingered the whistle which hung on the loop of silver chain across his left shoulder. There was no place else on earth he would rather be.

Three men entered the foyer beyond the potted palms and went upstairs.

Hicks ran his finger along the classified ads.

The pleasant steam sighed from the teapot.

The reassuring rattle of dishes came from the kitchen.

But beyond the shuttered windows the call of a bird came to Hicks' ears: an odd cry, thin and desolate.

He stood at the table and looked at the empty staircase out in the foyer.

Sigh, rattle, tweet: his senses came together and he unsnapped his holster as he started for the stairs.

His first impulse was to call for the sentries. Where were they? But better not: instead, he made his way toward the bridal suite. He rounded the corner of the hallway as the three men faced Leo's door. One of them was either about to strike the door with his shoulder or had already done so—Hicks weighed this only for an instant—and another of them was drawing a weapon.

Hicks spun against the wall, bounced across the hallway, struck the wall there, bounced again, and in this zigzag pattern opened fire.

A fusillade of almost twenty shots followed.

There was much discussion among the Elite Rifles, the press, and Tshombe's authorities as to what happened.

Clearly, Leo had opened fire from inside his room. All the bullet holes in his door had been discharged into the hall. Pogo, the poet, had leaped out into the hall at the far end and a bullet, probably one of Hicks' shots, had ripped off his left thumbnail as he clamored back inside his room. Mewishi, up one flight in the room next to Harry and Val, sprang out of bed at the first noise and sprayed his room with a Sten gun, destroying a case of Weldu's liniment put there for safe keeping. Harry secured Val in one of the large closets and managed to station himself behind the bed, his .45 trained on his doorway. El Paladín ran into that same upstairs hallway naked and armed only with a dagger.

A dumdum bullet struck Hicks in the chest early in the exchange of fire. Still, he managed to get off more shots as he fell. The three men, seeing Pogo, ran toward the falling Hicks and the stairway by which they had entered and two got away. The other stumbled over Hicks and as he scrambled up Hicks shot him between the legs, blowing his balls, entrails, and his assassin's heart into his brains and beyond.

The brave Hicks died of a strange and awful wound. The dumdum had struck the medals on his chest—Leo's precious awards and medals fashioned in Bond Street, made of good British gems and coins, of African carvings and sculpted bone —and had scattered these like hard confetti through the Sergeant Major's body.

There were only a few results of this attempt on the Commander's life.

Mewishi became Hicks' temporary replacement.

Pogo, the poet, was cited for bravery under fire.

The missing sentries, aware of what was in store for them, left the troop never to be heard of again.

And for the next weeks—until the end in Katanga—the Elite Rifles went out behind the Rex Hotel at around six every morning and drilled. Either Harry or Leo kept watch over this resumed discipline while in the adjoining streets the guard was doubled and sentries sat in the windows above or on the roof, cigarettes dangling from their mouths, their rifles ready, their eyes sharp.

† † †

J. R. Hoskins, who could sniff the political wind as well as anyone, gave a party for General Mobutu in Leopoldville.

Bedford covered the event for *The Times*.

Tribal leaders surrounded the buffet and regarded the
forks and cocktail toothpicks as small insubstantial weapons.

Because the party was held in the Mobutu headquarters inside the old movie house, two films were shown: one with
Cornel Wilde, one with Burt Lancaster.

There was a contingent of tribesmen who spoke in the
famous click speech and even Mobutu had difficulty following what they said.

"African code?" The Peacock inquired of this strange talk.

"Code? Oh, yes, absolutely." Mobutu laughed, feeling
some advantage over the American.

Mobutu set aside the latter part of the evening—after midnight—for talking business. The Peacock was very sleepy and
although he looked vivid in his coat of many colors he almost
nodded off. Hot coffee was served him. Mobutu, who had
napped that afternoon, took the floor.

"We want everything in writing," he told J. R.

"Come on now," J. R. yawned. "In the old days not a
tribal leader in Africa would sign his name to a white man's
paper."

"And we won't now," the General replied. "It's bad juju.
But we want a treaty—a full agreement—signed by you."

"Couldn't we swear an oath?" J. R. suggested, his eyes
dropping. "Wouldn't that be the old jungle custom?"

"Ah, yes, oaths," Mobutu announced to everyone at the
party. "The savages love oaths, do they not? Blood rites, wailing at the moon, walking on fire, flirtation with the cobra,
thorns in the flesh: all tests of bravery, allegiance, and true
devotion. No more, Mr. Peacock! Let us have written documents! We will have panels of lawyers! We will have courts
of arbitration in Geneva! Councils and legislatures! Seals and
notarizations! Writs!"

"This is a sad day for us all," J. R. Hoskins complained, but he was too sleepy to protest much and, besides, as always, one form of juju was about the same as another.

† † †

One morning as Harry sat watching Val comb out her hair a knock came at the door and one of Tshombe's officers materialized.

"You're to come see Mr. Tshombe," the officer said.

"Where's Commander Rucker?"

"Already in Mr. Tshombe's office. There's a meeting of— ah, several interests."

The officer stood in the room, hands behind his back as if at parade rest, as Harry dressed. For a few moments the only sound was the brush in Val's long hair, then the officer, who would not look in Val's direction, said politely, "You're really to come at once, sir, very urgent, I'm afraid."

They drove over by car and Harry tried to make himself a mental list of recent events, but finally gave up the effort. The Leopoldville parliament had been dismissed. Kasavubu, who at one time had thrown Tshombe into jail, had now turned on Lumumba, who was trying to make himself into a leftist martyr. Hammarskjöld was trying to sort out the foreign elements and expel them. Mobutu, behind the strength of his army, was bargaining and making private deals. The mercenaries were in several camps. There were hints that a large UN peace force would rumble in and decide everything.

As they drove along, Harry read the *Herald Tribune*. He had missed breakfast after morning drill.

On the second floor of Tshombe's suite of offices he was informed that the meeting had shifted to the basement of another building across the wide green lawn. A soldier in some unidentifiable uniform led him there and pointed him down a dimly lighted subterranean hallway toward a door flanked by guards.

The guards spoke only Swahili and French, so there followed some minutes of discussion and identification. Leo finally opened the door, snapped at them, and got Harry inside.

One of Guy Weber's henchmen was talking, so Harry opened a warm beer and looked around for something to eat. No hors d'oeuvres. There were two Turks—or were those Egyptians?—and the Swede was there along with a half dozen others. Everybody held a bottle of Simba beer, it was a minor party, and Tshombe was terribly nervous. In the center of the room, perhaps the object of conversation, but not part of it, was a scrawny man in a blindfold.

When Weber's man stopped talking, Tshombe's basso profundo began. "The world press, gentlemen, is a kite in the breeze! It's powerless, completely powerless, we agree on that, yet up there for everyone to see, so it has to be reckoned with!"

Harry emptied his bottle. Instant nausea.

The press is always romantic and personal, too, Leo added, sounding professorial. *It can never show ideas or movements, but it can always show actions and events and individual men!*

This theorizing passed unnoticed above everyone's head.

Meanwhile, Tshombe kept popping that crocheted skull cap on his head and jerking it off with growing agitation.

The basement room had no windows and stank.

"The question is," Tshombe boomed out, "not whether we're engaged in criminal behavior, but whether or not we want it published!"

The little man in the blindfold seemed impatient with the whole line of talk.

"Even if accused in this," the Swede put in, "it might also be turned to advantage in the newspapers. Who knows?"

Harry sat holding his empty beer bottle as a trickle of sweat edged down his body. The men around him grumbled both their approval and disapproval.

As the mysterious topic continued, a big shirtless black passed a new case of beer among the men and took up the empties.

Leo shot Harry a glance as the Swede took the floor.

Unlike Leo and Tshombe, the Swede was short on theory or complaint and long on practical advice. "Announce that the prisoner was shot while trying to escape," he said, and at last Harry understood they were discussing how to dispose of the little man in their midst.

"Perhaps and perhaps," Tshombe said, jerking the cap off again. He pointed a finger at Harry. "And what do you think?"

"No opinion," Harry concluded.

"The American CIA has no opinion?" Tshombe asked with a mean smile.

"I'm a simple colonel in the Elite Rifles," Harry answered.

Be criminals, at least, who demand an audience, who work on a grand scale, Leo advised again, a little off the subject. *I say this needs to be outlandish, talked about! We're not petty burglars sneaking through dark windows! We're major political rebels!*

For a moment Harry thought he might puke from the beer and heat.

Another uniformed black—Harry had the immediate impression he was Mobutu's man—began talking about sectional interests, how the western sectors would react, how the army would take it.

Then Tshombe turned and produced a .45 Army Special which he thrust at Leo.

"To business, to business," Tshombe said. "We're not only witnesses today, we're here to create confusion! Let there be many representatives, much credit and blame! Let there be points of view and philosophical discourse and argument!"

The pistol turned to ballast in Leo's hand.

The little man in the blindfold seemed about to speak, but didn't. Tshombe kept talking in a normal voice.

A tiny wave of Tshombe's fingers urged Leo to get it over with and everyone edged back.

Harry put down his second bottle of beer and watched.

"Troubles, deep troubles!" the little man in the blindfold began to say in a whiny rasp of a voice. "The colonial spirit forever, isn't that how it is? Except now the whites who come here to manipulate us get used and manipulated themselves! It's fair and just, if you consider! We've learned well, we've been taught and we've learned, and we're leaders in our own intrigues now, not merely victims. We're participants in our own downfall!"

"Shut up," Tshombe told him.

"And the Congo is a great stream!" the little man went on. "It surely is, it flows red, and the years wash it clean again. And the nation is like the river: it flows, it flows forever, and it takes all history with it!"

The little man seemed adream, but he was still lost in this rhetoric as Harry stepped out and took the pistol out of Leo's hand.

"Not Commander Rucker," Harry said, handing it back to Tshombe.

"He is in my employ," Tshombe said with his mean smile.

"Not politic," Harry offered. "Let a black do it."

"Indeed," the little man in the blindfold added, as if he could see through the cloth.

"Come on, Leo," Harry said, and he touched the Commander's shoulder, turning him toward the door.

As they left, the .45 was going around the room, passing from hand to hand. The little man in the center talked on.

Outside, the air was pure and cool. It was one of those days when the altitude of Elisabethville gave its visitors a true mountain climate: the breezes and sounds of the Blue Ridge, Savoy, Bavaria. For a few blocks Leo and Harry walked along in silence.

"Thank you, Harry," Leo finally said.

The following day they learned that two others had also been disposed of, aides of the little man in the blindfold, and true to the Swede's advice the story went out that all this transpired in an escape attempt.

The little man in the blindfold, of course, had been Patrice Lumumba.

Kasavubu and Tshombe had struck a deal—or so rumor had it—so that now enemies had become friends, alliances had melted, paranoia reigned, chaos was complete.

† † †

Rain poured down and the streets were awash: rivulets flowing into thick pools into gushing streams into tributaries which eventually flowed out of the mountains of Katanga into the watershed of the Great Congo.

Under the eaves of the wide porch of the Rex Hotel, Leo and Val entertained a group of reporters at lunch. They were having a typical Leo Rucker meal: steak with Worcestershire sauce. Sheltered from the cascade of water from the roof and looking out over the bog which comprised the street, the reporters ate slowly so they could ask Val endless questions.

Q: "Is it true that a massive UN force is gathering?"

VAL: "No comment."

Q: "Will Tshombe really go into exile in Madrid?"

VAL: "We don't know."

Q: "Who made the attempt on Commander Rucker's life?"

VAL: "Subversive forces."

Q: "Is it a fact that you have a psychopathic killer in your troop who killed a friendly platoon of boy soldiers just outside this city?"

VAL: "No, nonsense."

Q: "Is it true that the Elite Rifles have a CIA hookup?"

VAL: "No, but we're friendly to American foreign policies."

Q: "True that your unit tortured prisoners in the north?"

VAL: "Untrue."

Q: "Will the mercenary forces disband when Katanga falls?"

VAL: "Katanga is safe. Commander Rucker believes that future wars will be fought by brave mercenaries who believe in freedom and the craft of soldiering."

Q: "Are you pregnant by Commander Rucker?"

VAL mimicking Mae West: "Well, boys, I'm knocked up by somebody around here, that's for sure."

The reporters laughed and drank quantities of brandy and coffee as the rains poured down.

Later on that afternoon Harry appeared on the porch and a photographer lined everybody up for a group shot. Harry held a grenade beside his face, Leo tried to hold in his paunch, and Val, a regal smile on her lips, obligingly opened her khaki shirt to reveal her cleavage.

A French reporter claimed he had fallen desperately in love with her, that he would follow her forever like a dog, that he would kiss her every footstep. But Val explained, no, that she couldn't return his love, that she was suicidal, that she had joined this wayward and barbaric life in order to destroy herself, that life was too difficult. The Frenchman was moved almost to tears by her solemn teasing. She went on that she had read all the great existentialists, philosophers and novelists alike, and that her deep sadness and pessimism would probably never leave her.

"Triste, triste!" the Frenchman said, and everyone else laughed at his forlorn stare and lifted their glasses and drank a toast to the war.

† † †

Being a Christian gentleman, Dag Hammarskjöld felt guilty for his pleasure and satisfaction with all his pain and anxiety.

Among the things which made him feel very unhappy for feeling so good were his few possessions (African masks, marble writing stand, Gucci coat, Dansk silver), his few women friends (dowdy secretary, Greta Garbo, two wives of co-workers), and his own fair-skinned body (freckles, pink toes, round tummy, soft genitals, and the mole on his cheek).

About Val, that distant dream, he was unsure. She gave him guilt-pain-pleasure-warmth all at once and he couldn't imagine going to Africa, as he was now preparing to do, without trying to see her.

On a September morning he sat in his office on the thirty-eighth floor composing his last will and testament (a normal precaution, he considered, for visiting the Dark Continent) and trying to beat back thoughts of Val. He was a humble man, material things scarcely mattered, so his labor was short and by noon he gave the document to his dowdy secretary to type. For a time after that he stood at his window, gazing out over the harbor of New York, as he took his lunch; a Pepsi and a Peanut Cluster.

In the airport limousine, he took inventory: tickets, the brown valise, his notes. He had the uneasy feeling that his notes on the Katangan business were inadequate.

He searched through the brown valise for his diary, but found that he had left it at home.

The light died in the low clouds . . . Branches wrapped me in their peace. When the boundaries were erased, once again the wonder: that I exist.

Dag was taking a trip—in his usual earnest way—and once again didn't fully comprehend the fire with which he burned.

† † †

Leo announced that he was in a trading mood, and all over Elisabethville the arms sellers, the black marketeers, and the crooked quartermasters came out to barter. The lobby of the Rex soon resembled a county fair and Val, as accountant, made lists of weapons, vehicles, raw ivory, crates, oil drums, and hundreds of civilian items including cars, refrigerators, radios, rugs, and art objects.

Mewishi and his "finders" visited every warehouse, office, bivouac, and hiding place in and around the city confirming the existence and whereabouts of items up for trade.

The war had become a sale: Belgium had dumped its arms, business had been good for America, the mining profits were up, the rich had gotten richer in the inflation.

Harry became impatient with Leo's sudden new enthusiasms and told him so.

"I thought you hated the merchants," Harry complained.

"You're just jealous that Val's spending so much time helping me," Leo countered.

"That's not it. You just look like a shopkeeper these last few days."

"Harry, don't worry," Leo confided. "Let me tell you a secret."

They stood in the swarm of the lobby. Leo had a pencil behind his ear and a Czech arms dealer who had a cache of bazookas and mortars had jumped up on a wicker chair trying to get some bids going. Harry scanned the room for Val as Leo explained.

"We're not buying or selling anything," Leo told him. "But in a day's time I'll know where everything in the city is located. When the UN force gets here and things get frantic I'm going to swipe a dozen bloody lorries and take half the arms in Katanga back across the border to Ndola. Damned if I'll be caught underpaid."

"Then you're going to loot."

"Exactly," Leo said, his face brightening.

"Well, I'm not interested in that either."

"Harry, you are," Leo said, pulling Harry behind one of the potted palms. "We'll be rich! We'll have the biggest armory in Africa! This'll set us up for years!"

"Leo, I'm taking Val and pulling out."

"Taking Val? What's that mean?"

"You take the fucking spoils because I'm getting her to safety."

"She's safe with us!" Leo said, his voice getting higher than he meant it to.

Harry shook his head stubbornly.

"Listen, Harry, truly: we'll assign a whole platoon to her! Then go after the arms! There's got to be a million pounds' worth of weapons stored in straw huts and flimsy warehouses all over town."

"Screw the weapons."

"She doesn't want that sort of safety anyway! Ask her!"

"She wants to go with me."

"Where?"

"Switzerland."

"Oh, bloody Christ, Harry! Switzerland! A fucking cow pasture!"

"She wants to!"

"Chocolate! Cheese! The fucking Red Cross!"

That night the Elite Rifles held their last major celebration in the ballroom of the Rex. There were a number of traders, Jungle Bunnies, and assorted guests during the early part of the evening while the buffet was served. The unfortunate music that evening was performed by a violinist, a trumpet player, and a drummer who didn't seem on good terms with each other. But the meal was good—pork, wild fowl, lots of champagne and Carlsberg beer—and there was enough diversion so that Leo could concentrate on his argument with Harry.

"Naturally she's yours, but the baby's mine and, besides, the three of us have been through a lot together," Leo persisted.

"I guess so," Harry admitted. He felt terribly uncomfortable sitting there in the midst of a party talking over personal problems.

"We're all beasts, a pack of dogs, Harry, we don't want to be tamed. Let it stay that way!"

Weldu stood on one leg listening to the discordant music and swigging Sloan's. Harry watched him, trying to keep from listening to Leo.

"It takes courage to see the world as it really is, the veils ripped away and no niceties," Leo went on. "Nations are built on guns, not constitutions—only honest men can admit that. And we all mate for a few seasons of lust, not love. Only the strong admit that and survive."

"Leo, I don't want to talk about it."

"Suppose," Leo said, leaning across the roast pork, "Val wanted both of us, not just you alone."

"She's going to have the child in safety."

"Wait, let me finish. Suppose she wanted that arrangement? Think you'd have the courage to let her have her way? That's an important kind of courage: the willingness to let people go untamed."

"My mind's made up," Harry said.

"You think Val's going to be content with her parasol and shopping basket and the local housewives?"

"Don't talk to me, Leo."

Later that night the musicians, traders, whores, and all the rest were gone and Leo took the stage in the ballroom to tell the troop how they were going to steal everything in Elisabethville. "We'll take more out of here than Alexander took out of Egypt!" he proclaimed, and the men roared with enthusiasm. "A bonus for every man!" he shouted, and the men roared again.

With the falcon on his shoulder, a Carlsberg raised high, the men and Val and Harry all attentive, Leo made another speech.

So we're fools, some say we are, romantics who still believe in the necessity of extravagant acts, but let me tell you, men, the alternative is the introspective shit of merchants, men who twiddle with life, who collect things, who examine themselves and their objects and study life apart from living it and wonder who the hell they are and what they're doing! We won't become inactive, we won't become objects, we'll never stop fighting! So we're melodramatic, we're corny, we wear the chocolate uniforms, pin medals on ourselves, play at games, but by god we're no zombies, we're not bloody consumers, we're still alive!

The men cheered.

Leo stalked the stage, his eyes glowing: a man paunchy, small, desperate, intense, visionary.

So much of domestic existence has come down to one thing: a deadly consumer mentality! More goods! Bread and circuses and any bloody Caesar who'll give them away!

The men cheered again and Harry watched Val as she watched Leo perform. Her face was adream with belief.

The domestic life is a bacteria covering the earth! It breeds shops and apartments and idle, fat people! It's a killing disease, men, it kills off freedom and vitality!

Pogo and El Paladín led the rhythmic clapping.

Yeah! the men yelled. Yeah, yeah, yeah!

Cut-rate villas! Shopkeepers! Beaches and leisure boats and cabins and picnics! The whole world wants to become California, god help it! It's cancer and I lay it to one cause: there aren't enough of us to kill those fat, lazy bastards off! To keep them from domesticating the whole bloody world! Because domesticity isn't civilization, men, no, by god, it isn't! It's the very bloody enemy of civilization, it's turning us all into plastic and shit!

Yeah, yeah, yeah, yeah!

Val was ecstatic.

Mewishi passed the commander another beer.

I offer you all—

Yeah, yeah, yeah! The rhythmic handclap, deep as drums.

True individual power! It's a radical idea, men, it always has been and by most standards it's pathological and criminal! But let every man be a state within the false state of society! Let that be a moral and political truism which ravishes the bourgeois idea of what people think they ought to be!

Harry watched Val.

She was beautiful, but her lips were moving with the men's chant.

Individualism is anarchy, true, and it has some romantic and foolish traps, men, but we have to believe in great moments, not great mass-minded causes! Great personal dramas! Or we sink in the domestic herd! We acquire and consume! We worship the mundane, the fucking group value, objects, and we die!

† † †

Not far from Leo's camp near the Lukanga swamps and the Mkushi River in a field of elephant grass the Secretary-General lay dying.

The wreckage of his plane had burnt itself out, everybody else on board was dead, and Dag was in his painful half-sleep. A day had passed, perhaps more—time, already, had died—since he dragged himself out of the wreck.

He had finished all his prayers and was trying to come to grips with death, his old preoccupation, but pain was a distraction. He found his mind wouldn't work. He wanted to review his long journey, but couldn't. He tried to think of his family of warriors, poets, clergymen. He tried to contemplate guilt—that great fuel which kept him going—or the abstractions of theology or ambition, the secret vanity, but no use.

One becomes earth of the earth, a plant among plants, an animal born from the soil and fertilizing it.

His plane, blown off course, shot down, had brought him near the bungalow where Val had paced before the eyes of Leo's men, near the forest paths she had walked, the inlaid desk where she had composed her entries, and he felt her presence. He didn't understand it. A strange last rapture. In his innermost, savage last thoughts he conjured up her vision. He had never found her.

Blood, grime, sweat, earth—where are these in the world you desire? Everywhere—in the ground from which the flame ascends straight upward.

† † †

Harry talked Leo into keeping a lorry on reserve for Val's escape, bought another secretly and tried to arrange for a plane. The two-lane dirt road down to Ndola remained open —it appeared safe from Mobutu's onrushing army in the west —but Harry considered caution his first business. Tshombe's gendarmes and other mercenary groups just weren't holding. There had been some brief flurries of victory—one recently north of Kaniama—but the federals were coming fast. They occupied seventy villages inside Katanga, had murdered many white settlers in their advance, had raped fifteen Belgian nuns at a seminary, and had mistakenly seized thirteen Italian airmen flying for the UN, accused them of being mercenaries, beat them, shot them, dismembered them, and disposed of their pieces in the Congo River.

Harry read his little brown packets with dismay.

Tshombe was pleading with Adoula, head of the federals,

for a cease-fire, but Mobutu and the army seemed like a separate force over which Adoula had little control. Besides, the UN was angry at Tshombe because Lumumba and Hammarskjöld were dead and because two UN representatives had mistakenly been beaten up outside a private residence in Elisabethville, so the war—which should have been stopped by the UN peace force—was being condoned and accelerated.

Val was assigned Weldu as a permanent bodyguard. She also wore a .38 Police Special on her hip, covering it with one of Harry's fatigue shirts.

Colonel Alphonse Pakassa of the Congolese army issued a press statement on the unfortunate behavior of his troops toward the unlucky Italian airmen, saying, "You know how soldiers are."

At the end of the month Tshombe flew to Brazzaville trying to settle things with Adoula again, but, rejected, flew on to Paris the next day. His absence from Katanga seemed to prompt the UN to get into the fight directly. UN planes started bombing and strafing roads leading into Elisabethville.

Harry sent courier messages suggesting other possible courses of action for the UN, but the couriers didn't come back.

Leo received word, though, that Tshombe would fly from Paris to the camp of the Elite Rifles outside Ndola. Leo and an escort force were asked to meet him and bring him back to the embattled city.

"You're in charge while I'm gone," Leo told Harry.

"Thanks so much," Harry said. He also told Val he wasn't sure who would shoot him first: Tshombe's gendarmes who suspected he was really a UN spy, the UN troops who would probably roar into the city before long and consider him a

mere mercenary, some assassin sent from Adoula or Mobutu
—or, if matters became more complicated, even one of the
Elite Rifles.

Leo left town.

Rumors and fears: a quality confusion.

A note from the Peacock arrived ordering Harry to proceed
to Lisbon and await further orders. Harry ignored it.

Val suggested that they should go to bed and make love
until all hostilities ceased the world over, so they did this—
for an afternoon—with Weldu standing guard outside the
door, perched on one leg like a furious waterbird, submachine
gun ready, thoughts befuddled.

† † †

A week later, Val stood in the gathering rubble of the city.

A small shoeshine boy, perhaps seven years old, had
fashioned a broom from the palm leaves blasted from the trees
of a boulevard near the Rex Hotel and was sweeping the dirt
around his makeshift box of polishes and shine rags.

Val stood in the uneasy traffic—pedestrians and lorries trying to behave normally—and watched him. A bright sun beat
down and she was conscious of the warmth on her bare arms.

On the side of his box he had inscribed the words: NEVER
SAY DIE! He gave his observer a smile.

† † †

Last days and the battle for the airport.

A mild zaniness reigned as the UN troops who arrived to
assault the Elisabethville airport were Indian Gurkha soldiers
replete with turbans, swords, leggings, and their usual high-
pitched broken English on the walkie-talkies and shortwave
sets.

The engagement began with an almost courteous exchange of rifle fire in the afternoon, but soon mortars were brought up by both sides and gendarmes fell all through the night. Harry and his dozen or so Elite Rifles hid themselves in Leo's armored lorries, well covered from the shrapnel exploding around them, listening to the wounded moan and trying to see what the Gurkhas were doing. Once or twice Harry induced members of his squad to jump out into the open and take a couple of shots at the enemy, but mostly they all huddled in the safety of the armor. He wished Hicks was alive. Hicks was a good shot, could probably see those little bastards out there in the darkness around the perimeter of the airstrip, and would probably drop a few.

The thump of sixty millimeter shells went on for hours.

El Paladín suggested that someone should go for coffee, but Harry vetoed the proposition.

"It's only a few miles into town," Pogo the poet noted. "I'll go."

"Keep your head down," Harry told him.

With the airport secure—it was the only one for miles—the UN would begin to fly in troops and the war would soon be over, Harry knew, so he determined to keep the lorry where he lay as well as the other vehicles put aside for the sake of Val's safety. All *Les Affreux*—Tshombe's various lots of mercenaries—would be thinking of a way out. Already they were pacing the corridors of the Lido, Rex, and Hotel Leopold II striking deals and trying to arrange their last paychecks. Some, like Leo, had an eye on loot. Others would be turning their coats—perhaps taking heads on their own side to appear convincing.

Harry raised up, aimed into the darkness underneath a distant row of trees, and fired. After a moment, crouched low again, he heard a bullet whistle overhead as someone returned the shot, aiming at the burst of light which had issued from his shiny Mauser-Bauer.

Two or three mortar shells knocked holes in the roof of a nearby hangar, but luckily no blaze started.

A slow patter of rain began.

Around two in the morning he ordered the armor—their most precious possession—turned toward town. They abandoned the gendarmes and rolled through the darkness, the beating of their windshield wipers the only noise. Leo had returned with Tshombe, but wasn't at the Rex. Harry found Val, Mewishi, and Weldu playing a game of hearts by candlelight in the bridal suite, blankets over the windows to effect a blackout.

"Not much to the battle," he commented, pulling up a chair. "Can I take high score and get in the game?"

† † †

As mortar shells lobbed into the suburbs the next few days the animals came out of the bush and congregated in doorways, underneath cars, and in alleyways of the city. Clusters of monkeys occupied every limb of every unharmed tree. At night, the nocturnal cats slipped through the shadows and hurried toward new hiding places. Mewishi, whom everyone always believed about everything, claimed that he saw two lionesses and their cubs padding across a rooftop. Birds sent up a distressed clatter day and night.

In a parking lot near Tshombe's government buildings a small herd of various antelope and gazelle gathered, wild-eyed and terrified, and greater in number than anyone guessed were around.

† † †

At last the bags were packed, the Mauser-Bauer wrapped and taped ready for shipping, the inlaid desk loaded onto a lorry. Words and threats ensued. It was as if relationships had to be quickly defined—and violently—at the last possible moment.

"Goddammit, I'll kill you!" Leo swore.

"No, you won't kill anyone," Harry snapped.

"I'll *have* you killed! I'll send men after you!"

"No, you won't do that either. Because not a man in your whole dumb troop would take the assignment."

"Then I'll bloody do it myself!"

"Not you, Leo, because you're a goddamned coward!"

If he hadn't said that in front of Val, Leo thought later, it wouldn't have been so bad.

But they were standing on the stairway in the lobby of the Rex, going through the bitterness as if it were rehearsed and ready, the words waiting for them to say, and Val did hear. Leo's eyes fell into hers. She gave him a sad, distant, somehow unintelligent stare as if he weren't even there anymore, as if he had turned into a wounded creature of the bush.

"I am not," Leo managed to say, but it was awful.

† † †

A mere three nights later.

Leo lay on the sagging bed in the bridal suite of the Rex trying to block out thought and sleep.

The Gurkhas had been joined by Ethiopian, Irish, and Swedish troops—a mammoth UN force—out there at the airport and through the suburbs. But fighting had tapered off. A lull: oddly still and quiet like those last moments of twilight on an African evening before the cacophony of insects and nightbirds, frogs and small animals.

Leo's hand trailed to the floor, his fingers touching the magnum pistol on the rug beside him. From the next room came Mewishi's slow, steady breathing and Leo wished he could sleep, too. Like Mewishi. Or like Harry: a clever and somehow unthinking animal, instinctual, and seldom troubled.

Leo considered picking up the pistol—a cold, hard metal along the barrel there—and going into the bathroom with it. He could pull the shower curtain around him, he thought, and place the barrel against his chest. He didn't fancy a shot to the head. The heart, more like it: let the brain be alive to that last pain and breathless moment.

His thoughts turned. The bush, the forest, the savannah, the veldt, the highlands.

Nothing was ever explained out there, nothing was ever understood; dreams were inexplicable like the patterns of leaves; beauty was accidental like the orchid set in rot; death smothered everything, yet that was irrational and bloody wondrous, for life always came back, green, moving the last seasons of decay aside. It pleased Leo that both the slavers and the missionaries failed. Every exploit, every philosophy, each cause or movement became as fragile and as transient as the jungle's smallest fern.

Leo got up and paced the room.

War itself: it was chaos. No clear battle lines, no constant enemy, no firm objectives, no strategies, only political confusion and wild personal dramas. "Which I like," he told the dark of the room. Such meaningless confusion drove adrenalin through the veins at the speed of light. Wonderful.

Harry and Val: oh, bloody Christ in Wales, what to do?

Did Harry contemplate the nature of war, he wondered, and the elusive relationships of nature and death? Shit no, certainly not. Harry lived straight ahead, never examined his motives, took one event after another in a chain, and left all interpretation—even his bad dreams—to the spiritless drifters who could only ponder. A true adventurer: he followed his intuitions, never examining them; he listened to the murmur of the old slave trails or paid homage to the leopard in the hills; others calculated, worried, revised, but Harry just moved on.

No, death, certainly, Harry wouldn't think too much about. He'd play life against it, instead, move around it in a circle. To such men as Harry death was a true dance: it had no meanings, the melody was absolutely wicked, an intoxicant, and only the dancer who moved with grace could dance at all.

And Val.

Condemned to a life of a few odd inner complexities, Leo decided. Like me. She watched those games out in the bush like a voyeur. She wasn't an adventuress, only an analyst, falcons and men and weapons her symbols, the war a kind of liquor she craved, and she took Harry between her thighs— Leo knew it—with a sense of awe. He was her cat and she watched herself watching.

Leo lay down on the empty bed again.

He wished Harry hadn't called him a coward.

An image arrived: Val sitting in the back of one of the lorries, her writing pad propped up on her knees, jotting her notes.

She was always trying to write them down. Fix them in place.

Having walked around in their borrowed nightmares, she wanted to be the interpreter of dreams.

Lying there, his hands cupped over his genitals, Leo at long last drifted into sleep.

He slept for two hours.

And in a remote chalet far away Val was sleeping in the crook of Harry's arm, their bodies warm against the frigid Alpine winds whipping the shutters outside their windows.

A continent away. The sea, rivers, mountain ranges distant and apart.

Suddenly Leo awoke.

A cock had crowed.

There it was, once, twice, that old familiar barnyard noise. But in the dark middle of the night. He sat up in bed, a cold sweat over his body, listening. A dream? He listened long and hard, waiting for it to come again, but it didn't. Instead, he felt his skin come alive and with a shudder he sprang up and ran into the room where Mewishi was still asleep.

"Get up! Break camp!" he yelled, and he pulled Mewishi to his feet until they were both stumbling around in the dark.

In a frenzy Leo emptied the hotel. His men rolled their gear, found their weapons, turned away from their women and poured into the night. Before dawn they were packed up and gone: lorries, armor, Land Rovers rumbling through the empty streets, their headlamps dancing on the shanties and dirty stalls and buildings of the city, all loot left behind. Then out into the bush. No one saying much. Some of them confused and complaining. And Leo wasn't sure, yet sure enough: death hovered close, so goddamned near that he couldn't explain it or fight it, only run.

A cock's crow in the dark of night.

An ancient omen.

In Switzerland, Val heard it, too, and pulled out of Harry Veer's arms. In that far away land—cold and howling—she sat up in bed with a cry.

PART THREE

BIVOUACS

SWITZERLAND,
SPAIN, CHILDREN, GAMES,
WEAPONS, THE DOLDRUMS

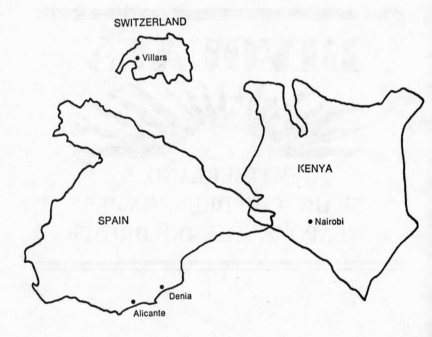

SWITZERLAND
• Villars

SPAIN

KENYA
• Nairobi

• Denia
• Alicante

FORBIDDING MOUNTAINS TAMED LIKE COWS: SWITZER-land.

Little shops lurked everywhere: shops for cheeses, skis, woolens, leather goods, cameras, books, and the ever-present clocks. The paths of the forests were neatly worn, covered with soft elastic pine needles, lined with rail fences, and adorned with drinking fountains and clusters of wild flowers carefully planted and groomed. The chalets and streets were clean and swept. In the cafés, all the rituals and amenities of drink and food were kept and observed; voices floated above the music, the odors of strong black coffee, proper beer, soft wines, cooked beef, and pungent fondues wafted around; one sat at windows framing extraordinary vistas, fingers around a good espresso or French brandy. Time slowed and the comfortable senses lost their sharpest edges. Val always seemed to have her thumb in a book, a pensive expression on her face. Harry took up skiing.

By the time Victor was born that first spring, Harry knew the slopes above Villars. The snow was too wet, but he skied every day, going up on the cable car and taking lunch at the Roc d'Orsay restaurant so Val could be alone to read and write while the baby had its afternoon nap. She wasn't always in a good mood and had several magazine assignments to keep her busy, so it was better when they spent most of the day apart. He bought good boots, skis and bindings—and an orange sweater with the small black silhouette of a falcon stitched on it. Sitting and resting at lunch, he watched the tourists and tried to be amused. Then, before going back to the chalet, he attacked the slopes one more time; there were times when he put his skis together, tucked his poles under his arms, and deliberately picked up too much speed. The game was whether or not he'd spill. He also traveled the unmarked and forbidden areas. The patrol was constantly warning and threatening him, but he usually smiled, drew them into conversations, invited them for drinks, and did as he pleased. One day he helped rescue a girl caught in an avalanche. She had two broken legs and he enjoyed his part very much. Afterward he invited some of the patrol back to the chalet where they managed to get drunk and annoy Val.

Skiing. A civilized risk.

In the forbidden areas in the late spring, trails turned into obstacle courses. Patches of brown earth opened up and the jagged edges of rocks appeared; the snow turned to ice overnight, so the early morning runs were treacherous, and in the afternoons the sun made a dangerous mush of it and more ground and rocks appeared. He pointed his skis downhill. A low-grade danger, but available.

As he promised Val, he took care of the baby most of the time. Vic looked like a noseguard, was fond of defecating in his diaper, didn't cry much, and he and Harry got along fine. They went up the mountain—on one or another of those manicured trails—every day. Harry bought a Fiat and a baby stroller which he pushed into stores, cafés, and various bars. Reading the sports pages of the *Herald Trib* or sipping a glass of Chablis, Harry could look over and meet Vic's sleepy gaze. The kid slept a lot. When awake, he seemed, like Leo, to be thinking things over.

Harry worked crossword puzzles in the newspapers—something he never thought he'd do—and read a few books himself. He started a book about Roger Ascham, born 1515, Elizabeth's tutor and England's greatest archer, and he thought of Leo. Archery was one of the sports the Commander claimed. Said he made his own arrows and strings, cutting the nocks of the arrows in the old way and setting the vanes himself. Once, down at the Ndola camp, Harry had seen some strings hanging from a nail: three skeins waxed together just so.

Val liked sex, but she was also busy and moody. They spent time every day making love and she liked it on the little sunporch on the south side of the chalet. Harry figured this was so the neighbors up the mountain would have a chance to watch. You want to display my talents, he accused her; sometimes in cafés or other public places she reached over and touched him between the legs. He liked it, but more than that she intrigued him. A weird horniness, he told her. Creative sluttiness, she replied.

She worked on a long profile of Leo Rucker for the *Observer* which Harry wasn't allowed to read.

Some days she spent entirely at the inlaid desk. (Harry's allotted writing space in the chalet was a bedside table with a wobbly leg.) He accused her of composing her memoirs. Sometimes he caught sight of her in her study, sitting there writing with very good posture. He held Vic inside the door once and said, "See, there's your mommy."

He didn't approve of moods and told her so.

One night past eight o'clock he went up and knocked on her door.

"Want some supper?"

"God, is food all you think about?" she snapped at him from inside the closed study. "We're both getting fat! All we've done for weeks is eat!"

Downstairs again, he made himself a sandwich. He thought about moods, including sexual moods, how people got into stages, and he wondered about Val, how she seemed a lot like Leo, who told them once, he remembered it well, *I have my seasons when I want to rut around until the heat's gone, but then months or weeks can pass and I won't give sex another thought.*

Harry knew he wasn't like that.

He wondered, in fact, if he'd ever cool off.

Maybe, too, Leo was lying. He's probably just like all other men, Harry decided, and his balls throb the same as mine; he yearns, though in a slightly different way, maybe, I'm at a loss to say exactly how.

He ate his sandwich and read.

And Roger Ascham said, "A bowe is not welle made that hath not plentye wood in the hand."

All books had lessons.

† † †

Leo began to disband his force.

He kept a skeleton group consisting of Mewishi, Weldu, El Paladín, Pogo, and a dozen underpaid newcomers who worked as porters and laborers.

The rest of the Elite Rifles scattered to spend their pay in the bars of Johannesburg or Salisbury or to take up duty as nightwatchmen or as regular army at obscure posts.

The camp went dark. And because the inactivity seemed to bring in the lonely nightsounds of the surrounding forests and swamps Leo was soon away on diverting trips, going to Durban or Nairobi for no good reasons. He drank more. And the malaria—his old dormant affliction—came back. For a period of time he liked spending money; he bought a fifty-foot yacht at anchor in the harbor at Durban, moved his books and private weapons in, got himself a television set, stored some booze and medicines, and took up residence. In Kenya he bought property—including some land he had once owned—and talked of building a manor. He traded off some armor and good used weaponry—the bazookas, an old World War II-vintage flamethrower—and got himself a Mercedes limo. In the apartheid countries he became relatively popular for a while, being invited into the homes of government officials and businessmen.

When sick, civilization calls its doctors. And when afraid, civilization naturally wants its barbarians. Everything's splendid until the Goths or the Mongol horde or the Simbas beat on the village gate, then everyone looks around for somebody crazy enough or mean enough or angry enough to go out there and hammer those evil bastards.

He was good for laughs some places and taken very seriously others. This mostly depended on the amounts of the booze and the fever, for he looked disheveled under the influence of either—and unconvincing.

In one of his lucid periods, though, he conceived of his future: he would go to the munitions manufacturers of Europe and America and strike deals in which he would become a middleman and wholesaler. Arms manufacturing, after all, was the world's second largest business—just behind oil—and everyone needed consumers.

"I'll provide the wars," he told a few representatives who prowled through Africa.

Talks opened up. He was invited to Brussels and Prague. Except for the fever—lingering, draining off his energies—he would have gone immediately, but even so he saw his destiny working out. His financial destiny, at least.

About Val and Harry and the baby—what did they name him, anyway?—he was brokenhearted.

"The reason I took up with that woman," he explained to Mewishi or some stranger in a bar, "was to have a child! And I got a boy child! A male heir! Heartsblood! But where the fuck is it? What's its name? Do I get him or not?"

Tears always came to his eyes.

Mewishi and the others heard his antibirth-control speech many times. *Another program set forth by idealists who don't understand the nature of this impoverished and bloody awful planet! My average savage wants sons, doesn't he? Also cattle and wives and territory! He lives in his shack, eats one spare meal a day, protects himself with homemade weapons, and suffers the bloody elements! His only wealth and hope for old age security or eternal remembrance are the products of his loins!*

He didn't like Durban with that dingy, lonely yacht bobbing out there in the harbor; nor the new Kenya with all its neons and British bullshit; nor the men who had heard his stories, lectures, and complaints too many times; nor Rena, the tattooed pro who offered herself; nor the creeping peace of his continent; nor life's hard losses of wife, son, and best friend; nor money and the paltry items it bought; nor time which made him fifty years old and fussy.

The fever got better, then worse. Is a fever, he wondered, part of my style? Fuck it, what bad luck.

His foul sweat covered dozens of hotel pillows and stank up his own bones and in a fit of decision he put up for sale all that he had recently bought: land, boat, Mercedes. Some of it sold and some of it didn't, but mere rearrangements suited him—the illusion of doing business.

He laid more plans: he would become a munitions wholesaler. And hire a private detective to find the objects of his obsession. And take a trip to Europe where the streets were clean cobblestone.

As soon as the fever went away, he told himself.

† † †

J. R. Hoskins visited the chalet wearing a fancy patchwork coat and long hair.

"How'd you two get so much money?" he asked.

"We have a savings plan," Val explained.

J. R. hadn't eaten much homecooked food recently, so devoured two dishes of fondue—dipping bread faster than either host or hostess—two loaves, four beers, three pieces of cake, and a jug of coffee.

"I read your *Observer* piece on good ole Leo," he told Val. "Very good data. In fact, I filed it as classified information and added a note which should establish you as an authority on mercenary activities."

"Think of us as the Swiss office," she said with a smile.

They played cards for a while after supper, then at midnight Victor appeared for his nightly feeding and J. R. watched

Harry administer the bottle. After that they drank a quantity of cognac.

"Leo gave me a letter for you," J. R. announced. "Do I say I couldn't locate you?"

"Give us the letter and say you're still looking," Val decided.

"Leo's making deals with the Israelis," J. R. revealed. "Oh, he's doing a lot of shit, but that's something we've picked up on. There's a mutiny and war in the Sudan. It's gone on since nineteen fifty-five, matter of fact, Arabs killing hell out of the blacks. We can't get information."

"I'll drink to information," Harry said.

"I reckon Leo wants himself a war," J. R. drawled, the cognac loosening his control. "Also, his ranch down in middle Africa is breaking up since his cutthroats don't have work."

"Is all that in the letter?" Harry inquired.

"Nope, the letter just says he wants to see his baby boy. It's a sad damned letter, since you ask, and made me want to cry."

He placed the letter beside one of the empty fondue pots where neither Val nor Harry looked at it or touched it.

After Val turned in for the night, Harry and J. R. played gin rummy. J. R. kept losing—he got down one hundred francs—and kept asking after Harry's finances.

"What's the matter? You need a loan?" Harry asked.

"No, no, money don't interest me—except as it corrupts," J. R. answered.

He asked Harry if he wanted to go to Madrid and serve under Tshombe who was in exile there, but Harry declined. He asked Harry if he'd like a job with an assassination team, but Harry assumed J. R. was kidding so didn't answer.

"So where are you, kid?" J. R. wanted to know. "You finished with active service?"

"Just on leave," Harry told him. "Being a father and husband."

"That's a full-time job?"

"Val's pregnant again," Harry said. "So far so good."

Over the tops of the cards fanned out before his face J. R. Hoskins studied Harry Veer, thinking, god, the career of such a young man is a marvel to contemplate, but here he is in this village banging a fancy cunt and warming baby bottles. I do not understand man's fighting soul, J. R. told himself; when I think I've got it straight, I don't; the call of the fucking wild misleads and confuses men same as anything else.

"Your play," Harry said, and the Peacock took a card.

† † †

There were nights Val and Harry seemed to stalk each other. He watched her with the old aching excitement; everything she said and did was a prelude. Once, before the weather turned too cool again they took off their clothes and moved around the woods outside the chalet. Val in moonlight: jutting rib cage, large breasts, her belly not yet divulging a new pregnancy, hairy mound, hard thighs: she lay down beneath the pines, her arms spread like wings, twisting her body sideways so he could look. They made love until the needles stung their skin, then he followed her back inside, through the dark rooms of the chalet, watching her movements as her body caught a slant of moonlight at a window or stopped in brief silhouette at the doors to the sunporch.

"Hey, wait for me," he called as he followed along, but she drifted out of reach once, twice, as he came near. At the bed, then, she turned and waited for him, kissed him, and pulled him down on the cold sheets. A faint, cloud-thickened moonlight illumined the soft hair of her underarm. Nipples erect and lovely. He mounted her again and they were both coming in the first movements.

Such good sex made him puzzle over the last months: she had been restless, writing out her secrets upstairs, giving him a good-humored but uninspired coupling most of the time, as if she were his tender caretaker. The old flame died, then came back. Fierce, wrenching fucks.

He watched her. She lay there like a panther momentarily quieted, her legs still open, the down of her body hair faintly aglow.

Had someone on that populated hillside of chalets seen them? The thought arrived and passed on.

"Come here," she said softly, and he slid into her again. Their eyes fixed. The black deeps of her eyes, down in there where even the moon fails, he thought, and where my Val hides and beckons.

He thought of saying he never wanted to lose her, but such words would make him sound like a husband.

"That's it, do me again, Harry," she whispered, and he felt his body beginning to obey, he loved it, he was scared to death he loved it so much.

† † †

A deck of cards, crimped at the edges. Slapjack. Wasn't that one of Harry's card games?

Forms, several and varied. Order sheets for bullets, medals, cloth, petrol, and Worcestershire sauce.

Val's letterhead stationery. Some with a UN emblem.

Leo cleaned out the mess.

Broken watches. Timex, Bulova, Omega, Rolex: the economic history of a career soldier in those silent faces.

A poem typed out on more of Val's stationery. The world hath neither certitude nor help for pain. Let us be true. The darkling plain, etcetera.

Photo. Mewishi with Val.

An old letter from mother. (Imagine that!) He recognized its worn folds and didn't open it, letting it lie there like an old piece of the heart's chamois.

El Paladín's prescription for jungle boils.

Sports clipping. Who the hell are the Denver Broncos?

† † †

Not long before the birth of his own son—Leo's little Vic was a year old and dominated the chalet—Harry became unaccountably restless. He peeked into the newspapers every morning, trying to find out who was hiring, if there were coded messages in the personal columns, and what some of the better-known contingents of mercenaries might be doing. He still rode the cable car up the mountain, but his enthusiasm for skiing had faded. He mostly sat in the restaurant on the slopes and watched people.

His attention began to focus on a rowdy group skiing at Villars that month. The leader was a big blond kid, perhaps twenty, with thick arms and a loud mouth. The group—there were five of them—managed to be in most of Harry's preferred spots. Their voices were metallic, their manner bullyish. Harry admitted to himself that he might have once been like that too, but this bunch annoyed him in some deep, irrational way. At the skating rink they hissed and booed the local hockey team. On the slopes they were noisy and rude. Harry's favorite waitresses at his favorite cafés gave them a wide berth.

That they were Americans annoyed Harry most. One of them had a twang in his voice—Texas, maybe—and they wore the shaggy hair typical of this period. They were in the small village two weeks, three, on and on.

One afternoon Harry watched them in a bar. For some reason which was hilarious only to them, the big blond kid was spitting on the floor and pointing down at it. The rest of them howled with delight.

Val was in her ninth month, big as a house, but had just been given a book contract and an advance payment and seemed in a much better mood than Harry. The book—which, finally, she would never write—was supposed to be about the Elite Rifles and Katanga.

In the evenings Vic was often left with a sitter in the chalet while Val and Harry gobbled French food at one of the hotels, usually the Sporting or the old Villars Palace. On this particular evening a flamenco guitarist was playing at one of the big local bars, though, so they went there. Val wore her beads and bracelets, a bright loose-flowing *kanga,* and jeans unbuttoned at the top. She looked beautiful and Harry enjoyed the fact that she received stares and attention—pregnant as she was—from every man in the room. They arrived late and were shown to a poor table beside the jukebox, but ate some good baked chicken and drank beer and were in a good mood as the guitarist finished his first numbers.

Then the five boys came swaggering in. They took up their places at the bar—noisy, as usual—and Harry seemed almost happy to see them.

"Someone you know?" Val asked.

"Not exactly," Harry said, finishing his dinner.

The guitarist took a break, came back, and finished another set. Val was surprised that Harry seemed content to watch and wait; he usually wanted to go back to the chalet after the meal, so she assumed he enjoyed the music and the brandies.

They talked about places to live. Spain, London, Texas: it was agreed they should have villas, flats, ranches. Val seemed informed about London prices, so Harry turned his snifter in his fingers and listened—watching Val's eyes and lips as she talked and looking just beyond her where the boys occupied the curve of the bar.

"Of course we're going to run out of money," she said, laughing. "By the way, did you ever tell your Uncle Peacock what he wanted to know?"

"No, nothing," Harry said absently.

The guitarist had finished his last show, the bar crowd had thinned, and the last drinks of the night were being served when the big blond kid ambled over and shoved some coins into the jukebox. The sound was Elvis Presley—no more offensive than anything else, but loud. As the blond kid returned to his admirers, Harry reached over and unplugged the box. Sudden silence.

A smile edged into Val's mouth and she watched as Harry pretended they were still very much in conversation.

"Go on," he urged her. "You were saying?"

"Saying what?"

"About the price of a good London flat."

"We finished talking about that," she informed him.

"Hey, butt hole," the blond kid said. Another of the group said something, too, but Harry didn't catch it.

"And where is it you wanted to live?" Harry continued. "Kensington?"

"Near the heath someplace," she said, going along with him now.

"So the kids can play."

"Right." The smile curved her lips.

"Butt hole," the kid called. "Plug it back in."

Harry shifted in his chair, so he could see all the boys at the bar. Each of them seemed to be trying to say something. There was also a young bartender—not having much fun with his job—who spoke in a voice high-pitched enough to carry across the room. He said in French that he wanted no trouble.

"Butt hole: *you*," the kid said, ambling back toward Harry.

"Oh my," Val said under her breath.

But Harry was on his feet with a big smile, hands in the air. "Hey, everybody, hey," he said in friendly ambiguity. Only Val understood that he had lost his temper.

The blond kid occupied the center of the room now, hands in his pockets. He was thick across the chest and shoulders, deeply tanned, smirking—as if all this pleased him, too.

"We're having this conversation," Harry explained, gesturing toward Val. "And so—" He reached down and picked up the cord to the jukebox, held it up, and pulled the plug off. "I want everybody in here to please leave. Leave the bar. Right now, please."

Incredulity on the boy's face. One of his friends at the bar broke into laughter. But Harry's smile had altered into something so harsh that the blond kid didn't join the laughter and two men in a booth nearby fumbled in their pockets, got their money up, and started out.

"You too," Harry said to the other kids at the bar. "Vacate the premises, please, will you?"

The bartender protested weakly. Meanwhile Harry turned slowly so that his pointing finger signaled a solitary drinker there, two others here, and a number of the night's customers began to obey. In the silence one could hear the sound of a car motor out in the street.

"And especially you, butt hole," Harry said to the blond kid, who tried to muster a tough smile.

The kid turned to his buddies, they exchanged smiles, then moved as a group toward Harry. But they stopped. Harry had produced the little Astra-Constable, its shiny chrome nose pointed their way. By the time the blond kid saw it, Harry had jumped toward him, feinted left, right, and kicked him in the groin.

"Don't go, after all," Harry told the others. "Stay and watch."

"Mister, come on—" one of them intoned.

Harry sat down on his haunches in front of the boy curled in pain on the tile floor.

"Where're you from, butt hole?" Harry asked him softly. "You're not from Texas, are you?"

"Up yours," the boy managed to rasp.

Harry sighed heavily. The pistol was held lightly, pointing at no one in particular, but the boys at the bar had frozen in place and two more customers edged out the front door. The bartender said something else.

Harry tucked the pistol out of sight beneath his folded arm. "No, if you were from Texas you'd have more manners," he said.

Val spoke Harry's name in a reasonable tone.

People outside the place peered through the windows.

"Piss off," the boy rasped.

Harry took him by the hair and banged his face on the tile. The second blow broke his nose and addled him.

One of the others said, "We apologize, mister, no shit," but

Harry hardly acknowledged him. Instead, he dragged the blond kid over to the bar—the others fell back—and arranged his face against the brass bar rail. When the kid twitched into consciousness, Harry reached into his neck and pressed the carotid artery—his old trick, it gave him a smile that he could still do it—until the twitch ended and the kid passed out again.

Val was standing, smiling nervously.

"Oh, heyyyyy," another boy groaned. "Don't, man!"

Harry seemed to know what he was doing, yet didn't. There was mainly the moment at hand.

Someone outside yelled for the police.

Harry put the boy's mouth on the brass rail, balancing it just so. The boy stretched out on his stomach, his neck arched up, mouth open, the rail propping up his head in a high and awkward position. Then Harry kicked in the back of the boy's head and broke out most of his teeth; the impact made a sickening noise and Harry and Val left before the police and ambulance arrived.

The next day, though, a delegation came to the chalet: two Swiss gentlemen in business suits, very apologetic, and a policeman who winked at Victor. They were sorry, it was all very unfortunate, but Harry was under arrest.

† † †

On fifty acres ten miles out of Nairobi another camp began to grow: large tents with wooden floors and roofs covered with leaves and *maputi*—palm branches. Leo decorated them with bones, skulls, rocks and fossils and planted wild flowers and cactus around them. His soldiers became *watu:* workers laying walkways and heating water for baths, gardening and throwing out corn for the warthogs and bushbuck who came to feed. "This isn't forever," he promised them. "We'll get back into the thick of it."

He put up one frame building, the studio, in which he kept his books and papers. They dug a cave into the side of a hill, put the generator there so the noise of the motor wouldn't be heard, and turned the remainder of the space into an arsenal: flares, Sten guns, dynamite, M-1s, mortars, cases of cartridges.

Northern Rhodesia was a political dogfight now, Zambia was coming into being in its place, and the Ndola camp was impossible. Leo put it up for sale. The bungalow embraced weeds and vines which crept out of the surrounding forest; the parade field became an undergrowth. In the harbor at Durban the yacht's paint peeled away in the sunshine and slime formed at the waterline. Leo's things, like his life, seemed to fall into disuse, and his enthusiasms for establishing a new camp faded quickly so that everything had a partial look: the tents not quite furnished, the flower beds dug up but not fully planted, the pump at the well not working all the time. He drifted into town most days, leaving Weldu and Mewishi and the others to their idleness. They made home brew in the cave and got fat.

El Paladín and Pogo baited leopards—which Leo enjoyed. They hung the reeking carcasses of gazelle and antelope from a tree in clear view of Leo's tent, and when the wind was right, blowing out over the valley and the distant Ngong hills— called, locally, *knuckles*—a leopard would sometimes come up at night and take a leap at it. They didn't shoot or photograph this, just watched. It gave them all a good feeling.

One day two neighbors from across the valley came to the new camp. They were both German: red-faced, decked out in leather vests and safari trousers, enough alike so they were probably brothers. The leopards, they told Leo, you will have to stop baiting.

"Why is that?" Leo asked.

"We are afraid they will eat up our dogs," one of them asserted.

"If you're afraid for your dogs," Leo told them, "better let us bait leopards so they'll get their bellies filled."

The Germans claimed there were never leopards in the valley before Leo and his men hung bait.

Leo said he didn't want to discuss the matter.

Lawyers will be called, the Germans said.

"If there's anything I bloody detest it's a dog," Leo finally told them. "Besides, when the leopards aren't fed they die off. And when the leopards die off the baboons increase."

The Germans indicated they didn't want to be lectured on wildlife.

When they left, Leo was furious.

After that he didn't allow his men to put up bait for more than a month and the dogs of the vicinity began to disappear. *Watu* from the neighbors told Leo's men this and everyone at camp began to keep score according to report and rumor. One boxer, two poodles, a pit bull, a prized spaniel: they loved it. "If I could find a leopard with his belly full of that domestic meat," Leo said, "I'd strike the beast a special medal! I'd give him the Victoria, the Medal of Honor, the Iron Cross!"

Wild animals are slender and intelligent and beautiful! They have a high social order and laugh and play games! All that is ever needed of a domestic animal in contrast is that he's fat and greedy and oversexed!

† † †

Deep in the Nigerian palm jungles and their mazes of lagoons and indolent creeks north of the Niger delta, a young army officer dreamed of good armor.

He was drunk on palm wine. In fact, he had just finished the whitish residue at the bottom of a gourd of wine and he dreamed, babbled, and plotted not too coherently.

He staggered to the edges of that deep trench surrounding the city of Benin, a relic of ancient defense dating back to the old medieval kingdom.

If I had good armor, he told the forest, I'd build a new kingdom from here to the Cameroon range, from the Udi hills across the oil rivers to the Bight of Biafra.

Palm wine soured in his dark beard.

Biafra. I'll devise a coat of arms with two leopards, he decided. I'll be a millionaire, shipping oil out of Port Harcourt. My mother will open a French restaurant in Calabar. If I get armor.

He imagined his heart's desire: a big Saracen armored lorry mounted with machine guns, carrying rockets and cannon. With a white mercenary—courageous, but, more important, mechanically minded—to operate it.

The young officer tumbled into the trench and rolled to the bottom with a smile on his face.

And a white woman, beautiful and wicked, he told himself, at my side. And a wise man to tell me all the truths of my ambition.

Little did he know.

† † †

When Leo visited Brussels and Paris to confer with representatives of munitions manufacturers, he came into the company of a French film director, Louis Starkie, and the actress Ramona. The two had traveled together for some years, had

made films set in Algeria, and had turned to intellectual con-
templations in the way so many movie people did—without
benefit of history, philosophy, or much literature. Starkie, who
was graying and distinguished-looking, believed that Eisen-
stein somehow lived before Plato and that the cradle of western
civilization was located somewhere along the American west
coast. Ramona touched her breasts when she talked and her
basic theme was that Africa was a wild and wonderful place,
that everyone should live there and go naked, and that animal
instincts should prevail.

Both of them found Leo exciting and authentic.

Starkie announced that he would film the Commander's next
war, and Ramona insisted she could bring Leo sexually alive
again.

They arranged evenings around Paris so Leo could express
himself.

*Any life that exhibits strong vitality is doomed! The large
beasts of the savannahs are somehow too free and powerful to
be let alone! Reasons are always found to put them on game
reserves, to tamper with their mating, their food, their paths,
their spirits! They're an affront! They're not barnyard creatures
and man is! But let me tell you: when they're gone and man
has only tameness to ponder he'll despise himself!*

Starkie shot several thousand feet of film with Leo as pro-
tagonist: sitting on the little white balcony overlooking the
Boulevard St. Michel, throwing daggers at the cork wall of an
apartment near the Invalides, walking in St. Germain, posing
at the emperor's tomb. Leo's voice over all this: glories of the
soldier's life, the code of honor, exploiting the dark continent,
and such subjects.

The friends of the director and actress enjoyed Leo and the
Commander fancied himself on the screen. He grew his mus-

tache longer. In the darkness of Starkie's studio off the Boulevard Raspail they viewed the takes: a closeup of Leo, Leo making a point, Leo smiling. Starkie contemplated splicing in shots of war, tanks and infantry, exploding bombs or diving planes, and he and Leo stumbled through their views of film aesthetics. They also ate a number of crepes, drank cases of wine, and tried to decide what to do with Ramona.

"She's stricken with you," Starkie complained.

"I'm burned out," Leo confessed, but the concept of a ruined warrior appealed very much to the director and he always suggested that Leo should take Ramona on a long trip.

"Also introduce her to the men who sell arms," Starkie suggested. "She likes all sorts of adventurers."

Following this advice Leo invited Ramona to the Restaurant Ledoyen with two Belgian gentlemen. Ramona preferred to call them "gunrunners" and looked for double meanings in all that was said. One of them advised Leo that it was perfectly all right to sell himself as a middleman in African wars, promising heads of state that he could deliver untold quantities of ordnance, but that he should always make certain he was the best armed among his allies.

"Protect your own reputation," the man said. "Why give some steelie your only antitank weapon? Keep it and use it! Be sure your own men have the automatics, too."

"Naturally," Leo said. "I'm not a beginner, you know."

Ramona asked if this was a secret meeting.

"Secret?" the Belgians asked her.

"You're speaking to Leo in code, right?" she persisted.

"No, not at all."

"Does anyone suspect what we're doing here?" she whispered.

"Perhaps the maître d'," Leo suggested.

After midnight Leo and Ramona walked up the Champs-Élysées toward the lighted arch. The sound of drummers was in Leo's ears, though Ramona was still chattering about strong men. A faint mist fell on the streets and the late-evening lights played in the delicate pools as Leo tried to imagine what it must have been like coming back from Austerlitz, leaving Russia or Egypt and returning here, flags whipping the air, frenzied voices, the reality of war zones traded away for the urban niceties; he didn't like cities—and somehow the better the city the more he disliked it. Paris was illusion: all beautiful and wrong like icing on a cake.

"What're you thinking?" Ramona asked, squeezing his arm.

"You wouldn't know if I told you."

"Don't be too cruel. Just a little."

He was afraid he couldn't perform with her, but did his duty. In the wallowing maw of his hotel feather bed, he had to find her and pin her (she was a real acrobat) and all of a sudden he was gushing away. Afterward, he stood naked in the middle of the bed—ankle deep in softness.

It's all right to be afraid out there, he told her, *but don't linger on the problem! Take Harry. He was never afraid of being afraid, though when the time came to fight I reckon he pissed in his pants same as the rest of us!*

"Of course he did!" Ramona shouted.

It isn't true I'm a coward! I was always a tactician, not a bloody hero, but I was there: I've seen a hell of a lot of wars and had their fever and their fucking fear! Goddamn the man who says he's seen hell any closer!

"Leo, darling, I love you!" Ramona shouted.

A profound melancholy came over Leo the next day. He went out to Orly and sat around on plastic benches until he could get a flight; hours went by and he neither ate nor slept nor read the newspapers nor even thought about anything; his mind went blank with depression. Ramona's perfume was on his clothes—which he hated. Beyond that he had the vague terror that he might grow old living in cities such as Paris, walking boulevards or sitting in parks or sleeping on such beds.

He felt once, briefly, that when he was airborne, winging out over the Mediterranean toward Africa again, his emotions would come under control. But they didn't. His mood deepened and the awful hours in the airport turned into weeks, months, years; he didn't even count or keep up, though he wondered once or twice if he had possibly set some records for pure pain.

† † †

"That boy's mouth will never get right," J. R. admonished Harry.

"I'm sorry, I really am."

"And a *pistol!* Jesus! Nobody here totes a pistol!"

"I don't know what came over me." Harry was so properly contrite that the full burden of responsibility seemed to fall to J. R., who had come back to Villars to straighten matters out.

At first Harry had claimed diplomatic immunity. Then a Swiss judge asked outright for a bribe. Then the parents of the boy who lost his teeth on the bar rail flew in from Ohio. Harry's status with the American government was reviewed, defined and argued in a series of telegrams, phone calls, and official letters; a notice of eviction came to the chalet; a deposition was taken from the ski patrol noting that Harry was a disobedient sort who strayed off the correct slopes; little Victor wouldn't accept his potty training; the deadline for Val's first piece of book manuscript passed; and finally immunity was declared technically impossible. But J. R. Hoskins paid off the boy's parents, the judge, and had the incident struck from Harry's file.

"You're still on the inactive payroll," he informed Harry. "But take care! A pistol in an Alpine café! Jesus, you're not in Houston!"

"I wasn't going to shoot any of them."

"What if they attacked you while you were beating up their pal?"

"Well, I might've blown off a kneecap or something."

"A pistol in Switzerland! Jesus!"

Harry's son, Jocko, was born in Spain, then, in a clinic in Denia down the coast from Valencia. Harry and Val bought a small villa with a pool and guest house on the Cabo de la Nao looking out toward the Balaerics, the shadowy outline of Ibiza out there on the horizon. Below their cliff was a patch of beach hidden in the rocks—some forty foot square—where Vic, tanned and thick in the chest, waded into the blue water when he was scarcely a year old. Jocko liked sleep. There was a maid who fixed paella on an open fire near the guest house. Val planted a garden of bright flowers beneath the canopy of almond blossoms.

All was pleasant again, except Harry's nightmares resumed.

He dreamt the awful dream he called his extravaganza.

Otherwise, fine: they drove the coast from Valencia to Alicante taking meals in little seaside restaurants, went to the bullfights in Ondara and Benidorm, visited the ancient mountain stronghold of Guadalest tucked in the jagged hills. Val seemed contented at the villa, spending her time on its garden and upkeep, going to the market with the maid and children, swimming, dieting, and caring for her looks again. She looked wonderful, Harry thought, if a little too much of a contrast to the plain village women who slouched around in their black mourning clothes.

Harry lifted weights, traded in the Fiat for a Jaguar sedan, and bought two motorbikes—a Triumph and a Honda which he tried to induce Val to ride. He also set about establishing a small armory out in the guest house. At first it contained only his personal sidearms and ammunition, but it grew. Soon three other heavy rifles occupied the rack with the Mauser-Bauer and several pistols—everything except the Astra-Constable which had created the stir in Switzerland and which was now kept in his bedside table—materialized in a display case out there beyond the pool and garden. He bought a loader for his several calibers of cartridges and even complained that he had no grenades or explosives.

It became known in the village that they went around unclothed at the villa on the cape—the boys, too—and that they swam naked in the cove. But they were accepted as foreigners and other foreigners invited them to dinners they didn't attend or to the club at El Tosalet for tennis and greeted them with smiles on market days. They were such handsome people, some said, that any social oversight or unfortunate rumor would be forgiven, and to the natives strong sons were proof of family solidarity and well-being which was much admired.

Once or twice a week men or boys would pause in cars or bicycles on the road near the lighthouse there on the cape hoping to get a glimpse of Val's naked body down there in the private cove. This annoyed Harry, but Val said they didn't bother her—and, anyway, she said, nobody ever stopped at the right times.

And Harry's dream came again and again.

"Tell it to me," Val urged him, but he didn't want to.

He used to never dream, he said, and when he slept he saw only a peaceful sheet of white; he was never even interested in his dream life, but this one dream came so often that he finally did get interested, thought about it too much, in fact, and got concerned.

"You've opened up your nether life," Val told him.

"Maybe so. I might as well tell you about it."

He was an old knight, he said, white-haired underneath a shiny helmet, the leader of seven or eight young companions armed with broadswords; it was the end of a long day's siege of a castle beside a lake; the fighting had waned—his army had clearly won the day—and he ordered their horses sent back to camp and announced to his men that they'd spend the night in the castle of their defeated enemy. A groom gathered the horses, then his companions called him over where two of the remaining enemies, squires of the lord of the castle, were backed up against some rocks near the castle's sluggish moat. They wouldn't put down their swords and surrender. And in the dream, considering what to do about these two stubborn boys, he stared down at his coat of mail—blue ringlets, a cold metal—giving himself elaborate study. Details everywhere: it was all very real. Then he walked over to where his young, hot-headed companions were toying with them. Everyone watched and laughed as the two squires were given lessons in the use of the broadsword. It was a mean sport, naturally, since neither of the two could escape, but no matter, they were brave, not one quiver of their mouths or an unsteady hand, and not one word of mercy asked. One by one the old knight's young war-riors stepped in to tease these two, then stepped back as others took them on. Then one of Harry's men made a clumsy move and took a slash on the arm, a nasty slice to the bone, and

Harry suddenly lost his temper with this stupid show, stepped in himself, and gave one of the squires a blow across the neck and shoulders which almost beheaded him. A sudden silence. Everybody stood there stunned. Then, recovering, taking their leader's example, they closed in and finished both the squires: a quick, neat butchering, metal on metal and flesh. Harry walked to one side, embarrassed, feeling he should say something in his defense. His men put the two heads on the stakes of the iron fence beside the drawbridge and everyone went inside the castle.

The dream then had a second major part.

They moved through the castle viewing their meager spoils and visiting the wounded brought off the field.

Dank rooms and hallways. A castle with many small chambers, narrow turrets and cramped hallways which opened into immense galleries and festival halls then narrowed once more into side rooms, small passageways, and closets. Floors of tile, a marbled rose color. Walls of gray stone with lackluster tapestries. Rough tables with pewter.

In a large gallery Harry moved down the rows between the wounded, then stopped at a window where he glimpsed the cold November lake stretching off toward the Alps. Then he moved among his men again, touching an extended hand, comforting where he could. They were moaning and crying with only a flagon or two for anesthetic, most of them with amputations or mortal wounds from lance or sword.

He came to a bedroom, then, the master suite, and there was the old lord of the castle, dying, a frail, white-faced bastard, and as Harry entered a servant held the old man up into a sitting position on the velvet-covered bed, and sitting there feebly in his black robe, as a kind of salute or curse, the old man lifted a death mask to his face—it was fixed on a carved handle—and held it there with a palsied fist until Harry passed through.

And in the last room of his visit Harry came toward a hard bed set in a large bay window overlooking the lake; he moved toward the figure resting there, lying in silhouette against the lake's twilight. Echoes of his own ominous footfall as he approached. He felt his age like ballast as he crossed that room: his hands veined and elderly and his back aching under the strain of the armor. Then he reached the figure and it had no chest nor stomach, just a cavity of gore, but it wasn't dead, the eyes opened, and there it was, unmistakably: it was Jocko, his Jocko, and he was thirty years old, say, as of course Harry had never seen him outside the dream, but it was Harry's own son.

Val touched Harry's arm, comforting him.

"I never understood before," he told her. "For that matter maybe I don't know now."

"It's an awful dream," she said.

"I don't think I'm superstitious," he admitted, "or I wouldn't tell it."

† † †

A year of games.

One learned the limits of Scrabble, the infinitude of chess, what properties were best in Monopoly (railroads were okay early in the game, but should later be traded off), and the character of poker. Everybody and everything, Harry decided, was divulged in games: Val, for instance, trusted any player with an inherent mean streak. And in the irrational patterns of his own chess maneuvers Harry saw himself.

"If Leo were here," Val said, "we'd also be playing back-gammon, obstacle course, and intellectual hopscotch."

"Not to mention eternal triangle," Harry added.

Competition, he remembered Leo saying, *is the highest form of civilization. Beyond it, there's only pure aggression.*

Games, then, day and night.

The boys grew up, Victor bullying little Jocko, so even that became one of the sports of the household.

† † †

Leo had his games, too—as a reclusive betting man. Sitting in a canvas chair in the camp outside Nairobi, pencil in hand, studious and lost, he went over various betting forms and newspapers.

In the afternoons Mewishi would get into the Land Rover and drive down to the New Stanley Hotel where he would send off a fistful of telex messages conveying Leo's hunches on some obscure heavyweight from Bristol or the Queen's Park Rangers or the rugby playoffs. Leo claimed that he used to be a wing forward in his svelte years, so rugby got most of his attentions. For a couple of seasons he followed the good South African team, winning four thousand pounds on them one time down in Ellis Park when they trounced Australia 25–3 for the championship.

The nearby cotton trees sent their airy particles across his face as he sat there in his betting chair.

And Mewishi enjoyed his duty. After sending out the Commander's wagers, Mewishi would go up to the bar on the mezzanine, sit there with a lime cooler and a copy of *The Standard,* and act the gentleman. He bought himself a fez for such occasions, keeping it underneath the seat in the Land

Rover, fitting it atop his head as he drove into town. He wished the Commander could be there, too; that they could be seen together sitting near the big tusks which embraced the door, drinking and talking, having sent money all over the world.

† † †

Val wrote an article on the city of Valencia noting its history and present character.

El Cid had driven the last of the moors from Valencia and when they were gone they were grieved, she noted, for they had been a tolerant people, artisans and warriors, and the Christians who came forward were poor replacements. It was also the last city to hold out against Franco's troops and like many good cities was always at its best at war.

A sexual city, like Rome or Alexandria. A hint of intrigues on the balconies.

A definite feminine character: both maternal and whorish.

Political, too: the sidewalk bars and cafés were usually packed with speechmakers, arms raised, and every bartender in town could mimic the dictator.

The common bribes thrived. Critics of bullfighters, for instance, were just paid off not to write anything ugly.

Pagan incense billowed up from the gray cathedrals.

Ragtag vendors wailed outside the fashionable *galerías*.

Old men traded Civil War stories for cigarettes.

A beautiful decay.

The jokes were dark and the drink was always *sangría*.

Death was the essential ritual and motif and their great fiesta—Las Fallas—literally turned to ashes.

Late at night some fat and middle-aged flamenco singer cried her song, Val wrote, and flamenco here wasn't the bright

and high-twirling tourist dance, but a doleful song like the
blues, the lament of a broken woman.

† † †

For Harry, Spain became tiresome and he couldn't capture
his dismay in such a romantic way. He began to complain, Val
told him, in the style of Leo.

"The Spanish beaches, the whole coast," Harry said, "caters
to every fat tourist in Europe. They come down here on those
chartered planes just to trample the sand. Everything gets pol-
luted by bodies, the stench of paella and beer—and all because
of those short little holidays!"

Beyond the beaches, of course, was a poor countryside:
scraggly earth, those familiar white mongrels at the sides of
the road, bent peasants, tumbledown *fincas,* and the dictator's
sullen army of Guardia Civil walking around with their plastic
hats and capes. The Mediterranean was wasted; centuries of
carpenters had used up the timber and generations of fishermen
had cleaned out the sea. The sleepy towns were overgrown
with tourist hotels and shabby *apartamentos.* The famous rock
at Calpe—which once looked as regal as Gibraltar—had cheap
buildings all over it and looked like a big brown crustacean
covered with parasites.

Even the bullfights were sad. Occasionally Harry saw a
novicio rammed against a barrier and knocked silly, but the
pageantry of the *corrida* was gone, there was neither terror nor
real valor, and everyone in the stands looked appalled.

One night Harry eased out of bed and paced the darkened
house. It was a moonless night as he went out to the armory
and slipped into a dark sweater and pants. He snapped on a

holster and fitted the Astra-Constable under his left arm. A knife in the belt, a black handkerchief, a Navy stocking cap: all ready.

He stopped by Val's bed, then by the boys'. They curled in such beautiful sleep that he cursed his restlessness, but he went outside again—it was near three A.M.—and rolled the Triumph down the driveway and half a mile down the cape road before getting on it and kicking the motor alive. Soon the cool night air was in his face as he considered his plan.

The headquarters of the Guardia Civil down in Alicante was a big stone monstrosity with a large inner courtyard surrounded by offices and barracks for the men, officers, and families of the corps: a rabbit hutch of a military compound replete with nurseries and arsenals. It sat in the midst of a busy commercial section of that city with lots of traffic outside and lots of crying babies and nagging wives inside, so that in the early hours of the morning one could go over the wall in the rear of the complex, go along the shadowed *naya* of the inner courtyard, and break the padlock to the arsenal.

Before dawn there was a guard change—Harry had watched all this and kept times—and that seemed the right moment to escape. There were only a few questions: whether to go in armed or not, whether to create a diversion at some point, what to do if seen and caught. Harry thought on these as he cycled down to Alicante, passing the rock at Calpe, the dark sea at his left, the black handkerchief around his neck flapping in the breeze.

Then he didn't think about anything further.

He went over the wall, hoisting himself into that military ghetto, moving through an empty latrine area—god, the odor—then into a narrow passageway which opened on the courtyard. He sat there in the darkness for a long time—perhaps thirty minutes—wanting to smoke one of the old Celtas which he found in a pocket, but not stirring.

A simple burglary. And an old fashioned breathless wait with lots of uncertainties. Anticipation and danger. Unknown factors. He was enjoying himself.

What if he had to kill a guard, he asked himself, to get out of there? He dismissed the problem.

He waited.

Beyond the courtyard wall he could hear the voices of the guards and their footfalls. They were out there with their plastic bonnets as straight as straight, clumsy rifles bulging underneath their capes. Franco's stupid little home army.

When their footfalls died away and he knew they were at the other end of the compound, he slipped around to the door of the arsenal and knocked off the lock. Inside was a room with a dirt floor smelling of bluing and oil.

The dynamite was being used on roadwork up around Villajoyosa and kept here for safety until the engineers called for it. This wasn't a country careless with its explosives and Harry knew he shouldn't be greedy, but he wanted a box for his very own. He switched on his pencil flashlight, pleasant sensations coursing through him, his pulse hammering along. The door edged open, a cool pinpoint of air touching Harry's cheek, so he shut off the light again while closing the door. Careful, he told himself. But he grinned in the darkness. Again, he waited and thought over his situation.

There were three or four guards out there around the perimeter of the compound, none of them expecting anything—much less that someone would try and break *out* of their headquarters.

If Leo were here, Harry knew, he'd complain that this wasn't at all well planned.

Waiting. Thinking what to do with the box if a guard jumped out unexpectedly. Harry turned on the flashlight once more, found his treasure, hefted it, sucked in his breath.

Outside the door to the arsenal, Harry made the padlock presentable again, then hurried along the length of the *naya* with his burden. Some dreary captain might climb out of bed upstairs, he realized, and gaze down into the courtyard trying to catch some poor guard sleeping on watch. Best to hurry through the remaining steps. Harry moved through the shadows and once—ever so slightly—his tennis shoes squeaked on the tiles.

He stopped in a doorway, looking outside for guards. Nobody near. Then, quickly, on to the next doorway. The weight of the box was a strain.

Then, some extraordinary minutes.

Harry stood in the next doorway looking through a narrow crack where the door stood slightly ajar. A sentry was there. His back was turned to Harry, he stared off absently into the night, and they were some four feet apart, separated by the thick wooden door, yet so close that Harry got a whiff of the beer and nicotine on the man. Harry took a brief inventory of possibilities, considering an attack, how best to do it. The man was isolated from the other guards, around the corner of the compound wall, out of earshot, standing there alone and probably half asleep.

Then, a subtle turn of the guard's cheek.

A frozen moment.

They waited, both of them, breaths held, for a few supreme seconds: the guard felt Harry's presence, no doubt of it.

The man felt Harry as the hunter in the bush feels the leopard, as Harry had felt that mystic javelina years ago in South Texas; fear reeked on the man and Harry's advantage over him grew so strong that Harry wanted to burst out laughing.

The guard wouldn't turn around all the way. The hairs on the back of his neck were erect, his knees had turned to water, and he didn't want to confirm what his nerve ends told him.

Then he was gone. He hurried away, leaving his post.

Harry edged the door open with his shoulder, glanced down the length of the outside street, and stepped into the light.

Three blocks away he boldly tied the box of dynamite and caps onto the rear of his motorcycle, kicked the motor over, and started home.

† † †

After this he cursed himself for his recklessness.

Normalcy: that's what he wanted. He wanted the sun to come up over the terrace in the morning, the sea regular and calm, the unities of toast and coffee, Val with little Jocko on her lap, Vic bouncing a ball, the secure sounds, sights, and habits. He said it to himself like a litany: I'll go another ten years and won't lose my head, promise, and time will stitch me together, my dreams will soften, I promise, and maybe the fire will die away and Val and I can live in the embers, she'll change with me, I promise, I won't do it again.

He watched Val come up the path from the cove surrounded by a flight of butterflies; golden in the sun, all of them, the butterflies swarming like a bright nimbus. I won't risk myself again, he swore.

The garden was redolent with new blossoms, and across the way, decked and entwined with bougainvillea and roses, sat the armory. Promise. Another ten years, even more. I do promise.

He didn't even want that goddamned dynamite.

† † †

"We want the Elite Rifles active," J. R. Hoskins drawled. "The time's comin' when our policies need to be so flexible that—well, we can withdraw an American force, say, yet still have a clandestine group in the field."

"My men are scattered all over bloody hell," Leo answered.

"Get new ones. Or, if you want, we'll share our files."

"What files?"

"We've got files on all the men who ever served with you," J. R. revealed. "I think we still know where most of 'em are."

Leo gave J. R. a stare. Exasperating, this bunch, but they always were efficient.

The verandah at the Norfolk Hotel had been remodeled and Leo couldn't bear it. It was referred to as the Lord Delamere Terrace—or some such—and the safari types were everywhere with their Colpro suits and suntans. There was a great cuteness about "going on safari" which Leo sniffed at—including the term itself. The concept included such niceties as safari boxes, porters, the proper clothes, the correct gear, and the whole British ornamentation. It was even bad taste sitting on this sanitary verandah, Leo felt, except that in the company of an American it didn't matter and, besides, the Peacock was a monument to bad taste of all sorts.

J. R. Hoskins ordered a T-bone steak with chips and waved his empty whiskey glass at their waiter.

"We'd like you buzzing around the Arabs, but anywhere on the continent is okay," J. R. went on. "You've got a good nose for trouble, so we'll just follow your lead."

"Good of you," Leo murmured.

"And if you end up on the wrong side of the fence, that'll

still work fine. You may shoot a friend of ours now and then, but that'll look convincing."

"Absolutely," Leo agreed, sipping his cooler.

"We'll renovate that shabby yacht of yours sitting at Durban," J. R. continued. "We've got a nice budget item for that job: special facilities. We also have an apartment in Salisbury we'd like you to use. For that matter, anywhere. Half a piazza in Rome, if you ever want it."

"Did you ever deliver that letter for me?" Leo asked.

"No, couldn't locate them."

"I don't believe you."

"We can also get you better deals with the arms manufacturers, so you won't be trotting all over Europe introducing yourself," J. R. said. "And we'll build up your supplies here. But our relationship with Kenya is shaky as hell, so best you station at Durban or Salisbury."

"You know where they are now, don't you?" Leo persisted.

"Yes, in Spain."

Leo tried to conjure up a quick image of Spain, but couldn't. His mind tripped along.

"Oh, yeah, a place in Mombasa, too," J. R. remembered.

"You seen them personally?" Leo asked.

"No, never."

"I don't believe that, either."

"Tell you what else," J. R. went on, glancing around for the elusive waiter. "We'll even decorate you, too. Give you a bona fide American medal, services in Washington, and let you say a few words. You'd like that, wouldn't you?"

"You've been studying my file," Leo answered.

"Damn right. Got you memorized." J. R. grinned and brushed bread crumbs off his green-striped blazer.

"Where in Spain? Madrid?"

"Don't you cause them any trouble," J. R. warned, sounding like a Texas sheriff.

"I haven't got any trouble in me," Leo said. "I'm too old. And my heart's broken."

"What you need," J. R. said, visibly moved, touching Leo's sleeve in a fatherly way, "is a good war. You'll be fine."

† † †

Weldu ran away from the camp because he just couldn't accept his new status as a *mutu*.

He should have cleaned guns, skinned out the animals caught in snares for camp food, carved new pistol grips or walking sticks, banked up the evening fires, kept the gear in its ordered place, kept hot water for tea or shaving, all that. But there was no drill, no proper demeanor, no beautiful Val. Only Leo's promises that some future would occur. He took his pay, walked out to the highway, and bought passage on a local bus as far as it took him—to the edge of nowhere. Then he started out toward the Northern Frontier on foot, buying food en route, and sleeping at night underneath his camouflage-colored slicker.

He dreamt of his people, the Dinka, as he curled in sleep on the hard ground. They were always a nearly naked people with fur anklets, tall, with strong triceps and forearms; the women had high, dark breasts and flashing eyes. Like Weldu, they stood at ease on one foot, the other tucked up underneath. They herded cattle like the Masai and their land stretched from Uganda through Kenya into the Sudan, Ethiopia, and Somali. Gypsies. Free and good-natured. They liked themselves in full silhouette, standing straight and dark against a flat horizon.

On the fourth day out, Weldu was tired and worried that he had done the wrong thing. That night a bandit—or perhaps a boy teasing—ran by and jerked away the slicker. Weldu came up with his vintage .45 and fired a shot which reverberated around the open countryside like a cannon. The intruder kept running, dropping the slicker as he gathered speed. After that, though, Weldu couldn't get back to sleep and fretted that he had never been a proper warrior either as a Dinka or a mercenary. He had never actually shot anyone. Harry Veer had made an absolute fool of him in the Rex Hotel. In the famous battle which had taken the life of Sergeant Major Hicks, Weldu had only suffered the loss of a case of liniment. Before dawn he was walking again, leg-weary, soul-weary.

On the sixth day he came into the forests around Mount Kenya. He saw the wild bees, their legs yellow with pollen, and followed them higher and higher into the camphor forest with its ferns and leafy undergrowth. Toward evening he came on an old blind man who tended the bees and made a strong home brew out of their nectar.

"Sit down! Drink all you want! Have a rest!" the old man offered, so Weldu did. He drank two full gourds, then fell over in sleep.

The note of the lion and the cackle of the hyrax sounded in the forest.

The next morning Weldu got up, left his pistol with the old blind man, and went toward the high ground armed only with a *simi*—his long knife.

The mountain forest wore a deep gloom and a cathedral silence. Weldu was terribly afraid and couldn't reason out why he had come—and why, especially, he had decided to leave his pistol behind. He stopped at a stream, lay down on his stomach, drank, and when he got up he was somehow beyond fear. Death, like the ground fog, was all around him. And there was a great majesty about it which he hadn't understood before.

That afternoon he came back down the mountain and stayed with the old blind man again.

"Unbelievable up there," Weldu said. "I'm going back and tell my master about this experience."

"Your master," the old blind man said, "already knows these things."

† † †

Bad dreams were catching over the years.

Some nights Jocko screamed and beat the pillow and Harry would stumble into his bedroom, fumbling in the dark, until he had him in his arms. They'd sit on the side of the bed, Jocko in Harry's lap, Harry's head nodding in semisleep. Some nights Harry would remember the slender merchant who was his father and the creaking frame house on Brazos Street in South Texas many nightmares ago.

One night Harry asked Jocko what made him cry so.

"I saw a man come into my room and look around," Jocko said. "He had a bird on his shoulder and the bird scared me."

† † †

And on a day after a long summer in Spain, after the tourists were gone and the restaurants on the beaches had closed, Leo arrived. He was more overweight than ever, wore a scraggly beard, and his clothes—bits of uniform, jeans, leather—were so rough and worn that he looked like an old pirate come home from the sea. The man who got out of the taxi with him was a bent, distinguished-looking black man who wore a fez and who wouldn't be recognized until he spoke: Mewishi. They came up to the door of the villa, knocked, and were received by Victor—who stared open-mouthed, then ran away when Leo tried to scoop him up.

"What is it you want?" Val asked, sweeping downstairs as she heard the echo of men's voices in the foyer and the taxi driving off. But her words caught in her throat.

Harry was putting new tires on the Triumph and came through the kitchen with his greasy hands held away from his overalls when he saw Val in Leo's arms. Before any emotion could generate, though, Leo boomed out, "Harry, hey!" and came lurching his way, grabbed him, and gave him a bear hug. An old warmth came over Harry—and great relief. Leo was one of the two people in his life, after all, Val being the other, who gave him such rapport and here it was again. When Harry drew back and looked into the Commander's face Leo was wet in the eyes and Mewishi and Val and everyone else beamed.

Before supper Leo and Harry took a walk, shuffling along like two old men, putting one careful foot forward, gently, then another, heads down, until they came to the cliff above the little patch of beach. They could see the *cabo* and lighthouse.

"If a man steals an orange off a tree in this district," Harry said, "the authorities toss him in jail and forget him. But the local law's got a nice feature: if a man's really hungry, he can sit in anyone's grove and eat as many oranges as he wants underneath the tree where he picks them."

Harry cited this as an example of Spanish wisdom, but Leo wasn't impressed.

"Screw laws, even the good ones," Leo answered. *Law just protects property, Harry, and it's never more than the rhetoric of ownership and selfishness.*

"We've got to have laws," Harry decided.

"A bloody law that gives a few oranges to a poor man who's starving is no fucking big deal," Leo said, and he asserted that *legal language is a rationalization for power, the haves explaining the rules to the have-nots again,* and Harry couldn't muster much rebuttal, Leo being as strong and as much the same as ever.

Across the valley was another magnificnet rock looming above the sea, the mountain Montgó. Javea, the little village nestled on its far slope was settled by the Greeks, Harry explained, then this was all a Roman outpost, then Moorish.

"Harry, for Chrissakes!" Leo said, turning to him. "You *like* Spain?"

"We've been happy here," Harry contended.

"Yeah, Harry, sure," Leo said. "But I mean, are you really *happy* with happiness?"

"Hell, how should I know?" Harry answered, then he showed Leo the little armory out behind the swimming pool which the Commander was much more interested in.

Dinner that night turned into a series of inelegant stories which Val, looking queenly, encouraged. Harry told about working in the oil fields in Midland, Texas, where a sixty-year-old roustabout tangled with one of Harry's fellow football players. It was a fair fight as such brawls went, Harry allowed, and had a memorable detail. The kid, who was loud and strapping, went for the old man, missed, then got cuffed, kicked, and butted senseless. He was lying in the mud trying to see straight when the old guy strolled over to the tool box on the rig and selected a hammer. "Casual,"

Harry said. "Like he was picking a piece from a box of candy."

"Here now," Leo put in, "you didn't come to the aid of your teammate?"

"No buddy of mine. Just a pigheaded halfback snot who was to blame for what happened." The old roustabout ambled back over, Harry said, and we all thought, god, this is it, he's going to kill that dumb kid, but, then, sort of artistically, the old man stretched out the boy's arm and knocked off the right thumb. "Neat," Harry said. "One short little stroke."

"Let's hear it for the team," Val said.

"Daddy tells good ones," Victor added proudly, which got a look all around.

Stories, stories. De Sade loved narration. All crimes were juicier, he said, if they were told in story form before and after committing them.

After supper they smoked some hash. Leo was on his knees with the boys, slapping them around, a sort of soft, open-handed combat, with Leo explaining, "This is how the baby lion cubs learn to use their paws, see, they get bloody quick at this," and the three of them kept going like windmills until Jocko, clipped on the chin, retired for the night. The hash spun Harry around. He went out onto the terrace, took a deep breath of the salt air, then went to the kitchen where the maid and Mewishi were drinking Coke and playing gin rummy. Victor was watching and he patted Harry's arm. Everything softly whirling.

"Let's sack out for the night," Harry suggested, but this proved silly, there was TV to watch, the ever-present Spanish rerun of "Bonanza," so Harry left Vic and went in search of Jocko. Harry heard Leo's and Val's voices as he trudged upstairs.

The bed smelled like Jocko, rubbery like a clean tennis shoe, and soon Jocko's head was resting on Harry's shoulder.

Lying there with his son asleep against him, Harry thought, god, it hurts, I'm jealous as hell, I always have been, but what to do? He closed his eyes, considering, shit, I want to protect her, but she's the toughest of all of us. Val, my Val.

He slept more than an hour.

When he woke up he immediately knew that he'd find them together, that Leo would have everyone else in the house stoned by this time, everyone would be sleeping and the rooms silent except for the drugged breathing, and Leo and Val would be down there on the cushions somewhere. With such thoughts, he got up and staggered downstairs.

But they were watching television. Hovered around a bowl of popcorn and watching an old flick. Randolph Scott. And Vic, who was getting lanky, was sprawled out on Leo's lap translating the action for the Commander, Leo's Spanish being not so good.

"A piece of shit," Leo said of the movie.

Harry sat and watched, taking a nibble of the cold popcorn.

Val's eyes were almost closed in beautiful sleep.

Leo didn't look up anymore. He was listening to Vic translate the showdown.

PART FOUR

BIAFRA

PUBLICITY,
REFUGEES, STUDENTS,
DEALS, DEATH

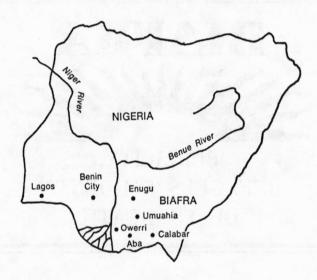

IN THE GATHERING DARKNESS THE BIAFRAN TROOPS formed a circle and opened fire at the surrounding mangrove jungle.

At first there were the reports of only a few rifles. With each crack of rifle fire limbs in the forest broke and snapped. Then the firepower increased. More men began opening up. Mortar shells exploded and trees toppled over in the darkness.

The jungle was shot away in a widening circle as the men grew frenzied. One brave soldier ran out a few paces and threw a grenade which sent up a tongue of orange flame. Another—very young, his chin jutted out in defiance—stood in full view on the hood of a lorry and sent out a long burst from his submachine gun. The men cheered him as he emptied his weapon and leaped back to safety. Those who had no real weapons ran to the edge of the circle and heaved sticks and stones into the darkness.

"There's nobody out there," Harry told Leo as they watched.

"I know it," Leo answered.

Commander Rucker and Colonel Veer had joined the Biafran force near Owerri. The Elite Rifles numbered only fourteen, but were greeted as saviors. They had armor, Sten guns, mortars, cannon, and an array of personal weapons while the thousand Biafrans had only two machine guns, a rifle for every three men, two creaking lorries, and two bicycles.

The men screamed as they fired now, yelling, "Yaahhhh!" as they emptied their guns. In the center of the circle where Harry and Leo stood, Colonel Jiggs Akpakpan distributed the ammunition. His eyes rolled insanely as he handed out grenades, clips of bullets, and mortar shells like a demented clerk. Once or twice he had the presence of mind to reprimand one of the men who came back for more that he was firing too quickly, that he should make his ammo last, and not be greedy.

Someone opened up with tracer bullets and the entire troop cheered. The good part of the fireworks had just begun.

A flare ignited along the edge of the jungle. More cheers. By its greenish light one could see the stumps of whole trees; a cloud of acrid smoke hung over everything. For a moment the men watched, dazed, expectant, and adream until the flare died and then when the darkness resumed—and their fear returned—they opened fire once more.

Leo decided to get into the action.

He began walking around the interior of the circle, saying, "There! Over there!" and pointing into the darkness. His sharp commands got immediate reaction and sights shifted, men aiming in the direction he pointed, and blasting away. "And there!" he barked. More fire. Colonel Jiggs' eyes rolled with wild pleasure, he broke into a bucktoothed grin, and he nodded his relief that the famous mercenary saw the situation.

Harry noted that about half of the ammo was gone.

One soldier went to the edge of the circle and jabbed out with his bayonet at nothing. "Yaahhh!" he screamed. Then, satisfied, he dislodged the bayonet and sent it whistling into the night.

Leo jumped up on an oil drum with his Sten gun and gave the jungle a blast. The men cheered wildly.

You know what we fight for, men? We fight—not for the fucking material necessities and comforts—and not to save our bleeding homes and families—but for poetry! It's that, men: poetry! The right to read and think and dream radical!

The men—with no sense of what had been said—cheered again.

Tracer bullets arched into the wilderness.

Ka-voom! Grenades exploded. Ka-whang! Mortar shells.

Colonel Jiggs gave Commander Leo Rucker a full salute.

Harry got behind the wheel of a Saracen and moved it into place along the perimeter of the circle. Around him, the Biafrans continued a sporadic fire, but mostly watched as the cannon leveled into place. A moment before it fired, silence fell. Then: Va-voom! They roared their approval as a ball of fire mushroomed out of the distant night.

Harry waved his hand in appreciation.

Another flare, the last one the Biafrans possessed, arched over the mangrove trees, but failed to ignite. A dud.

Sitting in the rear of Leo's lorry, Mewishi and the men waited and watched—having received no order to participate. Pogo the Poet composed a verse with the borrowed line, "In the rocket's red glare . . ."

Colonel Jiggs handed out the last of the grenades.

The Biafrans around the Saracen asked Harry, please, to fire the cannon again.

Meanwhile, a reckless platoon charged. They ran to the edge of the darkness, fired a few shots, heaved their sticks and stones, then turned and dashed back to the safety of the circle. They looked terrified, as if the night was their enemy.

A large white bird flew out of the jungle and was cut down. A burst of rifle fire, then feathers everywhere.

"Yaahhh!"

Va-voom! the cannon said, and the soldiers screamed with pleasure and terror. Leo was back on top of an oil drum making another speech, his words lost in the noise, but everyone enjoying him very much.

† † †

A simple war with only a few sides.

The southeastern part of Nigeria, Biafra, where most of the Ibo tribe lived, seceded from the rest of the country. Because this section had the oil and mines, the army in Lagos attacked to get these back. And in order to fight off the federals the Biafrans sold their oil and mineral rights in exchange for weapons. In this way, nobody got anything.

Except propaganda and publicity. Val became Leo's press agent, riding around in an armored lorry behind her inlaid desk writing about the adventures of the Elite Rifles and chatting with the international press representatives who came to do homage—much to Harry's unending annoyance. Colonel Ojukwu, the Biafran leader, who, years before, when he was only an ambitious lieutenant, drunk and longing for armor and fame, had tumbled into the ancient trench around Benin City, hired himself a public relations firm called Markpress. The firm had access to planes, communications systems and army facilities while the average Biafran regiment had no shoes, guns or field telephones. Colonel Ojukwu also had on his side a band of pacifists, led by a Scot named Smoate, who published *Peace News*. On the other side, Colonel Gowon of the Nigerian federal forces countered with a propagandist of his own, a German pilot named von Schwenk who composed Surrender-or-Die leaflets—in a strong, melancholy prose—and dropped them from his rickety, twin-engined, high-winged Fokker.

Words and photos everywhere.

Reporters poured into the country—Bedford of *The Times* among them—and filed reams of dispatches and profiles. Leo made innumerable speeches. And Starkie, the film director, showed up wearing a pith helmet and shot thousands of feet of film—mostly pathetic moments of refugees or babies crying, whatever he could arrange.

Apart from the journalism, it was a poor war.

Harry was issued some explosives and blasting caps, but the caps were electrical and there were no batteries.

"How can we blow up bridges and roads without detonaters?" Harry complained to the bucktoothed Colonel Jiggs.

"Improvise, improvise!" the colonel said, rolling his eyes.

Harry decided to try taking batteries out of the Saracens, using them to detonate the dynamite, putting them back into the armored cars, then making the getaway. Blowing up the second bridge on his schedule, though, he and his men got caught: the battery was out beside the bridge, the federals were suddenly coming down the road, the bridge was blown, but then the Elite Rifles could neither recover the battery nor move the Saracen without getting shot. The federals set up their guns on the far side of the swollen creek—smoke from the blast still settling—and took potshots whenever anyone appeared. Luckily, Mewishi had stayed inside the Saracen, so he turned its cannon around on the federals and fired a couple of rounds. The shots missed, but the federals retreated under the barrage and El Paladín ran out, plucked the battery out of the grass, and handed it to Mewishi as he sprinted back to safety.

"We can't go on that way," Leo said shrewdly, appraising the situation.

But the next week there was no dynamite and the week after that there was no petrol, so the Saracens were idle.

Around them, meanwhile, the Biafrans always seemed to be picking things up and transporting them someplace else. Corrugated tin went everywhere: atop minibuses, mammy wagons, the heads of women, the backs of donkeys. So did furniture, machinery, children, foods. Items left anywhere for only a few hours were stolen and so the landscape crawled with people's possessions—gourds and oil drums and rolls of cloth containing everything from cassava flour to cartridges to books to garbage. Their lean-to houses were dismantled and toted off. Pieces of cars went by. Guitars, mattresses, cooking pots, pets, banana stalks, rolls of wire, trussed-up chickens: every street was a supermarket of mobile litter.

And always out there somewhere the federals were advancing. Another town had been lost, another crossroads had been taken. Sometimes one heard the deep thud of the guns. Val wrote about this with all the noble phrases she could muster. Markpress stole her best observations and *Peace News* lifted these secondhand from Markpress.

"This country is too poor to make war," Harry told Leo.

"We'll concentrate our force at the airport," Leo said. "Make our headquarters at the airport hotel."

"There's not any hotel out there."

"Set up tents, then. We'll guard Ojukwu's getaway plane for him. He can't object to that. And if supplies start coming in, we'll be in a good position to deal."

"We're supposed to go blow up bridges and roads."

"There's no bloody petrol!"

"True," Harry admitted.

"So we stay at the airport where we can catch that first plane leaving when things go bust," Leo said. "Ojukwu's personal plane, if that's the one we have to take."

"Sounds sensible."

"Besides, if we hang around the airport maybe we'll actually get more petrol and you can take the troop out for an excursion or two. But you're on your own as far as the fighting goes—because my fever's back and I've got my own duties."

"Duties?"

"Speeches and such. I'm addressing the graduating class at the university on Thursday. Friday, if there's rain."

So the Elite Rifles came to be camped near a secondary runway at Uli Airport. And when Markpress, Val, *Peace News* and the resident press corps became effective, church groups and relief organizations began to ship food and petrol into Biafra—and into the Commander's fevered hands. Leo Rucker and his "band of valiant sympathizers" were also metamorphosed into liberal heroes fighting for the "starving multitudes" and the "people who only wanted to govern themselves" and against the "international oil cartels tampering in Nigerian politics." Even Bedford and the more legitimate correspondents—afraid to travel to the edges of the conflict— picked up such phrases and made them their own.

Val's words: the myths of her men. Wearing a simple Calabar frock and bandana, she sat behind the inlaid desk in the back of the armored lorry, an air-conditioner whirring, keeping her cool, Weldu standing guard, the sound of her typewriter clicking away. Armor plate above, around and underneath: Leo had her insulated and protected.

Only Harry became unhappy.

"You're not paying any attention to the boys," he complained. "They're running wild."

"They're doing fine," she argued.

"Last night they slept—do you even know where?"

"No, where?"

"In the ashes of the fire with the native kids."

"That's healthy."

"They're all covered with white ash this morning."

"A lot of African children sleep in warm ashes."

"They look filthy."

"Harry, I'm surprised at you!"

"I don't want the boys living like animals. Leo's got you in there writing day and night. You don't owe anything to Leo's war effort."

"I'm writing about you, too," she said.

"Well, don't."

The Biafrans liked Harry, Val, and Leo squabbling. The Ibos were a strange tribe who governed without chiefs, who honored the family above all else, who understood children, washing strung out on wire between the lorries, and arguments. And loved gossip: Val slept with Harry, but Victor was Leo's child, all that. War was even viewed as a sort of family feud: so-and-so's cousin shot our cousin, so now we'll shoot so-and-so's brother.

Leo traded, preened, gave interviews and commands, and made speeches; Val sat inside the lorry writing and being beautiful; Harry stalked around with quiet menace. The Ibos completely understood.

"Also," Harry told her, "you're writing lies."

"War is conducted with lies," she replied.

"You're not taking care of the boys!"

"Don't instruct me in motherhood! Or tell me how to behave!"

"They slept in the goddamned ashes last night!"

† † †

Commencement exercises at the university were hurried that year because the city was under attack.

The students had petitioned Colonel Ojukwu to allow them to form a battalion of their own. They were hot to fight for their new country, but their leader advised that they could best serve by finishing classes.

The student body president was Bayeke, a mild scholarly type who had worked his way through the college of pharmacy by playing and singing in a rock band. Eventually, he would be known as the King of Juju and would travel the continent as a pop music star. ("The King of Juju!" Leo would snort. "All mysticism turns to shit!")

Bayeke introduced Leo as the Commencement Day speaker. The day was bright and sunny, the palm trees sighed with a soft breeze floating over the campus, four hundred students and parents were assembled, and Leo was especially philosophic.

When everything is materially right, Leo told them, *and every steelie in Africa has two cars, a fridge full of chicken and beer, and the world smells like a rose and looks exactly like California, a great anxiety will be visited on people like a plague.*

The students sat rigid in their newly bought coats and ties, perspiration flowing, as their parents tried to smile. Far off, one could hear thunder—or the deep pulse of guns—and in a few minds there was the question of just how far away the federals were. Naturally, the Biafran Fourteenth Division was out there along with white mercenaries, but were the federals thirty miles away? Twenty? Less?

Anxiety is an unseen enemy eating at the soul of men. But there's an answer to anxiety. There is an answer to too much wrong civilization, too much plastic materialism, too much comfort. I offer you instead of mere anxiety—real fear!

Colonel Ojukwu, his black beard shining in the sunlight, tapped his swagger stick onto his open palm and gazed out on the unlistening audience. The president of the university sat nearby wearing the embroidered cap of a Hausa, worrying that the punch was getting warm, its precious ice melting while this man droned away. Around the marquee across the lawn, fat flies buzzed in the heat.

Convert your neurotic anxieties into fear and become real barbarians again! For only as man believes in adventure and risks death can he escape the plague!

Bayeke's eyes glimmered with hope and his pulse became a drumbeat. He found himself on his feet among his classmates.

Careful, you people of tomorrow! You can graduate yourselves into the little pissing moral considerations of the gelded suburban masses! You can fret over the boss, the garbage, the distant headlines, the football scores, and you can die of a strange anemia of the spirit!

Bayeke led the others in applause.

The sound awoke the elders on the speaker's platform and they clapped, too.

You'll have no blood to spill, no blood to get high. And you'll suffer a slow, weak, debilitating shrinking up!

Bayeke, his clapping hands held high, turned so the others could hear him and shouted, "The Cadet Battalion!" This brought a cheer.

Fear and blood! Recover the old instincts so long repressed and boiled away by a civilization which has betrayed you!

Bayeke and the eager volunteers of the Student Cadets began to make so much clatter that Ojukwu shifted left and right in his chair. As the ice melted in the punch under the beautiful marquee, they tore at their new coats and ties. One of them proudly showed the three deep scars high on his cheek: the old tribal markings cut deep in his flesh. Fists knocked at the air.

Civilization—a weakened, failed, hopeless civilization— has tried to embarrass you and reason you away from the mystic fire and the primitive blood! But I say walk on fire! Spill blood again! Enter the darkness!

The relentless sun heated their naked bodies in the afternoon: muscles, raging torsos, sinew black and frenzied leaped and danced. Some of the parents moved in the old rhythms. Over all this, Bayeke's high descant began to form: the high wailing screech of the forest.

Darkness will cleanse you! Fear will give you back the blood of yourselves!

Ojukwu's arms were raised and his bearded jaw quivered; his white eyes rolled back and his tongue licked at the corners of his mouth.

"Yes!" he cried. "Very well!"
Bayeke kept carrying on.
And the Cadet Battalion of the Biafran War was born.

† † †

The *harmattan* arrived.
Leaves dried up and rattled on the trees.
The rivers disappeared and as they did hyenas appeared
in great numbers to eat the dead fish in the last small rivulets
and pools.

Harry hated to leave Val and the boys at the camp at Uli
Airport because too many strangers were coming around out
of curiosity, but the back roads into the Cameroons had to
be investigated. Escape remained the first priority of such a
war, so he took a Land Rover and a few men—including
El Paladín, whom he could trust in a skirmish—and drove
into the mountains for a few days.

They paid off border guards on both sides, promising more
money and bribes if circumstances sent them that way again.

They checked the roadbeds—estimating what roads might
hold during the next rainy season.

While in the mountains they passed another mercenary outfit on the narrow road: a wild-eyed Hun in a white Mercedes
convertible which flew the skull and crossbones. Machine guns
mounted front and rear. Two armored cars following. A surly
band of cutthroats, Lebanese and European, and a woman
who looked like a gypsy. Harry's patrol passed them slowly,
only a few inches apart on the mountain road so that everyone
got a close look at each other. The leader sat in the back seat
of the Mercedes and when he turned his face toward Harry
he revealed the long, thick scar which started on his bald

head and made its way into his collar. No one asked directions or nodded the slightest acknowledgment.

Later on, Harry told the Commander what he had seen, but Leo just sighed and exclaimed, "Ah, war is an extreme form of show biz."

Yet Leo would hear of this man again and although they would never meet, their legends, years later, in the normal confusions of time and reportage, would intermingle.

† † †

In the high-winged Fokker Friendship flown by von Schwenk an old copy of *Newsweek* lay rolled and stuck in the pilot's seat: that same issue of the magazine in which, once, the Secretary-General had found Val's photograph. The copy was opened to the same page and Val's same slutty pose glared out at the German whenever he took controls of his plane. (Land Rover behind her, thumbs in her jeans, open shirt.)

Von Schwenk suggested to Colonel Gowon, leader of the federal forces, that this woman should be brought to Lagos and interrogated. "Ve need her," he stated. "Besides, I vould like to talk to her about ze aesthetics of propaganda."

Gowon was too preoccupied to listen to von Schwenk. The superior federal forces weren't exactly overrunning poor Biafra—first the *harmattan,* then the rains, then the wild-eyed Student Cadets had been factors—and von Schwenk, though important, was an obsessed romantic.

"I vill compose no more leaflets!" von Schwenk threatened.

But Gowon merely shrugged his epaulets.

Von Schwenk was, indeed, a terrible romantic bordering on the insane, but had lucid moments in which he seemed

merely stupid. He wore a long silk scarf and goggles. Rilke
was his favorite poet. There was hardly any cause for which
he wouldn't give his life.

Von Schwenk slept in the plane. In the evenings before
going to sleep he turned on the panel of lights in the Fokker
and in the soft luminous green glow examined that photo of
Val in the old *Newsweek*. On the little hotplate at the navi-
gator's table, he cooked his simple meal—usually sauerbraten
—while gazing into the curves and crevices of Val's image.
She had a true maternal appeal, he decided, and he associated
her beauty with the warmth of the hearth, the coziness of
home, and the smells of sauerbraten.

One day he gassed up the Fokker Friendship and flew to
Biafra. Deciding to give himself up and fight for the other
side, he radioed ahead, but his accent was so thick that the
Biafrans misunderstood and started sending up flak. Luckily,
they had only a few rounds of ammunition, and their aim
was far wide of the mark, so von Schwenk landed at Uli
Airport. Even so, as he glided down the runway El Paladín
fired a shot into the windshield. Von Schwenk emerged from
his plane with his hands trembling, uncertain if he would be
executed or celebrated as a hero, but obsessed with the
thought that he was near the fabled Val.

As it turned out, the regular Biafran army was indifferent
to his arrival because they had no bombs for the plane and
very little petrol, but Leo, mindful that it was good to have
another escape plane nearby, welcomed von Schwenk into
camp. The German immediately started hanging around the
lorry where Val wrote and lived with Harry.

"Just be careful to never do anything so I lose my temper
with you," Harry warned him.

Von Schwenk, who was used to war only at a great height

and distance away, was afraid of Harry up close. Torn between his need to be near Val and to keep away from her
lover, he turned melancholy, gray-faced, and crept away to
his old aircraft to sulk.

† † †

The heart of Ibo land was crossed with old slave trails.
They moaned, those ancient paths, and seemed to talk to
Harry. Wind in the trees picked up the echoes of the moaning,
the monkeys mimicked it, and it grew deeper and more pene-
trating as the weeks passed.

Harry stood on the beach at Itu, once, looking out on the
site of the old slave market. The jungles beyond spoke to him.

With what little petrol he could find, Harry kept on the
move throughout Biafra—usually getting back to Val and the
camp at night or after only a day of reconnaissance.

He came to scrubby villages mostly empty of inhabitants,
nameless places with litters of broken chicken coops, straw
huts and uneven fences whose people had fled and were out
on the roads throughout the region as refugees. He even saw
one place which had been hit by a tornado. Tornadoes blew
into West Africa much as they blew into Abilene, Texas, or
Durant, Oklahoma, and the devastation somehow made Harry
think of his Texas school days. Engineering, languages, football, women, ROTC. The only language he ever truly mastered
was border Tex-Mex and the only things truly learned, he
decided, were the four/three defense and how to drink tequila
with a salted fist.

In his way—which was not very abstractly—Harry began
to think about himself. He came to the conclusion that he
shouldn't fight anymore, that he should control his temper and
grow up and become a responsible father.

Meanwhile, he watched the war.

The Fourth and Fifth Biafran Battalions were in disarray. Once, just before Harry and his men arrived, a soldier who had paid a helpless visit to his starving family in one of the villages had butted his head on a palm tree in despair; he had done this several times until he had finally broken his skull. Nobody wanted to touch the body, so Mewishi ordered two of the men to take him away and bury him.

He saw an outpost along the Owerri–Port Harcourt road which had been overrun when the Biafrans took time out for breakfast and paid no attention to a federal advance.

An officer near Aba ordered his men out in the bush around the town to fire their weapons all night because the noise of friendly fire gave the residents in town reassurance.

At night, back inside the lorry with Val, Harry held her very close. He was afraid for her there—too close to the runways and vulnerable in an air raid. But Leo wanted to be near the spoils—which were pouring into the country from the Red Cross and church groups—and near escape vehicles and planes, so Harry gave in.

At last the rains came. All Eastern Nigeria became a bog and the federal forces stalled in their drive. Sheets of blinding water moved across the metal top of the lorry and in that comforting noise Harry and Val made love as Weldu stood guard, wet to the bone, and von Schwenk and Leo and Mewishi and the others looked out of their tents.

When the confining lorry became too much, Harry created other patrols. Back to the roads and trails, back to the moaning, which sounded like a deep undertow against the sound of the rains: he moved around listening, not thinking so much as feeling.

Roads swarming with refugees: village elders, children,

whores, merchants, soldiers defecting to join their hungry and misplaced families. The rains turned the roads into mire and a natural camouflage of mud covered everything, so that figures, lorries, trees, huts were all the same black color and thick texture. The whores held their palms up, hitching rides in exchange for their quick services along the way, and young girls and mothers took up the practice because they were too tired to walk on, too exhausted to care. Row on row of moving black faces. People buried their meager belongings in the bush along the roadsides and after a while they seemed to walk aimlessly, unsure of what town or village they had fled, unsure of their tribe, where they were headed. Cobras came out, slithering through the puddles, flies buzzed over everything, and makeshift bars selling a low-grade palm wine, home brew or any numbing liquid sprang up along the waysides.

Watching and thinking about himself in no particularly deep way, Harry got interested in the refugees. He still wasn't much for introspection. It just happened.

At Uli Airport he began loading the Saracens with food parcels. Leo didn't mind. The real money was in arms and the Commander's fever had somehow turned his thoughts to this simple corruption.

At the ramshackle refugee centers where Harry distributed what he could swipe off the planes, then, he saw a people whose skin had turned to jelly, like the slime of fish, with anemic, swollen bodies; the last strong men were digging huge common graves; others wandered like beggars reciting names from their lost families; flies buzzed around the bush lamps and crawled over sick and hungry people too weak to raise a finger and drive them off; old men lay talking to nobody in particular; priests hurried through the sacraments; nurses broke into tears at seeing the impossibilities.

Occasionally the Nigerian Air Force came over and dropped a few indifferent bombs. Casual attacks: just reminders.

When the Saracens had made their deliveries, Harry and the men picked up as many refugees as possible. People hung off the sides and sat atop the armored cars as if they were mammy wagons.

And the muddy roads moaned once more: an ancient, troubled sound which the surrounding jungle echoed back.

One day Harry jumped down from the Saracen when he saw a diviner sitting beside the road: an old man with chalk around his eyes, beating on a tortoise shell with a stick, throwing his cowries and muttering his incantations.

"Come on, old man, get up here!" Harry urged him.

But the diviner sat there, eyes glazed, saying, "Listen! You hear that? Listen!"

"You come on," Harry said, touching his arm. "The federals are right behind us and they might do you some harm."

But the old man suddenly stopped beating with his stick and his head fell over to one side.

Harry knelt down for a close look.

The old man was dead or in a trance, Harry never decided.

† † †

During the daylight hours when no planes were flying into the airport, Leo strung his bow while Vic, Jocko, and Dorothy the falcon looked on. They stood in the middle of Number Two runway. Stringing the bow became a production, Leo explaining each movement, and when he finished he allowed each boy to test the pull. Jocko couldn't do much with it at all and whistled through his teeth in appreciation. Then came the part only Dorothy understood: Leo tied a yellow cloth streamer, like the tail of a kite, onto one of the long Ibo arrows from his quiver.

Not far away the men in camp made busy, reassuring noises as they went about their work. A good stew was on the fire and its odors wafted out toward them. Harry was out on patrol. Weldu and Mewishi were standing outside the lorry where Val pecked away at the typewriter.

The rains had stopped for the moment and the runways were dappled with pools reflecting the gray sky.

"Now this is the good part," Leo explained to them. "We send Dorothy up, see, and she'll circle above us, watching all the time. When I shoot up this arrow and streamer she'll catch it and bring it back to us."

"Has she done this ever before?" Vic wanted to know. His voice was full of his mother's accent.

"Sure, lots of times. See, she's staring at the streamer now that her hood's off. She's happy to be playing the game again."

"What if she misses the arrow?" Jocko asked.

"She won't. The streamer helps her see it. But falcons have a sort of built-in radar and calculator which works in just the quickest of a quick instant. She'll see the arrow come out of the bow and she'll figure exactly where it'll reach the top of its arc. That's where she'll take it."

"Leo," Vic asked, "will you ever get married?"

Leo looked up from tying the streamer. Jocko, who wasn't interested in the question, stared into Dorothy's eyes as he had been told he shouldn't.

"I believe in friends, not husbands and wives," Leo answered. "Friends are better than anything else."

"Is Dorothy your best friend?" Jocko asked, joining the talk.

"Well, she's wild and natural and I love her for it. And, sure, she's a great friend."

Leo released the bird and the boys watched its upward spiral. It flew effortlessly, riding a soft breeze.

There's nothing like bow hunting, Leo told them, because the bow works as a natural extension of the arm, you provide the power yourself. And you figure the angle, he explained: making a mental triangle between your eye, the tip of the arrow, and the target.

He slipped the arrow into his bow with slow deliberation, knowing that high above them Dorothy was watching.

As the boys watched, he told them how in the Wars of the Roses the English archers were so skilled they could make the French advance or fall back at will, regulating the tide of battle, but the history lesson made the boys impatient. Dorothy circled in a wide, waiting arc, and Vic finally whispered, "Shoot, Leo, let it go!"

So Leo did. The arrow went sailing out and Dorothy, above it, tucked in her wings and fell with the pure speed of gravity to snatch it out of the air with such quickness that the boys were unsure of what they had seen.

"Goddamn," Vic muttered in awe.

"Do it again, please, do it lots," Jocko pleaded, and Leo said he would.

Dorothy came back with the catch, then, and settled on Leo's leather wristlet. The Commander spoke gently to her and didn't bother to accept the arrow from her beak for a long time.

"Do it again," Jocko persisted.

"One thing," Vic said, watching Dorothy. "If she's so wild why doesn't she just fly away and never come back?"

Leo prepared to send her off again.

"That," he admitted, "I don't know."

† † †

The Airstream trailer which served as Colonel Ojukwu's roving headquarters—moving between Enugu, Owerri, Onitsha, and wherever the federals weren't advancing—had stopped along the banks of the Nworie River when J. R. Hoskins found it.

Nearby was a frame house packed with children on pallets, old people sitting on benches—very much a refugee camp of its own. Some men had been gigging frogs along the river and had laid out their catch in the yard: two dozen skinny frogs with their white bellies turned up. The women stood beside boiling vats cutting up yams. No one paid much attention to the silvered mobile office parked beneath the cotton tree down by the river nor to the American in the pink jumpsuit who drove up with a courier's pouch to visit.

The Peacock was mostly involved in Vietnam these days, but was responsible for some of the data coming out of Biafra, too, so was making a rare visit. Harry was roaming around the jungles and couldn't be found. Leo had fever. Only Val was helpful and her prose was impossible to translate into officialese.

The menacing descant of the flies followed J. R. as he walked to the mobile home and went inside. There, Ojukwu sat in front of the air-conditioner scratching his black beard. He was all determination.

"We won't give up," he told J. R. "I have now sold half our mineral rights to France in exchange for planes."

"For the promise of planes," J. R. said, correcting him.

"But I believe they'll deliver," Colonel Ojukwu answered. "And—let's see—the other half to Belgium for small arms.

And another half to Pretoria for ammo. And the oil reserves to —hmm, slips my mind."

"Everything normal, I see."

"The Cadet Battalion is ready to attack Owerri, too."

"Oh, Biafra's going back on offense?"

"Absolutely. The mercenaries are doing a wonderful job, too." As he spoke and scratched, Colonel Ojukwu's gaze went blank.

The whirr of the air-conditioner and the cacophony of insect sounds from beyond blended the silence that followed. The leader of Biafra said something in Ibo under his breath.

"Word is," J. R. offered, "that you work for the mercenaries, not they for you."

Ojukwu's blank stare.

"Lyndon Johnson has asked me to convey a message to you," J. R. said, leaning close. "Are you listening?"

Clearly, Colonel Ojukwu was only partially there.

"The President is pleased that you have under your command a Texan—Colonel Veer—and one who has concerned himself with rescuing refugees and children. He thinks that's super. And he asked me to tell you—" J. R. Hoskins attempted to move his face in front of Ojukwu's gaze. "To tell you that our relief organizations are ready to give massive aid when Biafra surrenders."

Sounds of insects and air-conditioner. In time, Colonel Ojukwu's absent gaze hardened into determination again so that J. R. believed he might have understood the message.

Ojukwu stood up and began to scratch once more.

"Tell your president," the leader said, "that I have already given two cousins to the war! And I stand ready to sacrifice my wife's brother!"

† † †

The Student Battalion, the Biafran Fourth and Fifth, and the Elite Rifles did, indeed, recapture the city of Owerri—and claimed the only offensive victory of the war for their side.

Bayeke and Leo led the attack in their separate ways. The student rode in one of Leo's Saracens which had been rigged with a loudspeaker playing an assortment of rock 'n' roll music. He sang a few selections himself in that piercing wail which would later signal his rise to African stardom as the King of Juju. Leo, ever at the rear, conducted the best communications operation Biafra had ever enjoyed: von Schwenk in the Fokker flying ahead of the charge, Mewishi (fez, goggles, a big smile) spotting the action below, Colonel Jiggs on radio, all of them more or less relaying information and hunches to Bayeke and the various field commanders fitted out with World War II walkie-talkies.

Leo occupied the mobile control tower from Uli Airport—the one used to direct flight traffic. Two lorries pulled it to the outskirts of Owerri and there it sat primed for battle: bamboo underpinnings, a cluster of rusted car batteries for power, a maze of cables, and a revolving searchlight on top, which, because nobody could figure how to turn it off, El Paladín had generously shot out with a burst from his Sten gun. Still, the control tower had the best radio equipment and Leo liked the idea of being up there booming his voice above the carnage.

Surprise, of course, was the supreme weapon. A thousand college boys came roaring out of the bush like fans at a pep rally. Spears, clubs, machetes, a few rifles, fewer grenades. Underarmed and overzealous. The federal army mustered a few rounds of fire, but faced with such conviction were always in retreat.

"Ti-ya-ya-ya-yahhhhh!" came the sound of Bayeke's song from the loudspeaker as they rumbled through the streets toward Provincial Hall and the town square. "Yaahhh! Ti-ya-yah!" His music blared along without benefit of lyrics or melody.

That night a banquet was held: goat meat, rice, home brew, real bread—all the wonderful food left behind by the retreating enemy. The menu was announced over Biafran radio as a documentation of the victory. Markpress put out a special edition, Ojukwu came to address the cadets, Val was applauded when she appeared, and the fevered Leo got drunk.

Under the influence of home brew, his courage festered so that he said to Val, "Come sleep with me tonight up in the control tower."

When she paid him no attention, he kept on.

"We'll get the BBC on shortwave and listen to Felix Mendelspawn."

"You're potted."

"I am, true. And I've come into heat."

"The whole town's in an uproar."

"Not up there in the bamboo tower."

He knew, suddenly, that she was tempted. So, drunk as he was, he let the matter drop and joined the revelers for another hour. Colonel Jiggs was at the head table toasting victory, but also making a strange announcement: he would fight no more, he had converted to religion and would go into the bush. Leo staggered around the perimeter of the feast trying to make sense of things, but couldn't. Soldiers poured home brew into empty bottles that once held Star Lager. Bones of a barbecued goat lay everywhere. Tempted: she was, he knew it, this was it.

Later he took her hand and led her through the moonlight.

Neither of them spoke of Harry, who was out there somewhere like an angel picking up the poor, the maimed, the afflicted.

He watched her go up the bamboo ladder, trying to work up his excitement as he contemplated the roll of her hips. Inside the tower, he turned on all the equipment and the world's sounds flooded in: the BBC Third Programme, the American Armed Forces Network, belly dancing music, Lagos, Algeria, and various statics from the cosmos.

As she undressed, it occurred to Leo that they were all out of sorts with each other now: Harry was too sentimental, Val was too earnest about her new writing career, he himself was too mercantile.

Apropos of nothing, he said, "I'm not a soldier! I'm a bloody merchandiser!"

"Lie down here," she said. "Is this straw mat all right?"

It wasn't. Neither was Leo.

His impotence was accompanied by Brahms, selections from Ravel, and the soundtrack from *Brigadoon*.

There was nothing to do except lie in her naked arms and try to sleep, but that ended when the tower began to sway and move.

"God in Wales!" he cried. "What now?"

During their futile lovemaking, the two lorries had hooked up again and the mobile tower was being hauled back down the road toward Uli Airport for use in the night landings. The tops of palm trees passed by the tower's windows. The lorries barely moved, the drivers afraid that the important tower might topple over, so there was a gentle sway to their trip along that rough road. Val got up and went from window to window. Moonglow on her skin. Undressed and free, she was being borne through the night like a goddess of darkness.

"Sorry," Leo managed, sobered up more than he wanted to be.

"Don't be. This is nice," she said, padding around.

They looked down on the jungle swaying by; one couldn't see the tin-roofed huts, the refugees sleeping in the ditches, the litter, only silhouettes and shadows, everything dreamlike, soft and fair. It was all funny, too, Val insisted, and she told Leo to forget his poor performance.

Toward morning when they arrived at Uli, many planes circled in hold patterns above them in the sapphire sky. Constellations, a few small private craft flown by independent entrepreneurs, one big Hercules transport. The instruments inside the tower began to complain: get us down, come in, read me, calling, over and out.

Leo was barking into the microphone, pushing buttons, turning dials, and directing all the traffic before the ground crew at Uli got the ladder up and the regular controllers appeared.

† † †

Starkie, the director, and von Schwenk, the romantic, discovered Rena the Jungle Bunny at about the same time. After some initial sparring and arguing, an obvious compromise was struck: von Schwenk would become her lover and Starkie would film everything. He especially wanted shots revealing her extraordinary tattoo.

After a while, though, the Frenchman blackmailed von Schwenk: if not allowed to share in Rena's affections as an active participant, he would tell Val—with whom the German was still addled. It was a hard bargain. But von Schwenk agreed, not knowing that Rena and Val always discussed the men in camp anyway.

Starkie continued to film the Commander and wanted some footage of Harry, but could never find him.

"If he's out saving lives," Starkie complained, "then where?

And show me a life he's saved—a naked black baby, perhaps, or some old crone. Let there be photographic proof!"

At this time, too, there was a story going around that a leopard—of unusual size and cunning—had come down from the Udi Hills, disturbed by the gunfire and chaos of the war, to prey on those responsible. Starkie loved the story and was so eager to hear more of it that all the Ibos were happy to invent new materials for him. He wanted to film the beast—its giant tracks, at least—and weave a story around its existence. Also, in Starkie's mind the leopard and Harry Veer became tangled in a private mythology: creatures of the wild, one saving, one destroying. This would make a terrific movie, he told Val, as soon as the details of the script were worked out.

Meanwhile, the giant leopard, larger than a tiger, at least in the favorite Ibo versions, was presumably ravaging sentries and platoons of the advancing federal army. The leopard also took on other identities. Ojukwu's most loyal followers claimed that at night their leader changed into this dangerous marauder. Some claimed the leopard was that other mercenary, the one in the Mercedes who flew the skull and crossbones. In all stories the Leopard Cult was mentioned.

> Darkness of night surrounds us
> In our hearts we hear the drums
> Time is a shadow passing
> As the angry leopard comes.

Those lines, composed by Pogo, who fancied the leopard stories as much as Louis Starkie, were written in boldface on the straw mat in which he rolled himself and slept every night. Pogo, in fact, wrote two dozen separate leopard poems and decided he was destined to see the creature—which he claimed was somewhere nearby. Together with Starkie, then, he found a good bait tree on the periphery of camp, tied a rancid gazelle to a high limb, and began keeping nightly watch.

At the same time Val told her tale of being attacked by a leopard in a thorn *boma*. Only a few listeners tended to believe her story, but Pogo came to the conclusion that this was the same leopard and that Val was probably the object of his search.

Starkie tried to blend all these ideas and images into his crude art. Characters and objects flew into his head in vague outline, the footage piled up, and he kept the vigil with Pogo. They ate raw kola nuts out there at night and drank quantities of tea; the time was tedious and their imaginations soared. Pogo kept an old bolt action M-1 at his side and Starkie positioned himself nearby with cameras and infrared lights for night shots.

At last some leopard—perhaps, *the* leopard—arrived. It came into the clearing, circled the hanging bait, sniffed the air and looked sharp in all directions to see if things were right. A full minute, this first visit, then it trotted back into the bush. A half hour later it came to feed.

Pogo was mesmerized. It *was* large, its rosettes startling in the pale moonlight, and Pogo wanted to cry out to Starkie. He wondered if the Frenchman might be asleep because there was no sound of a camera whirring, not a leaf rustling, nothing, until the jaws of the animal crushed through the spinal column of the bait. Twice, three times, the leopard jumped at the bait—hanging, perfectly, a bit too high for easy feeding—and tore off bites. But where was Starkie?

Then the camera clicked on with a noise which sounded much too loud and the whirring filled the air around them.

"Oh, god, Monsieur Starkie!" Pogo whispered under his breath.

The leopard turned toward the noise.

Starkie, hidden in the foliage of his blind, kept his camera level and kept shooting film as the creature stalked him.

Leopards frequently maul men without killing them, unlike the lion, which usually dispatches its victims with a single blow or bite then drags them off to eat them. The leopard is sometimes content to show strength and mastery and Pogo hoped this was now the case as he bravely left his cover and staggered forward in the dark toward Starkie and the attacking leopard.

When he got to Starkie's blind, he saw that the Frenchman was gone. Blood everywhere.

With his M-1 ready, Pogo followed their sounds in the darkness. He could hear Starkie grunting and moaning—and, also the sound of the camera still whirring away. He jogged along, stumbling, resuming his stride, trying to keep pace. The sounds seemed to come from the limbs of the black trees above him; Pogo decided the leopard had taken its kill up high to eat it, yet the sounds continued to move ahead of him as he ran. On a vine beside a tree where he stopped to look and listen, a bright bead of blood caught the pale moonlight.

He called his partner's name. No answer.

The thought to turn back was overpowering. He was only a poet. A warrior only by merest chance: he had met Commander Rucker when in need of a job. Still, he was Masai—and clever with cats, resourceful, traditionally fearless. I'll go a little farther, he told himself. Only a little.

As he moved on, he saw the trees draped and aglint: film everywhere, crisscrossing the boughs above his head, shining black against the blackness of the night like a terrible celluloid growth, some hideous flower letting loose its tentacles. He pushed it away from his face and shoulders as he stepped inside its web.

A cascade of thirty-five mm ribbon: he saw his own face in it, saw the moon distorted and dim, saw—or thought he did—

impressions of the beast, of Starkie, ghosts and reminders. There seemed to be more film than a thousand cameras could hold: acres of gleaming darkness. Soon he became tangled in it; wrapped like a mummy, hearing only its crackle as it twined around him, he knew the leopard would probably return and attack while he was in this helpless state. But it didn't. Silence and emptiness all around.

† † †

Leo's fever got so bad that he filled out a will.

He noted that he would like his corpse donated to the Inspector of Anatomy, Alexander Fleming House, SE 1.

Money: to Val and the boys.

Personal Items: to Harry, who had sentiment for such as that.

Unused medals: distributed to whoever was left.

Quinine couldn't be found anywhere in Biafra, so Leo made a deal with John Peters, the top mercenary fighting for Gowon and the federals. In exchange for a couple of twenty-five-pounders—the Biafrans didn't have ammo for the big guns anyway—Peters sent over a case of quinine.

When Leo felt slightly better, he caught up on his correspondence. First he wrote to Ramona in Paris, telling her about Louis Starkie's unfortunate end. Another note went to J. R. Hoskins advising him that the war would surely be over soon. *Life as a mercenary,* he wrote to J. R., *is a grab bag: you never know exactly what you're fighting for until you've won it.*

Val wrote to Bedford, who was stationed at the Bristol Hotel in Lagos, saying, "Every day here is heavily reminiscent of the one before." Naturally when he received this Bedford became excited and started laying plans to visit Biafra for *The Times.*

Harry's diary contained the same simple entries: Down to Calabar with a load of refugees. Brought food back to Owerri. Over to Aba with supplies and medicine.

Mr. Smoate wrote in *Peace News* that many Biafran soldiers were Christian (he should have said they were without rifles, Leo commented) and refused to fire.

Markpress noted that inflation had run the price of a single chicken up to twenty-five dollars.

Colonel Ojukwu wrote a "Dear Sir" letter to the Chairman of the Board, General Motors, asking for armament, and, if that wasn't feasible, requesting that he intervene to stop the war, please, because of the starving multitudes.

Bedford filed an article with the *Financial Times,* quoting Lord Hunt and outlining the British position, which was: 1.) since the Arabs had closed the Suez Canal it would be beneficial to everyone if no oil installations were bombed, 2.) British-made arms were for sale anywhere in Nigeria to either federals or rebels, and 3.) Britain would continue, as always, its strong moral stance, offering to direct conferences, debates, or peacemaking meetings.

Pogo wrote two sonnets, one elegy, and a limerick.

Words everywhere.

Leo provided reporters and correspondents with juicy quotables. To the man from *Figaro: Psychologists study the strong man, they ponder him, that's how they hope to bring him down: they want to analyze him out of existence. They can't bear human intelligence or human will. They pity the artist and the criminal—both of whom, by definition, as far as I'm concerned, are superior animals.*

And to a kid from *Rolling Stone: The world is lunatic and gone. The only refuge is in a deeper craziness than it can imagine for itself.*

Words, all words.

To a columnist for *The Wall Street Journal: Power is always
personal, never social. Institutions never have power, only the
illusion of it. Individual men alone have power.*

† † †

An old Convair circled in the night sky above Uli, then
came in for a landing to find the field surrounded by Leo's men.

As the lorries rolled alongside the plane, Leo appeared in a
jeep and ordered the cargo doors kept shut.

"A new tax has been put into effect," he told a Biafran airport official who was present. "We get paid first. In either
British pounds or American dollars, please."

"Begin unloading," the official implored him. "These are
important weapons. I'll go into Aba and see what can be done."

"Nothing gets off the plane until my strongbox is filled with
bank notes," Leo said. "Five thousand British pounds or the
equivalent—double the price if you only got Biafran currency.
And if you try and screw us, we'll blow up the plane and
cargo."

"The General said we could trust you," the official whined.

"If you pay us, you bloody well can."

"There's not that much cash in Aba nor that much sterling
in the whole region," the man argued.

"Don't lie to me," Leo said. "Mewishi here will go with you.
Take the strongbox. If you come back with it filled, everything
will go very well indeed, but if you come back with Biafran
regulars I'll blow the plane and kill them all, same as if they
were federals."

The official sputtered and complained.

"Also, one more thing," Leo added. "If you're not back by
nine o'clock this morning I'll blow the plane as well."

"How can I get money before the banks open?"

"You *have* the bloody money! Go get it and give it to *me*!"

The official came back with the cash before daybreak, made a patriotic speech, and watched the Convair being unloaded. Apart from this blackmail, Leo took his usual 10 percent of the cargo, divided it between himself and Harry in the usual way, and sent the strongbox off to camp under the care of Mewishi and a full guard.

The problem of loot: there just weren't enough Elite Rifles to handle the take. It had to be sold off to middlemen, smuggled out on flights or across borders, and somehow protected if stored around Uli Airport. Leo always had convoys going here and there with hardware or cash and Harry wanted all the vehicles in the outfit, if possible, to distribute food coming in from the World Council of Churches or the Red Cross. Because of difficulties, Leo began to demand cash for everything. There were always arguments, but his men controlled Uli— the most active airport in the hemisphere, as Val described it— so in the end the Biafrans agreed.

The war was grinding down into the common horrors. Ojukwu proclaimed a scorched-earth policy—as devastating to his own people as to the advancing army. The federals weren't taking prisoners. In Port Harcourt they had murdered four hundred Biafran wounded at the General Hospital and there had been massacres in a dozen villages. The time had come to consider last things.

"How much in my account?" Harry asked Leo that night as the Convair was being unloaded. "Rough estimate."

"Almost a quarter of a million pounds," Leo said. "Giving or taking a few. And the same for Val. I've got three times that much, but then I'm paying the men and making the deals, aren't I?"

"That's more all around than I thought."

"Let's see, I've got two couriers taking money out now. Peters owes me for three pieces of artillery and I know I'll get my money, he's honorable. I got payment in advance to stay and defend Owerri when the next assault arrives. Our lorries are full. All our storage is full and we've got no more room in our hiding places. So there's more every hour."

"And there's the Peacock."

"True. He's a love."

"I think we should put a slice in trust for the boys," Harry said. "Would that be all right with you?"

"Sure, Harry," Leo said. "That's very responsible of you."

Their eyes met. Harry didn't pursue the subject because Leo was touchy about things ending again and especially touchy about Victor. Best to leave it lie, Harry decided. Family matters would be settled sooner or later. But would it be the same as Katanga or would Leo do something rash this time?

"Responsible of you," he had said, but there was a tinge of bitterness in his tone which set Harry thinking.

† † †

When the rains slacked many Biafran battalions folded and all roads east filled with refugees again. Time itself was collapsing.

Harry and his men concentrated on medical supplies—and powdered milk when they could conveniently carry a load.

In Owerri the refugees had blown open the door to Provincial Hall and all the wayward had flocked there for shelter. Harry managed to deliver a lorry filled with medical supplies and recruited a few deserters as orderlies. Val volunteered for service, but nursing wasn't for her and she quit after two days. The whole city boiled with bad nerves, everyone expecting attack and evacuation. Rumor was everywhere. French arms were coming in, including heavy guns flown in by way of South Africa, to counter the new Russian 122mm guns recently put in use by the federals. The enemy was forty miles away and charging. Generals were being assassinated. Uli airstrip was in the hands of pirates. Harry stayed too busy to check even the more probable rumors.

Val sent him a message urging him to get back to camp and stay there. His answer: "Soon."

Hard work was penance and oblivion.

Then the outskirts of the city came under fire once more and the rumors turned into certainties: the federals.

Bayeke came to Harry and announced that they would please like to borrow a lorry or two—and perhaps a Saracen, if a driver could be provided—because the cadets were going out to meet the onslaught.

"Do you know the road conditions out there?" Harry asked him.

"I imagine," Bayeke said, "they're soggy."

"I've got a reliable intelligence report," Harry bluffed. "The roads are impassable, so you won't bring our vehicles back if you take them. They'll be bogged down to the axles in no time."

"What does Commander Rucker say? I'll ask him."

"Commander Rucker has fever and a bad case of greed and doesn't give a shit."

They stood outside a rough field hospital and listened to the crickets. Rain dripped off the leaves around them and the skies remained ominous. Bayeke heaved a great sigh.

"We have no reliable intelligence reports," Bayeke admitted. "I hadn't even thought about the roads. But if the Student Battalion doesn't fight now it never will. And none of the regulars have the spirit."

"What ordnance have you got?" Harry asked him.

"Every third cadet has a rifle. We've got a dozen mortars, a dozen MAG machine guns, two or three workable Bren guns, a grenade corps with fifteen grenades, some dynamite and—the rest is all knives and clubs and wire."

"No armor?"

"There's never been any armor except for the mercenaries."

"No big guns?"

Bayeke shrugged.

"I'll donate one Saracen," Harry said. "Leo won't like it, but there it is. You'll have to scrounge petrol."

"Could we please have a merc driver?"

Harry looked at Bayeke in the gathering darkness as they listened to the crickets. He didn't look like a soldier or a rock star. With a little imagination he resembled a shoeshine boy: thin, smiling, nervous, quick hands and eyes.

"I'll ask for volunteers," Harry told him. "That's the best I can do."

Together, Harry and Bayeke went down to the local brothel: a row of broken-down lorries and mammy wagons up on blocks, their wheels gone, draped with tablecloths and sheets and containing brass beds, straw mats, bare foam cushions and all the coarse amenities of the city.

None of the Elite Rifles presented himself.

On the way toward the bars—stalls of that same corrugated tin siding and palm leaves serving mostly home brew—they met El Paladín. When Harry asked him to volunteer, he implied a challenge he didn't really intend, saying, "Right, señor, they need a real sonovabitch."

"Thees ees the won," El Paladín boasted. "I'm a keeler."

Suddenly, Bayeke and the Spaniard were revving each other up, trading foolish enthusiasms which made Harry want to walk away. But he stood there listening. Macho. Soldier talk. Camaraderie. The lust of the hunt. He stood listening to them as if he viewed them down the wrong end of gunsight: far distant and doomed.

Two days later the cadets of the Student Battalion would be dead and scattered. El Paladín's head would adorn the stump of a thorn tree on a hillside overlooking Owerri; the Saracen, as predicted, would be half buried in mud, its side blown by a direct point-blank shot from a 122mm; mangled students would be crawling through the bush for miles and miles, their wounds green with flies; and Bayeke, their leader, the singer, would be one of them; he would ride a twisted limb down a swollen stream, his eyes glassy with fright, but he would make good his escape; feeding himself on wild fruit and succulent leaves, he would begin to run after that, running to the eroded beauty of the Udi hills. Years later when he emerged, gaunt and mysterious, his high-shrieking voice would have altered; there would be a terrible pain in it which no one wanted to hear, yet did; he would evoke from his listeners—the young girls of the continent—dread and desire and such mixed feelings that they would partially cover their ears, letting only a little of his unholy music enter, and spread their fingers over their eyes, peeking out, as if they were trying to hide from him, yet find him; as if they feared his every thrust and gyration, yet wanted to bring their bodies to him and burn themselves into his flesh and go inside him where there was nothing more terrible or more true.

† † †

The mobile government in the Airstream trailer parked at Umuahia and began preparations to defend the city with makeshift determination.

There was a shortage of sand, so the bunkers were built with bags of sawdust from a local lumber mill. The sawdust wouldn't stop a bullet, but General Ojukwu's offices looked snug. Petrol and oil products were nowhere to be found, but it was discovered that coconut milk worked very well as brake fluid and a mixture of diesel and grease served as engine oil. Buckets were converted into the deadly *ogbunigwe*—crude land mines. And the new recruits, mostly kids, were given wooden rifles carved and polished so that they resembled the real thing.

At Uli airstrip, Weldu was promoted to sergeant and put in charge of training recruits from the nearby villages. The boys were clever at inventing booby traps, but each one was different from the next so that no one knew how to avoid getting hurt and a rule was required that such creativity had to cease. The new recruits also insisted that they could fight bravely with their machetes, that they didn't need anything else. Weldu stood on one leg, smiling, and listened to this manifestation of local pride, then he had Pogo drive one of the Saracens onto Number Two runway.

"First platoon, ready!" Weldu called. "Attack!"

A dozen frenzied fighters ran headlong at the Saracen and began banging on its armor with their knives. They crawled all over it. One boy's blow rang with a terrible vibration, hurting his arm, and he fell to the ground writhing and pawing as if he had a mortal wound. Another fell off and hurt himself.

"Second platoon, charge!" Weldu barked, mimicking the Commander as best as he could.

The next wave poured over the sturdy Saracen. One eager recruit with a poor aim almost chopped off his cousin's arm.

"Fall back, retreat!" Weldu yelled, after they were mostly exhausted. Sullen and perspiring, they all went over and sat underneath a cluster of palms and regarded the Saracen with hate. There it stood with a few bright new scratches on its metal.

"In the great battle of Umuahia which is coming," Weldu said, striding among them and trying to get Leo's lecture tone in his voice, "there will be such armored cars as well as tanks manned by the federals. Their object—since they will be **armed**

—will be to blow your asses off. What should your strategy be, then, toward armored cars and tanks?"

The eager recruit who had wounded his cousin shot his hand into the air.

"Yes?" Weldu asked, though he was prepared to answer his own question.

"We should attack them only with bombs and grenades," the recruit announced.

"Good thought," Weldu said. "Unfortunately, you will have no bombs or grenades. You will very likely, at best, have sharp knives."

The recruits paid close attention.

"Your strategy," Weldu said, "will be to avoid confrontation at all costs. When one of those comes out of the bush, scatter and hide. If lucky, you won't be found."

"And one of them might run over a land mine," another recruit said hopefully.

"Absolutely," Weldu agreed. "There's always the chance of victory."

At this point Commander Rucker came toward them, hands behind his back as he marched, looking stern. The recruits expected him to be angry about their failure to subdue the Saracen, but Weldu knew that Leo was just going to address the troop.

Our code of honor, men, is this: wear something vaguely military so your families know you're proper warriors and not just hooligans!

The men stood in uneven file, chins against their chests as Leo moved back and forth in front of them. The shade from the palm trees was pleasant.

Keep your weapon shined, if it's nothing but a long knife or spear! Claim that you're fighting for spoils, if accused of any

high motive! And when it comes to rape and pillage, men, it's
all right if you're not too sure what pillage is!

Detecting no irony, the boys under the palm trees stared
straight ahead into their doubtful futures.

† † †

A tinge of bitterness in Leo's voice.

There were things they hadn't spoken of: the old grievances,
the boys, the future the three of them had together or apart.
Harry began to suspect Leo of possible cunning. The Commander had already been given full charge of the lone jet
fighter in Biafra which was designated, everyone knew, to fly
General Ojukwu to safety in the last hours, and, besides, Leo
knew all the unruly schedules and flight plans at Uli. He could
arrange escape and he could arrange—easily—for someone to
be left behind.

Val had already asked if the boys shouldn't be flown out.

"No, we'll all go when the time comes. Don't worry," Leo
told her. But what was on his mind?

As a precaution, Harry went to von Schwenk and made him
a handsome offer for reserve space on the old Fokker. Von
Schwenk was sympathetic, especially since the mission involved
transporting Val to safety.

"But you're the ninth, maybe the tenth to ask," von Schwenk
said.

Nevertheless, the German accepted a down payment.

Troubled, Harry went back on the road in the single lorry
he now used to carry on his mission with the refugees. Another
thought came and went: that Leo and Val, somehow, had been
together again. If not to sleep together, something. Vexed, his
bad dreams came back. The Extravaganza. The old knight, the
deaths of the young squires, the wounded in the great gallery,

the old lord of the castle. About there Harry forced himself to wake up.

One night after the dream he got up from Val's side and put on his fatigues.

"Where're you going?" she mumbled as he went outside the lorry.

A moonlit night. He passed a sentry with a greeting and looked out across the airstrip. All the night's planes had come in early, so everything lay quiet and peaceful.

Then he saw the shape. Until that time, he hadn't believed all the stories, yet there it was—or seemed to be. The big leopard. Its silhouette moved across the dim horizon of the runway—feline, distinct, no doubt of it—and in its graceful lope Harry recalled every terror, sweet and wrenching, he had ever known: the javelina, the night at Wahling, the rundown service station with its Pepsi sign in another land long ago.

"Keep alert," he told the sentry when he passed again.

The sentry, hearing the alarm in Colonel Veer's usually calm voice, stiffened and held his automatic against his thumping chest as his eyes scanned the darkness.

† † †

Then von Schwenk decided to bomb Lagos.

The plan originated along that row of dilapidated mammy wagons and lorries which served as the local brothel. Von Schwenk, the camp cook, and Mewishi had gone there after their usual late meal served in the Fokker—meat and cheese and such delicacies as they could scrounge. Mewishi had lately become one of the more elite of the Elite Rifles; he wore his fez constantly, seemed concerned with his uniform and appearance in a time when clothes were scarcely worn, and took complete interest in machines, vehicles, and especially the aircraft which von Schwenk allowed him to visit and care for. He considered himself to be the air force branch of Leo's troop: a mildly eccentric vanity which everyone, even the Commander, indulged. After all, the war was dragging on and men of such long service and loyalty needed diversions.

Mewishi didn't take his pleasure at the truck stop that evening. He stood outside talking to some of the girls, preening a little, while the camp cook whooped and yelled and the melancholy von Schwenk—in the rear of a separate lorry—worked out his fantasies in a threesome composed of himself, a white girl named Anastasia, and Rena the Jungle Bunny. Mewishi's need was strong, but his sense of position and rank were stronger and, besides, his old chocolate-colored uniform was still handsome and the other whores were impressed that he stood around with them.

It was Rena who asked why the capital of Nigeria had never been bombed.

"Indeed, why not?" von Schwenk asked, pulling on his pants.

The question drew more attention and elaboration as everyone walked down the street to the bar stalls. As the evening wore on, drink made action imperative.

"May I go?" asked Anastasia.

"We will all go. Zis requires a full crew," von Schwenk answered.

The cook, who was mainly experienced with explosives, volunteered to rig up some bombs.

Von Schwenk told Mewishi that a supreme moment was at hand: the Commander's valet would this night take the controls himself. He would fly—once they were airborne—von Schwenk would navigate, the cook would be bombardier, and Rena and Anastasia would do that which they did best.

An hour passed as they went in pursuit of petrol, but they finally confiscated a few drums and went out to Uli to prepare the flight. At the cook's suggestion, two of the petrol drums would be converted into bombs by lashing them with several sticks of dynamite. Fuses were found—Mewishi remembered —in the neatly stacked gear of the deceased El Paladín.

"We'll drop two of these," the cook reasoned, "unless we need the fuel in one to get back home."

"Where exactly in Lagos does Gowon live?" Mewishi asked, thinking ahead.

But von Schwenk wanted to bomb the reserve oil tanks surrounding the lagoon. "Let there be fireworks!" he said. "The people of Lagos are children! They love a good fireworks display!"

Their enthusiasms revved up with such talk.

With giddy anticipation, Mewishi fitted himself into the copilot's chair and von Schwenk, filled with gesture, passed him his silk scarf and goggles, saying, "Here, wear these. Be an ace."

Contact. Flaps and rudder tested. Engines on. Oil pressure up. Val's photo in the magazine prominently displayed. Booze and *bangi* ready. They went down the runway, speeding by the flash of bush lamps which lit the way, and into the night sky.

Rena revealed the tattoo of the phoenix and the action began.

At the roof restaurant of the Bristol Hotel in Lagos that evening sat three distinguished drunks: J. R. Hoskins, and Jackie Patterson, and Bedford of *The Times*. As well as possible under the strain of the Peacock's nonsequiturs, they were carrying on a serious conversation about Third World countries and the multinational corporations—though, in fact, J. R. was pumping them for information he could include in some woefully tardy reports which he owed to his bosses and they were really trying to find out how the CIA was involved in the war. Their ninth or tenth rounds of martinis, rum colas, and gin fizzes had passed when the sputtering engines of von Schwenk's Fokker caught their attention. A moment later, the plane passed some twenty feet over their heads.

"Why do you suppose they're flying so low?" Bedford inquired out of his fog of fizz.

"Pilot error," the Peacock said.

In fact, Mewishi and von Schwenk were trying to locate a suitable target in the darkness. Lagos at two A.M.—and under wartime curfew and blackout—wasn't easy to see. The harbor, they guessed, was over there where there weren't any lights at all. There was probably the lighthouse, they concluded, but where were Victoria and Ikoyi islands? And where were those big oil tanks or the ships at port? Having reached Lagos by dead reckoning, they had circled a few times too often and their sense of direction was gone. Only the cook, fully ena-moured of both Anastasia and Rena, seemed unconcerned.

As the Fokker made its wide circles over the city it man-aged to buzz the roof of the Bristol twice more, so the drunks became ever more interested. It was J. R. who suggested that it might actually be an enemy aircraft. Jackie Patterson, the senior war correspondent, became excited at this and decided to take notes, but could find no pencil or paper. Bedford went to the edge of the roof, rested his chin on his fists, his elbows propped on the parapet, and thought of Val. He had tried every diplomatic ploy which would allow him to visit the eastern sector and see her, but all had failed. He wanted to cry. Meanwhile, the Fokker circled.

Then the thud of an ack-ack gun commenced.

Men of the Nigerian navy aboard the oil tanker *Apapa* in the lagoon had awakened to danger and their one gun—World War II vintage, a monument to rust—was made operational. Or: a coverlet was thrown off and two or three rounds of ammo were finally located.

Ka-pow! Ka-pow!

The noise attracted the residents of downtown Lagos, most of whom came out from the doorways and from underneath cars where they had been sleeping. Some looked out windows, others turned off lights, others took cover, but the men on the roof dared danger and watched von Schwenk and his crew at about eye level.

The flak from the harbor exploded harmlessly far above the plane.

"They haven't got the range yet," Bedford said from his observation post.

Inside the Fokker, Mewishi was still at the controls. He sweated profusely, but seemed to enjoy himself as von Schwenk and the cook determined that because of all the circling they should probably only drop one bomb.

"But we can't find the harbor," von Schwenk complained. He peered down into the blackness. "And if we don't find it soon, we'll have to turn back because we'll need the fuel in both drums."

At that moment the *Apapa* sent up the only flare they possessed. The sky above Lagos turned bright orange, so that von Schwenk and the others suddenly had a clear view of oil storage tanks, ships, docks, and buildings along the shoreline.

Until the flare went out, there was increased ack-ack fire, then the available light and the ammo supply ended together. The people of the city watched and listened. The drone of the old Fokker—like a German buzz bomb sputtering above their heads.

Rena by this time had become the sexual champion of the airplane, having outlasted them all with energy to spare, so she was given the honor of lighting the dynamite fuse. Mewishi banked the plane softly—he was doing a remarkable job—and glanced over his shoulder as match touched fuse. Then von

Schwenk and the cook rolled the oil drum back to the side door. Above, a canopy of stars and the cold universe; below, some splendid targets.

But the drum wouldn't fit through the door.

"How'd we get this in here?" von Schwenk inquired.

But the cook and Rena were too terrified to think of any other door or hatch because the fuse had already quickly burned down between the sticks of dynamite where not even the quickest, bravest finger could reach to snuff it out.

"Let's be logical," von Schwenk suggested.

The cook began to unlash ropes as fast as he could.

Mewishi had just glanced up at Val's photograph above his head.

Anastasia was taking a douche.

On the roof of the Bristol Hotel, the Peacock had just yawned and stretched, saying his good-night, as the Fokker banked toward them for a last time. Then his head jerked around.

The plane went up in a ball of fire. A miniature mushroom starting in midair: dazzling, like a magnificent rocket, far more spectacular than any ignited at any festival held in Lagos. People cheered in the streets. Bedford dropped his gin fizz off the roof. The Nigerian Navy—four pajama-clad seamen and a beribboned duty officer who aimed the ack-ack—took credit for the kill.

The nose of the Fokker was blown forward with the explosion and Mewishi, intact behind the wheel, eyes wide, mouth agape, clutched the controls in a long, arching fall toward the lagoon. He regretted his new vanities as he fell earthward: the fez, his infatuation with machines and planes, all the white man's postures and objects which he had tried to adopt. He regretted that he had served the Commander, that he had been a soldier at all, that he had wasted years in strange lands. Val's photo shimmered before his eyes as the chunk of metal in which he rode floated toward the water. He regretted knowing that woman, too. He didn't like her. At the very last second of his life before he entered the lapping teeth of the waves, he was all regret.

† † †

Before the great battle of Umuahia an arms vendor sat around the campfire with Leo drinking the Johnnie Walker he had brought up from Pretoria. The men were glutted with booze, strong nostalgia, and fear. Hank Wharton, the vendor, stood and named all the glorious wild flowers of South Africa and the sound of their names made the Commander weep.

The Cape Coast Lily, Sea Lavender, Snake Flower, Blue Flax, Wild Marigold, Karoo Violet, Wild Cineraria.

"Oh, god," Leo wept. "Pronounce that one again."

"Wild Cineraria!"

"Oh, god, that's beautiful."

Painted Lady, Red Afrikaner, Butterfly Morea, Falling Star, Belladonna.

† † †

"You know that you might have to die for the Commander," Val said to Weldu one of those evenings before the fall of the city.

"Why do you say that to me?" Weldu replied.

"Because it's true, isn't it? There's no way to stop the federals now and we're not sure there are enough planes for all of us."

Weldu stood on his good leg outside her lorry and drew from his pocket a small bottle of Sloan's. He took just a sip, returned it to its place, and watched his mistress. She had been inside at her desk for hours. Now she pushed a strand of hair from her face and turned toward the twilight breeze coming across the runway; it was hot, very hot, and a bead of crystal perspiration hung above her beautiful cheekbone.

"I think you said that to strike fear in me," Weldu told her.

"Do you really think that of me?"

Weldu paused, knowing he had already offended her.

"Perhaps you didn't mean it that way," he allowed.

"I certainly didn't," she said softly. She opened her collar and let the breeze cool her.

After a silence, she said, "I wish we had enough petrol to run the air-conditioner. I can't breathe." She looked at Weldu and his face was a mask.

She went back inside, strapped on a .38 police special, then went for a walk. The pistol against her hip, tapping lightly, felt good as she crossed the runway and turned down a small stream which flowed from the nearby hills. A worn path lured her on, so in spite of the gathering darkness she went.

She *had* meant to upset Weldu and he had caught her at it. Why did I do it, she asked herself, yet she knew: war, politics, games, lovemaking, daily existence were all good theater and she loved the drama. Drama opened the pores and let air into the brain and blood.

Anything that plays: people in a room, the language, men, events. And the stronger the confrontation the better.

She had been writing at several projects those weeks in the lorry and nothing had turned out. The old assignment on Leo, the one for which she took the advance back in Switzerland, couldn't be done. She had then started an adventure novel: awful. Then a novel about a young English girl in London: boring. Wretched poems. Travel articles no one would want. She couldn't even turn her hand to those insipid news releases Leo and the poor Biafran ministries wanted her to do. All her writing had come to an impasse and she knew deep down that she just wasn't called to the craft, that she'd be doomed to embarrassment or worse if she kept on.

Meanwhile, she craved excitement and knew how to get it, though, at times, with Weldu just now, for instance, her usual technique failed. A simple formula: beauty was power—and power always created eddies of action and whirlpools of emotion which were fun to watch.

She came to a place where the stream bent back on itself, creating a little peninsula of mossy grass. A nice glade: palm and cotton trees and a pocket of night darker than the sky overhead. Placing the pistol within reach on the bank, she peeled off her shirt, crepe shoes, jeans, panties, and waded into the water. Down into that murky stream, down and down, waist deep and refreshing; she let her body and thoughts float.

Week on week, episode after episode, she had possibly been creating a real-life book, she decided. Because of her, Harry was back in Africa where he never really wanted to be; and Leo felt he had another chance. They were jealous, too. She knew it. And things were going on: Leo was making plans to take the boys and her away, she knew, perhaps leaving Harry without a plane or an escape route except through the dangerous eastern roads into the Cameroons. Yet, Harry seemed perfectly aware of all this and ready.

Drama and confrontation. Perhaps something awful.

She wet her hair and smiled.

Darkness fell quickly as she put her clothes on over her wet body. She liked the way the cloth clung to her; she looked good. The pistol was cool in her hand.

As she went back up the path, she gave a thought to the leopard said to be stalking everyone. But then she was thinking of Harry: how he bashed that poor boy's mouth in Villars; the way he looked at her in Spain after Leo arrived; how she held his hand in the jeep that time in Elisabethville, his eyes glazed and ferocious; how, so long ago, he slipped those shiny talons on his fingers as he moved across the moonlight to her bed. Lately, he hadn't been himself—running here and there playing medic and savior. But Harry was all shadows and nightmares; he lived where the beasts lived, she knew he did, he'd come back to that. Those memories made her pulse hammer in her wrist.

Over the runway a canopy of stars had appeared.

Walking toward the lorries and tents, she knew the guards had already seen her. They were watching the roll of her hips and the jut of her breasts in the damp shirt, she knew, and she thought, god, I'm a bitch, I really am, and I don't care.

"We've been worried about you," Weldu said when she got back.

"I took a dip in that dirty stream," she answered. "Heat me some water for a proper bath."

"The night traffic will be coming soon," Weldu said. "Lots of planes. Maybe we should keep regulations.'"

"Have the men hurry."

She went into the lorry where Harry's big Mauser-Bauer stood in the corner beside the lamp.

Harry was in Umuahia. Helping.

Leo was probably over at airport headquarters making sure he had his cut of the night's loot.

"I'll go with the strongest one," she said in the confines of the lorry. "I will." And she slammed the .38 down on the top of her inlaid desk and began removing her clothes again. A button popped off her shirt and rolled down into the darkness beneath the desk where she couldn't find it.

Weldu, she decided, was insolent as hell.

She put on her robe and waited to be called for a bath. As she waited, she remembered that Vic and Jocko had gone with Pogo over to the airport canteen where they liked to play pinball. Her thoughts were momentarily confused; she wanted Harry, the bath, something. She feared—what? The abyss of small feelings. She wanted something to happen very soon and to be very important.

† † †

Bedford flew into Enugu, which was occupied by the federals, then started down the road to Owerri in a taxi en route to the heart of Biafra—wherever it now located itself—and to Val.

On the way, stopping here and there at small villages, he began to hear stories about Harry Veer he didn't believe. Scores of elders, wounded, children—every refugee in the sector, according to sources who were obviously exaggerating—had been saved by this gentle mercenary. Food distributed, first aid stations set up, transportation provided. Bedford remembered sitting around the lobby of the Rex back in Katanga hearing different tales. But it was Val he wanted to see.

They came to a roadblock after dark where he was given a bad time by a minor official who refused to look at his credentials.

"This is a press pass. And, here—a letter from the chief of communications in Lagos."

"You are not talking to me," the official said stubbornly.

"You want a bribe, right?" Bedford finally thought to say.

"Suddenly," the official told him, "you have found the international language."

Tired and irritated, Bedford climbed into the taxi and they started bumping down the road again. His stomach was upset —a mild dysentery—and his wallet was lighter. The driver, he suspected, was drunk on palm wine. Besides, for the first time he began to feel that his journey was over, that he had stayed too long in Africa, that things were not what they seemed any longer, and that a reporter, for all good intentions and perseverance, would come to lies, fabrications, myths untrue and sadly unimportant; was Harry Veer, the mad-dog killer, suddenly a saint? which side was right? was Val all he remembered or did he travel into disappointment again? He had always been an adaptáble man, but now he felt he should be riding in a solid London taxi, not this rattling disaster, going along the Mall, marking his old habits and familiar places. Snooker and ale. The Fleet Street pubs. Certainly not this junky jungle and faraway assignment.

"Turn back," he told his driver.

"Wot? Wot's that?"

"Turn around. We're not going on just now."

The puzzled driver stopped, questioned his rider to make sure, then obeyed. But as the old taxi edged back and forth in the road trying to turn around, a wheel became stuck. The driver changed gears, gunned it, then stopped altogether.

"I'll get some big rocks and branches and slip them under the tires," Bedford offered.

"Wot? No use! No petrol either," the driver said, trying to manufacture a grin.

"In a ditch and out of petrol?"

"Sir, for dis I gonna have to ask more pay."

"You want my money, too?"

Frustrated, Bedford started out walking back to the road-block. This trip, he realized, was a vast mistake. Val, the war, all of it.

The night was pitch dark so that after a while the correspondent of *The Times* couldn't help stepping off into that muddy ditch himself. He went in the ditch several times, as if drunk, until his shoes were heavy with the thick mud of the region, and his steps slowed. He began to shuffle along with his hands out before him. No moon, no single point of light;

this, too, was a mistake. Life became a mistake, a game played badly and foolishly, so that he wished he could be given one more chance, one more beginning.

For a moment he thought he had lost the road, but then he was sure he was on it. He decided to get down on his knees and crawl, feeling for tire tracks—the road was deeply rutted —so that he wouldn't stray into the jungle around him. So for a long time he crawled until his clothes were caked with mud, too, and his every weighted movement cursed him.

Then he came to the leopard. His fingers, trembling, reaching out into the blackness ahead, found its gigantic paw. For a split second he didn't know what it was—such a soft, comforting fur and strange sinew—and then he knew he was a dead man.

† † †

The day before the battle Jiggs, now a religious leader and medicine man, led his troupe of dancers out of the bush to worship Val. They were a dirty, naked bunch and when they leapt their breasts and genitals bounced and their sweat mingled with dirt and became an exotic slime on their black bodies. Gypsy fanatics: they roamed, begged, prayed, danced, and seemed to have a grave good time.

They associated Val with the Ibo goddess Ala, who was queen of the underworld, closely associated with ancestors, responsible for law, punishments, Ibo morality, and a feminine spirit who possessed all men in both life and death. Val was good-humored about this designation and put on a long frock for the occasion. She came out on the tailgate of the lorry, opened her arms wide, and let her hips sway with the rhythms of their crude drumming—which they took to be a blessing and an approval.

The group was mostly hungry and ate several meals through

the day. But Leo seemed not to mind. He felt they were good luck, so he served up beans and cassava bread in large quantities.

The day's top entertainment was provided by Jiggs, who went into a trance. Members of his own group filed in front of his glazed eyes and were told that they would have fat babies, inherit money, own good cattle, and such happy predictions carried through the afternoon. Slivers of wood were put through Jiggs' sides and arms to show the depth of his trance.

But then he told Pogo that he would die a poet's death and the mood altered. Nobody wanted their fortune told after that.

A pretty girl in the entourage sprinkled juju holy water around the edges of the camp as a favor. It was supposed to keep out evil spirits, thieves, the enemy, and the stalking leopard. Weldu, Jocko, and Vic walked with her as she gave her performance; she was much admired for her style of incantation—a high, pleasant song—and her dainty breasts.

An elder with the group passed around some good *bangi*. African marijuana, a whole ounce for everybody, and a little silver short-stemmed pipe.

Still, Jiggs wouldn't come out of his trance and as dark was falling and the men had to get back to work at the airport—120 tons of supplies were due in that evening—Val became interested in his prophecies again.

"Leave all that alone," Harry advised her.

"I want to hear how everything comes out."

"No you don't."

As she knelt down in front of Jiggs, the troupe began to sway and dance once more. She stared into his colorless eyes. The strips of wood still pierced his arms and sides, but there was little blood. She rested a gentle hand on his knee to let him know she was there.

Jiggs' head rolled and lolled as the frenzy of the dance increased. Words formed. Swahili, so Leo came over to translate.

Harry thought of that diviner at the side of the road. The whole show annoyed him and made him nervous.

"What's he saying?" Val wanted to know.

He was telling of an island in the sea. The Island of War. A great fortress on a cliff. Naked white women at the sea shore. A big battle and a victory for one of Val's men, but he would see a black flag and a child would destroy him.

"What of my other man?" she asked in a whisper.

No answer.

"And what about me?"

Silence.

† † †

Although there was no unified command for the defense of Umuahia, Ojukwu and his generals did get together at a party hours before the federals appeared. They offered a number of toasts (Rena received one dozen, Bayeke one, von Schwenk none) and divided up the arms and equipment at the brigade, battalion, and platoon levels.

Each Biafran soldier, they declared, would face the enemy with no fewer than three bullets for his bolt-action single-shot rifle. The fifteen officers would each be issued a Madison automatic rifle. Thirty CETME automatics, captured from the enemy, would be put into the hands of the sharpshooters of Leo Rucker's Elite Rifles. There would also be Colonel Veer's Mauser-Bauer, one Browning, three Winchester shotguns, five working mortars with three rounds each, sixty grenades, two Saracen armored cars (donated by Rucker), one Saladin "Red Devil" which two of the generals would occupy, two jeeps, three Land Rovers, forty bicycles, one 1951 Harley Davidson with sidecar, fifteen hundred slingshots, and assorted spears and knives.

Trenches had been dug all around the city.

Barricades of corrugated tin, oil drums, and bunkers lined with sawdust-filled sandbags would insure that Umuahia was a fortress.

One hundred land mines—the *ogbunigwe*—were in position. These would surely destroy all federal tanks.

Since there was no ammo, the six machine guns in the district would not be used. Ditto the two howitzers. Ditto the Biafran air force.

The order to invent booby traps was rescinded since "such traps tended to be destroying friendly personnel" at an alarming rate. Those who gave their efforts toward such inventions were duly thanked in a radio announcement from headquarters.

An hour before dawn, Ojukwu sent for Leo.

"Think we ought to have some reserves ready?" he asked, trying to be casual toward holocaust.

"Good thinking," the Commander said.

"We've got a battalion at Aba."

"I'll send for it."

"And another at Itu."

"I'll send for it, too."

"And by the way," the Biafran leader said, his expression going blank as if he had just vacated himself, "I suppose you should have the jet ready from this hour on."

"You want to be ready to skip out?" Leo asked, making sure.

Ojukwu muttered something in Ibo. The Commander waited for him to touch the earth again, but he didn't. For an hour or more, Leo enjoyed the cooled air of the Airstream trailer, then he left. When he emerged into the new day he could hear the rumble of guns.

There was nothing of consequence the federals could shoot or destroy, so they burned the cassava forests, the palm groves, a few mud huts, chicken coops, ungainly piles of corrugated tin and oil drums which sheltered their enemy, and eventually worked their way toward the center of the city where they expected genuine opposition. But the Biafrans were no more trouble than the elephant grass—which the federals also burned—though they were just as abundant. Weldu's brave recruits ran and hid, as instructed, but they were all duly found. Harry's planned coordinated sniper attack didn't materialize because the federal tanks and armor roared by with such speed that the Elite Rifles realized they were surrounded in seconds, so began to fend for themselves. All vehicles of defense, including Leo's prized Saracens, took direct hits from antitank guns—weapons most Biafran regulars had never heard of.

Leo wisely took off for Uli. When his Land Rover reached the airport, he radioed Aba and Itu for reinforcements, and the battalions in those cities, unfortunately, came in a hurry and were on the scene before the federals had completely lost their taste for slaughter.

Pogo, hidden in the top of a palm tree, soon found that he was a couple of miles behind enemy lines. He pondered his choices. He could stay there in the foliage until harvest. He could take an occasional shot at an important-looking federal officer and die a hero's death—instead of the one predicted by Jiggs. He decided to stay and think a little longer on his predicament.

Meanwhile, the federal MIGs were busy bombing the roads on the far side of town where the remnants of the Biafran force were in hurried retreat. One of the lorries they destroyed was the one in which Harry and his men planned to rendevous in the event of defeat.

The Airstream trailer was driven to safety while Ojukwu, sitting beside the air-conditioner inside, stared out dumbly at nothing. His mother was at the wheel of the Ford LTD which pulled it along the road back toward Uli Airport. She was a plucky woman, bent with the years, devoted to her son and good cuisine and would one day own and operate a French restaurant on the Ivory Coast much as General Ojukwu dreamt and hoped she would.

Inside an empty oil drum, cramped and frustrated, Weldu struggled to remove his clothes. So dumb getting in here, he told himself. Stupid. He couldn't see what was going on, couldn't fight, couldn't even undress. All around him were the shouts of federal soldiers, the rattle of tanks, the occasional crack of rifle fire. At last he tore his chocolate-colored sergeant's shirt down the middle of the back and slipped it off his arms. I'll stand up now, he told himself, and step out of my britches and come out of the barrel all in one move.

His plan was to transform himself into a naked crazy man. If the federals caught him with anything other than their uniform on, they would surely shoot him, he reasoned, so better to be naked. Except for his bottle of Sloan's Liniment, then, he emerged from the oil drum without a shred, went into his act, and hoped for the best. His head twitched, his eyes blinked heavily as if he stared into a withering sun, he walked in circles.

After a few minutes, he took a long swig from his bottle just to fortify himself.

Harry made his way into the forest where he began to feel safe. By sunset, he had calculated his position and had decided to walk all the way back to Uli—or at least beyond the federal drive, if, indeed, it ever ceased. He was pissed: Leo had jumped in that Land Rover before things got hot; the Biafrans were too weary and ill-equipped to go on with this charade; and his own plan to use the Elite Rifles as a sniper corps had failed. Yet this wasn't bad. The mangrove and palm trees gave him thick cover and no man was his equal out here. He had the Mauser-Bauer, a good pistol, knives, even a grenade.

Careful of cobras, he told himself, and you'll be all right.

After dark, Pogo edged down the trunk of his tree. His hands shook with fright, but he kept to the shadows and after a while began to have confidence in his escape. He skirted the main square—from the frequent bursts of fire, he assumed there was an execution squad at work—and the buildings downtown and moved across a gully filled with banana trees. A big decision was his weapon: whether to keep it or not. Passing a culvert, he deposited the rifle in the brackish water of a cement pipe, then moved on, more quickly now, across a vacant lot toward the outskirts of the city. Only then did he hear the clanking noise following him. But he didn't look back and tried to imagine he had done the right thing getting rid of the rifle.

He stopped, once, hid behind a tree and looked back. Nothing. But something, he felt, was coming after him— clanking and rattling.

Gasping for breath, he picked up his pace. Then he decided some federal would see him running and shoot him, so he slowed again. He jumped a small picket fence and continued on. The clucking of chickens. The moo of a cow.

In a stand of bamboo, he paused for another look back. And there it was: a tank. It came out of the night and crushed the little fence he had just cleared, clanking toward him, its treads beating a senseless metallic rhythm as it crossed the barnyard through which he had just come.

He turned and fled.

Down a hedgerow, across a small wood, through another field. He stopped to rest again. Waited. Listened. The thing was still coming.

Saplings went down before it, its gears shifted, its motor hummed deep inside.

Pogo reached a dirt road where he broke into his last full sprint, but the tank edged up the shoulder and gained speed behind him. Desperate, Pogo flung himself into the woods again. He passed a mud hut, the skeleton of an abandoned lorry, perhaps a man—some shadowed figure standing in the yard. Now he walked, unable to run another step.

The tank came on, its meaningless clanking growing louder.

At last Pogo was walking in not too straight a line, wandering in a field beneath the rising moon. He knew by this time there was nobody inside the tank; the thing alone was after him. A machine. He tried to say something to himself, but his voice was gone—just a mere wheeze against the oncoming noise. His pace slowed and stopped, so that he seemed to be waiting for it. Then it was on him. Its treads gathered him up and took him inside where it began to grind him up; his bones and muscles, his heart and brain made into mush by the wheels and pulleys and creaking axles; then it moved on, still clanking, using Pogo's body to lubricate itself. It became a shadow, noisy and ominous, against the light of the moon.

Weldu was stopped by two surly federal soldiers who didn't know what to make of him. The tall one wanted to bash him with a rifle butt, but the short one wanted to know what he was drinking.

Weldu talked with his tongue hanging out of his mouth, making slobber and nonsense.

When the short soldier reached for his bottle of Sloan's, Weldu pulled it away and hid it underneath his arm like a child.

"Wot you got? Gimme dat now!" the short soldier barked.

Weldu's drool was convincing. The tall soldier thought he might bite like a mad dog.

"Smells like whiskey liquor!" said the short soldier, turning it up and taking a long drink. Meanwhile, Weldu made a show of wanting the bottle back.

The two soldiers finished off the Sloan's Liniment in a matter of seconds. Loot was loot.

To stall for time, Weldu began relating a story with his tongue out. His words made no sense, but his gestures were ornate and won the attention of the soldiers while the drink did its work. The story concerned a long journey into the faraway mountains, the meeting with an old blind man, a great knowledge, and there were just enough discernible phrases so the soldiers didn't turn away.

Before long the soldiers were in convulsions, writhing on the ground with stomach pains. When they died, Weldu took the shirt from the tall one and the trousers from the short one and dressed himself as a federal. He put on a helmet, belt, and laced his new infantry boots. Then he put a rifle over his shoulder and began to march. His step was so sure and direct that he passed many other federals, including some officers, who failed to issue an order for him to halt.

Seventeen hours after having gone into the forest, Harry emerged on a road. Clearly, the war hadn't come this way. Women strolled along with baskets of yams on top of their heads. An old furniture maker sat in his stall tapping peacefully with his little hammer. A Coca-Cola sign appeared. He felt conspicuous in his fatigues with his rifle strapped across his shoulder; he pulled down the bill of his cap and adjusted his dark glasses as he walked. Burrs and thorns adorned his clothing, but Harry had a feeling of accomplishment, having stuck in the bush so long, and before long, at a crossroads, he saw coming from another direction a familiar figure taking long strides, saying, as he came closer and the cadence became more distinct, "Hep, one, two, and a hep, one, two!" It was Weldu.

Harry spoke to him as he passed—Weldu looking neither right nor left as he marched.

When Weldu recognized Harry's friendly voice, he sat down in the middle of the road with relief and exhaustion.

"Oh, sir, what about the others?" he asked Harry.

"There are damned few others," Harry answered, "and it's every man for himself."

† † †

Soon the federal forces would cross the Imo River at two points, sweep back into Owerri, shell the little town of Madonna and Uli airfield, attack Aba, and scatter the last of the poor Biafran army.

Ojukwu, his mother beside him patting his arm, would issue a statement that, yes, he was leaving the country, but would soon return to lead a Biafran guerrilla action. Jiggs would become an oil executive. Bayeke, the exile, would sing on.

In the camp beside runway Number Two there were many visitors. Leo entertained airport officials, figures from the defunct air force, even the guards who stood watch over the planes which, now, were out in the bush around the edges of the field, covered with palm leaves and hidden from the nosy

MIGs which made daily passes overhead. Leo gave one official a lorry filled with Lux soap, three kinds of beer, Johnnie Walker Red, sugar, salt, tins of tea, palm wine, bicycles, canned Spam, and bags of cassava flour. Another received British pounds, amount undisclosed. A guard received American dollars—the only currency he would accept.

Leo made a great show of protecting the two-man jet fighter which everyone knew Ojukwu planned to use for his escape, but actually Leo had his eye on a Beechcraft—said to be broken down, but in truth long ago repaired—which would take out a pilot and four passengers. Jocko and Victor had virtually taken up residence in that plane, stored not far from the camp of the Elite Rifles. Their toys, assorted candies, and Dorothy the falcon, hooded and docile, were inside with them. Even the pilot was ready and waiting: an Ibo named Sidney, to whom Leo had donated a completely stocked bar and grill which Sidney's parents now operated in Aba.

The Commander was fun to watch. His deals had flair. One day he even traded off his last case of Worcestershire sauce. That other mercenary, the one with the Mercedes, was dickering for Port Harcourt or all the palm-oil rights in the region, such very big dreams, and he'd get none of them, but Leo was tuned to the correct frequencies those last days of the war: he had the hard cash and the goods a fleeing and beaten people needed. His manipulations were small, but poetic.

Finally, there was a luncheon. A white table cloth, champagne, cold sturgeon to start, with Val, Harry, Sidney, Weldu, and the Commander making the toasts in that room behind the hangar at Uli.

Leo presented Weldu with a medal.

He then presented Val and Harry with their Swiss account books. After this, the dead were remembered with several toasts. *War, like hell, always has an interesting cast of players,* the Commander said, raising a glass to Mewishi and von Schwenk. Sidney, much impressed with this display of rhetoric and loyalty, took one more champagne than his limit.

Last assignments were then announced.

Harry and Weldu would drive the remaining vehicles, the Land Rover and the armored lorry containing Val's desk and various expensive small arms, across the eastern mountain border into the Cameroons. Leo would fly Val and the boys to safety and everyone would rendezvous in Nairobi at another pleasant lunch such as this one in a few short weeks.

Harry stood up, raised his glass, smiled a thin smile which meant he found this not too amusing, and replied, "Got any other ideas?"

Leo stopped drinking.

"It won't work, Leo," Harry went on. "For one thing, the border into the Cameroons is closed. The federals circled that way a week ago. My information—and yours, too, probably —is that we're totally surrounded."

"Are you sure about that, Harry?" Leo asked, trying to muster some consternation.

"Besides," Harry said, "I wouldn't go if the border was clear. Val and the boys are my responsibility."

"There's only one plane and it's mine," Leo said flatly.

"Horseshit," Harry told him.

"You are under my command and you'll do as I say," Leo claimed.

"Horseshit, again," Harry repeated.

Val, smiling, looked at first one and then the other of them.

"I won't let you take what's mine away from me a second time," Leo said more plaintively. "I just won't, goddammit!"

"Are the boys in the plane?" Harry asked Val.

"I think so," she said.

"Then we're going now. Sidney, go clear for takeoff."

"I won't let you do this," Leo said. "I'll put you under arrest first."

Sidney stood up, then sat down again.

"Go do as you're told, Sidney," Harry told him.

"Weldu," Leo snapped. "Put Colonel Veer under arrest."

Actions after this seemed in wild slow motion. Weldu and Sidney rose, bumped together, and started around the table in different directions. Val stood up in surprise. Leo grabbed Sidney's shoulder, speaking sharply to him. Harry threw Weldu against the wall.

"You're under my command, too," Leo was explaining to Sidney when all this ended. "So sit down."

Weldu complained about his leg which had somehow become tangled behind him when he hit the wall. "I think it's broken again," he wheezed.

Sidney, seated once more, folded his hands on the table.

"Enough," Leo spat out, red with anger. "You can throw the whole bloody airport guard against the wall next—because I'm fetching them!" With that he started for the door, but Harry produced the Astra-Constable and leveled it in Leo's direction.

"Harry," Val said, pronouncing his name in much the same way she once did in that bar in Switzerland, reasonably and soft with just the mildest touch of pride.

"You won't use it," Leo said bravely, yet he didn't make a further move to leave the room.

"Get up, Sidney," Harry said, "and go clear for takeoff. Turn in your flight plan and make all arrangements."

Harry fired. A half empty bottle of champagne exploded not three feet from Sidney, who was immediately up and out of the room.

"Oh, sir, it is broken," Weldu moaned. "The big bone."

"Bloody Christ in Wales," Leo said.

"I'll go pack," Val suggested.

"Go ahead," Harry told her.

"You might as well take the strongbox," Leo said, still not moving to the door. "You're robbing me anyway."

"We'll get together, all of us," Val promised him. "You'll see."

"You're taking my only true son!"

"Don't talk like that," she asked him.

"Get going," Harry said softly.

"The strongbox is under the floorboard in the driver's side of your lorry," Leo told her as she went out the door. "Load up your bloody desk, too," he called after her. "And—" But she was gone.

He sat back down at the table. He and Harry listened to Weldu moan. In a minute one of the airport guards stuck his head through the door and asked about the shot, but Harry explained they were celebrating.

"Could I please have something to drink?" Weldu asked, trying to arrange his broken leg into a more comfortable position.

Harry poured him a glass of champagne. Leo poured his own.

"You and your bloody refugees," Leo said. "Your whole behavior made me sick, if you want to know."

"It occurred to me," Harry told him, "that if all the people on our side died we would have lost the war."

"Well, that's a hell of a sorry way to think," Leo said angrily.

"Could I have another glass?" Weldu asked.

"It's all gone," Harry sighed. "I shot up the last of it."

They sat there for an hour waiting for Sidney or Val to report back during which time Leo said, "I haven't been a coward in this, Harry, I just want you to know that. If I hadn't been unarmed, I'd've gone out the bloody door and fetched the guards."

"Okay," Harry answered.

"Goddammit, you had the drop on me."

Then Sidney came and announced that everything would be delayed because it wasn't safe to take off in daylight.

"Some MIGs in the area, sorry, sir," he said, addressing Harry.

"We'll wait," Harry said.

"Could I please have my Sloan's?" Weldu asked.

"Bring this man his Sloan's," Harry told Sidney, who was more or less standing at attention. "And a doctor to set his leg."

Leo sat at the table looking at the dried food in the plates and the broken glass feeling much the same as that day at Orly. Depression and pure pain. Moisture poured from his face: sweat, tears, the juices of his last energy, he didn't know. Flies buzzed around the ceiling.

Eventually, a medic showed up, made a lengthy apology for having no morphine for one of Commander Rucker's men, then pulled Weldu's leg straight and tied on splints. Weldu was several strong sips of Sloan's to the good and felt no pain.

An hour went by in appreciation of Weldu, his capacity for that drink, the story of how quickly it killed the two federals who stopped him, and then related stories of the battle of Umuahia and the losses over the long haul of so many good men.

In his melancholy, Leo attempted to be philosophic. *The criminal,* he said. *Think of the word itself. It presupposes a nice moral culture with little deviancy.*

Neither Weldu nor Harry had any idea of what he was trying to say.

Later on he added, *The bloody psychopath needs his due. Let him murder for us and fight every war, see, we need his craziness, we really do, or we'll have to go on giving our darling sons.*

Harry was very tired of listening to Leo and glad when Sidney appeared at the door again.

"Men are waiting with bush lamps the whole length of the runway," Sidney reported with a grin.

Harry got up and stuck the Astra-Constable in his belt. "I don't ever want to see you again, Leo," he said. "And neither does Val."

"Good-bye," Leo sighed.

Harry and the pilot walked side by side to the Beechcraft where the faces of Victor and Jocko peered from the lighted windows. Val had gathered clothes, gear, her papers, Harry's rifle, the strongbox, and all the plane could hold. Even Dorothy the falcon was still aboard. Down the length of the runway, as reported, the Ibos had lighted bush lamps so the way was clear. Moths and insects swarmed around the lamps, but the men held them patiently as the motors roared and Harry entered the plane. As the plane sped by them and lifted off into the darkness each man holding a lamp stretched out his free hand and waved.

PART FIVE

OBLIVION

THE SOUTH SUDAN, NAIROBI, LONDON, MOMBASA, LAST MOVES

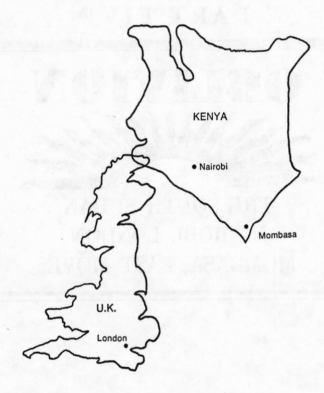

KENYA

● Nairobi

● Mombasa

U.K.

London ●

CHANGES OF ADDRESS.
New camps, flats, houses, apartments. Leo settled in East Africa and mostly remained. Val, Harry, and the boys went to Texas, traveled around, then settled in London.

After Biafra, Leo tried Nairobi again, first the camp out on the Langata Road: the same tents, bones and fossils, wild flowers, and the same German neighbors. But the camp echoed its own strange emptiness and Weldu's lack of enthusiasm for life as a *mutu* and rainy seasons which seemed to last forever brought them into town. For a while Leo had rooms at the Norfolk, but there were kids in jeans, businessmen in new, ill-fitting safari jackets, ladies with blue hair. So he bought an old plantation house south of town: a marble foyer, wide undulating hardwood floors, walls with white ovals where trophies once hung, and a green horizon of coffee trees which were leased to a corporation. Too big, a mausoleum. For a while after that he stayed at a flat near the university and went out to the estate on weekends—and then mostly to take one of his frequent inventories of the arsenal which he had moved from the campsite.

A legend—partially his, partially not—followed him around the city and won him some notoriety and a few acquaintances who wanted to show him off at the polo matches or buy him a Tusker at the Thorn Tree Café or engage him in long conversations on military history or other boring subjects. Women, too: a few spinsters, a few flirtatious wives, a widow. Idle times. Hours in bookshops, food with Worcestershire, notes from strangers to other strangers pinned to the hotel bulletin boards.

After a time he heard of a war that had lasted years between the Arab rulers in Khartoum and their black subjects in the South Sudan, rebels who called themselves *The Anyanya* —meaning cobra venom. Someone said that a mercenary was fighting for the blacks, taking Arab heads and keeping them in a basket. Others told him there was a mutiny in the army. The black tribesmen were Dinka mostly—Weldu's people— and in the end it was Weldu who wanted to go there, convincing Leo that they should hire a plane, fly up to Juba, the principal southern city, and look things over.

"I think I want to go home," Weldu said. "Maybe to fight, maybe not, I don't care."

Leo offered him the armored lorry—Val's desk still inside— which was going to rust out at the old camp.

"You can drive it up there and fight with it or trade it for cattle, if you want," Leo suggested. "That'll get you started."

"I do thank you, Leo, very kind," Weldu said in accepting. His leg had never been right after having been broken that second time; he couldn't stand like a Dinka anymore, but

he wanted to go back to some of the old ways. Leo, he said.
He didn't call him Commander anymore either.

As cities went, Juba was a toilet. White plaster buildings on
white sand with a few scrub bushes around and no facilities
so its inhabitants urinated against the walls, defecated in its
gutters, slept on its rooftops, cursed its isolation and their
own. There was a war, yes, but a filthy and undefined one:
Arab columns had sometimes rolled into villages and mas-
sacred everyone hoping to get a few rebels. There had been
a purge in the army. Some assassinations of Arab officials and
generals. Reprisals. But there was no one to see, no newspaper
accounts, neither Arab spokesman nor tribal chief available
for information or comment. Besides, the rumor of the other
mysterious mercenary was true: it was the one with the white
Mercedes flying the skull and crossbones.

Fuck it, Leo decided. Let that one have the war. Wherever
it was, if anyplace, profits were probably small.

Leo and Weldu got drunk a last time together, but Weldu
was sullen and somehow distracted. They never really looked
in each other's eyes or shook hands, then Weldu was gone.

Leo caught a flight back to Nairobi with two hunters, Glen
Cottar and Jens Hessel, nice enough chaps who didn't require
that he sober up and let him sleep in the back of the Piper.
They seemed to know about him, though, and stuck him in a
taxi at the airport and sent him to the plantation where he
slept another few days—or a week or month or longer, no
difference.

Weldu stripped himself naked except for the traditional
anklets of fur and the razored bracelets and began to wander
with his new-bought cattle. As time went on, his leg became
stronger and he was able to run again. He went with cousins
and friends to kill zebra: surrounding them, they charged

and wounded as many as possible, then ran the cripples down, butchered them, and devoured them raw under the soft light of the moon. In the Dinka language there was no verb meaning *to have* or *to possess;* they owned no land individually; the land was God's and belonged to the tribe as a whole.

Although he always wanted a wife, Weldu never found one. He became a witch doctor, the same as his father and all his grandfathers, and it was remarked among his people that if he had no peculiar powers, yet he had common sense, had traveled far, had seen men at war, and had therefore seen the eye of darkness.

† † †

Harry, not Val, ended up with a desk.

His was in Grosvenor Square halfway between the offices of the American consulate and the flat used by J. R. Hoskins when he visited London. At the desk Harry sorted papers, working on that great mosaic of data coming out of Africa. When he and Val first came to London, he hadn't worked at all. He felt he owed nobody help. But time became a bother and eventually he decided he had responsibility: he might save a life out there, he might extend his rescue mission a little, or discover some small truth in that catalog of time and names and wretched politics.

"I can't stand your hours!" Val protested. "You're so bloody normal!"

"I don't mind it," he said, touching her hair, and he didn't. It was normalcy he wanted, nothing else. The rhythms of recuperation.

Meanwhile, Val put on weight. She tried diets, but with the energy of old excitements drained away, her body idled; in turn, she was plump, then drawn and pale looking, then plump again as the diets affected her nerves. She also put away all her papers and never wrote again. A talkative recollection of Africa became her pastime and her girl friends—the wife of a diplomat, the wife of an editor—didn't believe most of her stories.

Every day that Harry put on a jacket and tie and went to his little office she disliked him more. Vic and Jocko, who didn't understand their father, yet liked him, saw their mother's attitude and became distant and difficult with her. Jocko called her fat. She didn't know how to regard Victor at all, so became oddly seductive and coy with him, which he despised. He told her not to touch him.

"I'd have an affair if I still had my looks," she told Harry once.

"You look wonderful," he said, bungling as any well-meaning husband would.

"So I should have an affair?"

"No, I didn't mean that. I meant you look great to me."

"Let's go someplace else and live."

"If we went, you wouldn't like it any better."

"I'd like Africa."

"There's no place for us there."

Money interested her, but she hated that about herself. Her muscle tone was gone. She wished she could play tennis.

At night she sometimes got out of bed and roamed the house, passing the painting by Winterhalter hung in the marble foyer, passing the doors to Jocko's and Vic's rooms, feeling a sick warmth which could be Leo's fever, she thought, or a kind of sexual nausea or the exotic remains of old memories.

One morning she slammed her fist down on the breakfast table rattling the sensible dishes. "Goddammit," she wailed, "why didn't Daddy teach me tennis when I was young?"

Jocko told her she wouldn't look good playing tennis.

Vic crunched his toast and never looked up.

† † †

Leo got arrested for standing in the median on Uhuru Highway giving drunken lectures to the cars passing by.

Consumers, listen! The world is in its deepest darkness and only a hideous light can make any difference now!

After the Kenyan police released him, he walked up and down Government Road, Kimathi Street, Biashara Street until arrested again. He hadn't shaved in a week and in his grizzled condition kept talking about the *acte gratuit* and other matters the tourists and shopkeepers didn't understand or want to hear.

A small boy, one of those who hung around the downtown section parking cars and giving directions to tourists for a few pence a day, called Leo *mzee*—old man. The caption startled Leo, so he went to his flat, shaved, rested, and sobered up. Am I old? His hand seemed steady enough. Am I a coward, as Harry once said?

It's all right to feel fear, but don't be afraid of feeling afraid, men, that's the thing!

I've been stopping people on the streets, he told himself. Jesus Christ in Wales.

J. R. Hoskins came out to see Leo. They had lunch in the sterile coffee shop of the Hilton, and The Peacock, dressed in a seersucker suit with pink shirt and burnt orange tie, offered Leo a pension.

"I don't need the money," Leo said. "I need something else, don't know what."

"Remember I told you we have a house in Mombasa? You can go there, if you want to," J. R. offered.

"I might do that."

They walked around town together. Ivory and jade trinkets in every shop window. Purses and shoes made of zebra. Throw rugs of a lion's hide and mane. *Individual character is radical, even pathological and criminal. We're not supposed to stand apart from the herd.* J. R. listened to Leo rave. The man made little sense and needed help.

"Take that house on the ocean for a while," J. R. urged him. "There's a view of the beach."

"How big is Victor now?"

"He's a real ramrod," J. R. drawled, smiling somehow more than he meant to.

"And Val and Harry?"

"Doing fine," J. R. lied.

"Even if they ask me, I'm not going up to London to visit," Leo said conclusively.

Domesticity isn't civilization, it's the blood enemy.

"You all right?" J. R. asked him. "I've got to leave you now and go over to the consul's office."

A bacteria covering the earth.

"Use that house. Get in touch with our man here."

Killing off human freedom.

"Goo'bye, now, Leo. I'm leaving you."

† † †

Harry became aware that he was dead.

He couldn't tell how or where he began to know, but distress became certainty. Some men, he decided, who had seen the beast up close just came to the knowledge naturally.

The boys were passing the football out in Hyde Park. Vic could throw a spiral now. He had a hell of an arm. And Jocko could jump like a gazelle and catch it in his belly like a good flanker. It was a Sunday afternoon, windy and sunny, kites above, traffic flashing through the trees from over on Park Lane. Harry saw himself as if from a great distance, as if through the scope of a powerful rifle, cross hairs fixed on his own warm corpse as he watched his children, as he loved a woman grown slightly plump. A retired soldier out of season behind a few tatters of paper on a desk.

He tried to remember good things: that odd delight as he stood before the tarpaulin in the jungle. Anything. But memory was unkind. The lobotomy of peace had come to him. He couldn't cheer his son's catch.

At night his fierce dreams had turned into a strange whiteness, a blank, and he realized his nightmares wouldn't come true exactly, that his boys would grow up safe and dull and bewildered—especially about their peculiar father, who was trying very hard to stay in control of himself.

† † †

Giraffe and wildebeest along the Mombasa highway.

Leo's hands gripped the wheel of the Land Rover which was beginning to rattle with age now; he thought of all the vehicles, equipment, and pieces of ordnance he had bought, sold, or traded. He'd never do any of that again.

He and Weldu had brought the Land Rover and the armored lorry with Val's desk and all the light arms out of Biafra and even in that—he hated the memory of it—he had been a sort of coward. They had hired some of Jiggs' gypsy religious group to help, had paid extraordinary bribes to scouts, border guards, and enemy officials, and even then Leo had hidden in the back of the lorry, down underneath the inlaid desk with a .45 and scarcely a breath as they crossed the Cameroons. Weldu had been ashamed of him. Was that why Weldu was so sullen at the last, he wondered, and would hardly say good-bye to me and wouldn't call me Commander anymore?

The old Land Rover was loaded with the remains of Leo's arsenal now: submachine guns, two lightweight mortars, Sten guns, cartridge belts, grenades, a half ton of ammo of all sorts. Back in Nairobi, the estate was boarded up and as a gesture to convention—perhaps he remembered it from a movie—he had covered all the furniture with sheets. There was no more camp out on Langata Road. No flat near the university. The pages bearing his name at the Norfolk Hotel registry, he decided, were already turning pastel with age. He speculated: will I be in a history book? will Val write about me? *The press is always romantic and personal.*

Driving through Tsavo, he thought of the elephants. A lingering drought had brought them together to die; they were trekking across the savannahs on the ancient routes, shuffling toward their burial in this old expanse of ground. Perhaps only mass death is of consequence, he ruminated; the single man's last breath is such a puny sigh. In the bars of Nairobi one always heard talk of the elephants' graveyards, their long march across half of Africa, the way they strolled together into their oblivion. A hush among the drinkers during this talk. A holy subject among drunks, elephant death.

Leo arrived in Mombasa, as planned, after dark. When he had a couple of drinks, he unloaded the Land Rover, moving the ordnance inside the beach house and depositing it on the tile floors downstairs. Then he went up, turned on the ceiling fans, took a bath, and finished the Johnnie Walker.

He found some mail. Among the letters, one from somebody named Ramona. Postmarked Antibes. He couldn't remember anyone by that name. Nothing from London.

That night he slept on a rug because his back hurt. In the morning, sunlight slanted across his face and he heard the call to prayer sung from the minarets. He went up a narrow flight of stone stairs to the roof and looked out at the island city: the mosques, Kilindini Harbor off to the southwest, the ancient Portuguese fort, the beach across the way. Half naked blacks, turbaned Indians, Arab women swathed and veiled already crowded the streets in those first minutes after dawn. *Bacteria covering the earth.* He watched for an hour as the streets filled to overflowing, then he went down, dressed, and made coffee. There was a note stuck to the refrigerator stating that occupants of the house should not be disturbed when Arabs entered the courtyard to pick fruit from the palm trees, as a lease for same had been arranged. There was no sign anywhere that this was a house used by American intelligence, not even a single *Time* magazine.

After finishing his coffee, Leo went out for his first reconnoitering.

Everything would be carefully worked out.

No mistakes. Maximum effort.

In the old harbor were Chinese vessels, a German schooner, and several Indian dhows unloading rugs and spices the same as they had done a thousand years ago. Beyond, the towering walls of Fort Jesus, built by the Portuguese. A great massacre there once: the Oman of Persia laid siege and after thirty-three months only thirteen of the original 2,500 people inside the fortress were still alive. Always a bloody place, this island. The reeking missionaries never did well here, Leo remembered, and all the island's rulers, the Zenj, the Portuguese, the Mazrui family, all the rest, were bloody slavers and damned tough. I could live here, Leo decided. There's sufficient blood in the stones. The Indian Ocean blows in a brine of death, a foul smell.

He walked all day. In the Old Town quarter he bought himself an embroidered skullcap and dark glasses.

Hindu and Jain temples, mosques, crumbling cathedrals.

At the end of the day he sat in a café overlooking the white sand beaches. It was a festival day of some sort: bands playing, people in bikinis with loose costumes over them, an assortment of colored flags catching the sea breeze, fireworks, the beginnings of a night of celebration. Probably some obscure religious observation. He had a full supper on the terrace of a hotel, then looked over the rim of his newspaper at the celebrants as he made plans. When the stars were out, he strolled down onto the beach and measured it off step by step: two thousand meters from the rocks around a cliffside at one end to the hotel beach at the other.

His thoughts flew away.

Best moment in his life: when Victor, awed, watched the falcon snatch the arrow from the sky.

And the worst time ever: when Harry had called him a goddamned coward more than a dozen years ago. *I am not!* he had replied—like a pouting child. He wished he had killed Harry, yet was glad he hadn't.

Standing in the darkness of the beach, Leo listened to a dumb Indian music drifting through the night: the cry of a flute, the tin sound of a horn, the plunking of a sitar. He trudged back up toward the road above the beach and walked to his house.

Get creative with madness, if possible, because such madness will finally be healthy.

He began preparing himself that night, refusing sleep or a

drink or anything to eat. Around three in the morning he parked the Land Rover near the hotel beach and walked back to the house again. He thought about leaving a note, but to whom? The American Peacock? Val?

If I make it to the Land Rover, he wondered, what then?

Before dawn, he began to dress. Beneath his helmet, the embroidered skullcap. Dark glasses. Fatigues and paratrooper boots. Cartridge belts. Canteen with water, as if embarking on a very long desert crossing. Two knives, one bayonet. Grenades like jewels strung in a heavy necklace. A .45 and a Luger. The Sten gun and ammo. The 7.62 assault rifle. The little portable mortar and six rounds. An M76 submachine gun. Too heavy, all this, but he would dispose of pieces as he went along. He clanked when he walked. Also waddled. He made his way upstairs in the house just to view himself in a mirror. There he was: a baggy, noisy beast of burden. The image in the mirror gave him a smile, a sad one, and yet he saw how vain and ridiculous military hardware and a soldier's artifacts were.

† † †

Val awoke at three in the morning, the night pitch dark, and knew she had dreamt of the black flag.

She touched Harry beside her, got up, wrapped her quilted housecoat around her, and made her rounds through the flat. The boys were all right. In the kitchen she made herself instant coffee. It's Leo, she decided. All this time and the prediction wasn't about Harry at all; his dream had become hers, time had scrambled all the psyches ever to touch each other, but Leo was somewhere somehow in jeopardy. Her bones felt brittle as she sat in the harsh fluorescent light of the kitchen, as if she might freeze and break apart, and the coffee cup went cold in her hand.

I've made a terrible mistake, she told herself. I can feel Leo from thousands of miles away; I should've stayed with him. The black flag was his; Harry is going to nourish dullness like a religion, I'm going to feed on memory like a narcotic, and Leo is my lost love, my intellect, my father, my commander, my husband, my leopard of the hills.

She began to cry. Her life was over.

† † †

When he appeared on the crowded beach just before noon, the first bathers who saw him laughed out loud. He looked like a walking military junkyard, clanking and clanging down the rocks beside the cliff.

There were more than a thousand bathers on the beach that late morning as he began to sweep them before him. Weighted down with ammo and all his weapons, he couldn't move fast, but didn't have to. Astonished stares as he opened fire; they were all thinking, god, an odd little soldier, all baggy with packs and rattling when he walks, and then they died. Their eyes filled with a strange disbelieving pain as he moved through them and then they broke like a herd, running ahead of his fire. An Arab girl in a bright red bikini was blown right out of it, stripped by his submachine gun, undressed and flying off in a slow-motioned erotica. One brave boy in cut-off jeans came at Leo with a rubber float after he was wounded, waving the toy overhead like a club until he was cut in half by a burst from the M76. A group of kids sprawled in the sand, boys beside their motorbikes and girls with their halter tops loosened; he emptied on them at close range because they seemed too cool to move. That finished the M76, so he set up his mortar and lobbed a few shells at the crowd screaming and retreating down the beach; the shells exploded beyond them, driving them back toward his spray of bullets from the automatic rifle. Almost casually, he strolled down the beach, walking near the surf where the sand was packed hard underfoot, pumping bullets into the wall of bodies ahead. They were beginning to pile up and tumble over each other. Another mortar shell: Cinzano bottles, Fanta signs, surfboards, beach balls floated in the air above the blast. Human parts. Screaming. They ran toward him, confused, as if they wanted to die. Leo dropped an empty cartridge belt as he moved toward them and let fly the last mortar shell. Ka-thunk! A young man with a spear gun came running at him. Leo let him get very close before blowing him away with a round of .45 fire. The spear went whistling by. Another kid tried throwing a stone. A burst from the .45 amputated his right leg at the knee. Bless the brave at heart.

Leo stopped under a canopy where moments before a crowd drank beer and listened to the jukebox. With the Sten gun, he dismantled the beach café: tables, bottles, chairs, Wurlitzer. Shards of glass, plastic, and the broken black discs of the records everywhere as the music stopped. Then he moved outside again, across another few feet of beach, stepping on a sandcastle as he kept firing.

Two policemen dressed in their khaki shorts ran toward him from the boardwalk. One seemed armed with only a silver whistle. Leo fired once, twice, with the .45 and missed. Then the Sten gun: the idiot somersaulted backward, legs and arms akimbo, when struck. The other one circled across the street, out of range.

In a little boat basin near the hotel, Leo found a huddled

group of bathers hiding. He showered them with grenades. Boats, bathers, mushrooms of water in the air; when the smoke cleared, he saw that he had sunk the lot. With his dwindling ammo, he took a few potshots at the windows of the hotel across the way. Guests, who stood there gaping, dived for cover. With one of his last bursts he took out the tires of two cars stopped on the pavement above the boardwalk. Boats, hotel, cars, jukeboxes: he enjoyed all that. Screams and voices yelling as the last bathers retreated across the lawn of the hotel. He had chased them the length of the beach. Lighter now with his ammo mostly gone, he spun around and fired off the last of the Sten gun's ammo in a wheel of flame.

Around the curve of the beach sat the fortress in the far distance. Flying above its ramparts was a dark flag. Dropping the Sten gun, he staggered across a few more paces of sand and produced the Luger. A child sat cross-legged with a small bucket and spade right at his feet. For a moment their eyes met, then Leo aimed and pulled the trigger. The Luger misfired. Nothing. He was checking the weapon when he heard footsteps behind him, someone running toward him, and turned.

The policeman was perhaps no more than eighteen or nineteen years old: a black kid, frightened, his lips drawn tight, the one who had run out of range across the street moments earlier. Leo looked into his face before he ever saw the pistol—and it was something light and pathetic, an old .22, perhaps, dark against the dark hand which held it. The young policeman was running at Leo full speed and firing as he approached, so that bullets were whizzing by. Jerky, frantic scattershooting. Leo leveled the Luger, but again it misfired. *Acte gratuit.* "God in Wales!" Leo cursed, and he fumbled for a knife. But the young policeman, still running at him headlong, had one more shot, and fired it from no more than six feet away.

The shot, like so many things in Africa, was curiously on target, accidental and deadly. It struck Leo in the heart and dropped him. He was on his knees as the young policeman swerved away from his knife and rolled out of his reach in the sand.

Leo took only a moment to die, pain and sadness and love of Val and Harry tearing at him in equal parts as he tried to get a breath, but couldn't. Then all around him a maze of movement and sound settled in: slowly, people came out of the shops and off the hotel terraces; they buzzed around him like uncertain flies around carrion; they spoke different languages, yet their voices rose in greater and greater excitement until they became one sound, a wail of confusion and fright; smoke from the burning canopy drifted on the wind and rattled the leaves of the palm trees along the beach; from far away, the thorns and leaves and weedy undergrowths of the continent shuddered and replied; pathways and streams, attacked by the rich jungle foliage, moaned softly in response; the savannahs answered with their doleful notes; the rivers whispered in their courses.